THE SALTED SCEPTRE

THE THRILL OF THE HUNT
BOOK FOUR

HELEN HARPER

SERIES RECAP

Tattered Huntress

Daisy Carter is a low elf living in Edinburgh, eking out a living as a delivery driver. She is dispatched to Neidpath Castle to deliver a parcel to Hugo Pemberville, a celebrated high elf who is famous for treasure hunting. When she hands him his parcel and waits for his signature, he recognises the silver ring in her eyes that indicates she is a user of spider's silk, a dangerously addictive drug that Daisy takes to control the wild magic inside her. Hugo's demeanour changes instantly and, with considerable rudeness, he tells Daisy to leave. Before she does, she spots some notes about the location of a special, long-lost locket necklace.

Upset at Hugo's attitude, Daisy suggests to a belligerent troll named Duchess that she leaves her current habitat in favour of a more pleasant one under the bridge at Hugo's ancestral home. When Hugo discovers that Duchess has taken up residence there, he calls Daisy's boss and ensures she is fired because of her drug addiction. To retaliate, Daisy uses the information from the notes to find the necklace before Hugo does.

Daisy takes it to a man called Sir Nigel. Impressed that she found it, he offers her a place in a treasure-hunting competition to find some chests of Jacobean gold. Daisy later realises that the locket on the necklace was enchanted; having opened it before she handed it over, she is now supposedly the boss of two very annoying brownies, Hester and Otis.

Daisy and the brownies join Sir Nigel's treasure hunt to find three parts to a magical key which, when combined, will reveal the location of the treasure chests. There are numerous other competitors, including Humphrey and Eleanor, a friendly couple who are somewhat lackadaisical about the hunt.

The first key part is located in northern England. Daisy would have found it first, but she is delayed when another team is attacked by a giant snake. She saves them but in the meantime Hugo and his team of Primes find the key part. Hugo initially thinks Daisy engineered the snake attack in a deliberate attempt to harm her competitors, though he soon realises the truth.

The second key part is located in the north of Scotland, in a concealed chamber behind an underground cavern called Smoo Cave. The entrance to the chamber is unlocked by another competitor, Gordon, a sorcerer who appears to have an uncomfortable relationship with Hugo.

Daisy discovers she is claustrophobic and panics when she is underground. Unable to continue searching for the key part, she falls through the ground in the cave and is knocked unconscious. When she awakes, she is challenged to a fight to the death by a one-eyed creature known as the Fachan. The Fachan eventually decides that she is not a worthy opponent, but he gifts her a sentient sword called Gladys and shows her the way out of the cave.

Suffering from spider's silk withdrawal, Daisy starts hallucinating. Hugo finds her and helps her recover, and his attitude towards her softens considerably. She re-joins the treasure hunt for the third key part, which is located in one of many houses owned by a rich man known for his unpleasant behaviour. With the help of Hester and Otis, Daisy discovers that the man has been keeping magical creatures captive. She releases them, sneaks into the house and finds the key part. Before she can retrieve it, though, Humphrey appears and takes it.

With no key part, Daisy can no longer participate in the treasure hunt and only Humphrey and Hugo remain in the competition. She is suspicious about Humphrey and spies on him when all three key parts are put together and the location of the treasure chests is revealed. They are on the tidal island of Cramond, near Edinburgh, and Daisy quickly heads there to wait.

She witnesses Humphrey attack Hugo with a terrible power known as blood magic and steps in to save him. Humphrey escapes, while Hugo and Daisy are trapped on the island as the tide comes in. They are forced to shelter there for hours, during which time Hugo reveals that his best friend died as a result of a spider's silk addiction and Daisy confesses that she takes the drugs because otherwise her magic will overwhelm her.

Eventually they make it safely back to the mainland where they recover the treasure and ensure that Humphrey is arrested. Daisy is offered her old job as a delivery driver – but she decides to become a full-time treasure hunter instead.

Fiendish Delights

Daisy is working as a freelance treasure hunter, but most of her commissions so far have involved little more than lost-and-found searches. That changes when a young girl, Sophia, manipulates her into searching for a doll she had recently lost. Daisy tracks the lost doll to a witch called Mud McAlpine, but he will only return it if she gives him a freshly cut toenail from a troll.

Daisy, Hester and Otis travel to Pemberville Castle where Duchess the troll is living. Daisy reconnects with Hugo and he agrees to help her retrieve the doll. With one of Duchess's toenails in their possession, they return to Mud McAlpine. Starstruck by Hugo, he breaks the ward on his flat so they can enter.

Once they are inside, he conjures up a magic scroll that will lead to one of the mythical thirteen treasures of Great Britain. Almost as soon as the scroll appears, Sophia shows up and reveals herself to be a fiend called Zashtum. Daisy learns that fiends are evil beings created through the misuse of blood magic, whose ultimate goal is to gain more power for themselves. They cannot be killed, only banished by powerful witches.

Zashtum fights Mud, Daisy and Hugo for the scroll. Eventually Mud manages to banish her, but he is critically injured and the scroll is destroyed. However, Daisy saw enough of the words on it before it burned to start hunting for the treasure.

Daisy, together with Hugo and his group of treasure-hunting Primes, travel to a rural cemetery in Wales where they believe the treasure is buried – but they uncover nothing more than an old dragon's tooth.

Daisy manages to interpret more of what she saw on the magic scroll and they return to Wales with the sorcerer Gordon Mackenzie, who agrees to help them. Gordon and Hugo have a long-standing disagreement resulting from Gordon's search for Lady Rose, a high elf who vanished thirty years earlier. The elvish community has long suspected that Hugo's parents had something to do with Rose's disappearance.

The team locate the treasure, a gold and silver chess set, but before they can remove it from the cemetery a dragon appears and snatches it away. Aware that the dragon could be in danger from fiends that are still hunting for the chess set, Daisy and Hugo resolve to retrieve it.

When they travel to a nearby town to find the dragon's lair, they are confronted by a fiend, Baltar, who seems to think he's met Daisy before. He has the opportunity to kill Daisy but chooses not to; Daisy does not understand why.

Daisy and Hugo discover several potential locations for the dragon's lair. Their relationship is deepening, but Daisy is losing control of her magic and having to take more and more spider's silk to stop her powers from spilling out. Because of this, she chooses not to act upon her feelings for Hugo; however, she does agree that once the chess set is safe, she will spend three months with Hugo and his team to learn to control her magic properly. Once she has achieved that, she can start weaning herself off her addiction.

There is no dragon at the first lair. Daisy is separated from Hugo and the brownies and meets the Fachan again. They are attacked by three fiends, including Baltar. Using Gladys, the sword that the Fachan gave to her when they first met, Daisy kills Baltar. She assumes that Gladys has special powers that forced him to die.

At the next lair Daisy reconnects with Hester, Otis and Hugo and they find the dragon who took the chess set. Daisy realises that a fiend has used magic to impersonate Hugo and fights him. The fiend reveals that he is Athair, the most powerful one in the country. He could easily kill Daisy but he lets her go, whispering to her that she is his daughter.

Hugo and Daisy turn the chess set over to Sir Nigel at the British Museum. He tells them that it is possible for a fiend to kill another fiend; because Daisy killed Baltar, she starts to believe that what Athair told her might be true.

Skullduggery

Daisy and the brownies have been living at Pemberville Castle for several weeks while she trains with Hugo and his team and attempts – unsuccessfully – to develop control over her magic. The side-effects she is experiencing from her addiction to spider's silk are increasing day by day.

At a party she is approached by the sorcerer, Gordon Mackenzie. He asks her to hunt for a tiny magical golden skull that he believes will unlock the secret behind the disappearance of Lady Rose thirty years earlier. Aware of Hugo's wariness about the matter, Daisy says she will think about it.

The following day Daisy breaks into Assigney mansion, the abandoned home that belonged to Lady Rose. Once inside she discovers a letter addressed to her from Athair in which he encourages her to search for Lady Rose.

Back at Pemberville Castle, Daisy and Hugo share a close moment, although it ends abruptly when her wild magic gets the better of her. Hugo admits that he thinks his parents might have been involved in Lady Rose's disappearance, and eventually they decide to hunt for the golden skull together. Despite experiencing some setbacks with a local will-o'-the-wisp along the way, they locate it beneath a cursed stone near Doncaster.

They return to Edinburgh to hand over the skull to Gordon. Daisy and the brownies enter his house but their meeting is interrupted by Athair, who has disguised himself as a postman. Daisy loses control of her magic and there is a blinding flash of light from the skull. Somehow, both she and the brownies are magically transported back in time to 1994.

Realising that she is penniless and trapped in the past,

Daisy takes advantage of a vampire infestation in the city. For every vamp she kills, she can earn £500. She engages the help of a young homeless witch, Tracey, who uses her skills to concoct an anti-vamp spray. When Daisy tracks down a group of vampires, however, it becomes clear they are being controlled by a fiend called Vargas. The vampires are dispatched while Daisy and Vargas fight. Daisy tells him that her father is Athair; in return, Vargas tells her that she can learn to control her magic if she expels all her power out of her body in one go. Daisy then kills him.

She and the brownies leave Edinburgh and travel north to Pemberville Castle and the Assigney mansion. Daisy meets two-year-old Hugo and his parents. Athair is also visiting in the guise of Rose's doctor. He asks the Pembervilles to encourage Lady Rose to leave her home for some fresh air. Fortunately, he does not yet recognise Daisy so she follows him when he leaves the castle and tracks him to Culcreuch Castle. Hiding in some bushes to spy on the castle, she realises that she isn't the only person lurking around: Hugo has also travelled back in time.

Now they are reunited, Hugo and Daisy go to the Assigney mansion. Although it is heavily warded against intruders, Daisy manages to get inside. She meets Lady Rose and tries to explain the situation and warn her, but she is thrown out of the house. Soon afterwards, the fiend Baltar appears. He directs a sorcerer to break through the ward and appears desperate to get hold of something inside, which Rose is hiding from Athair. Daisy and Hugo battle Baltar and, in the process, Daisy expels all of her magic and collapses just as Hugo's parents appear. Eventually, with Baltar still alive, the entire group – including – Rose manage to flee.

Daisy wakes up in Edinburgh after a long period of unconsciousness and realises that she finally has control of her magic. Lady Rose presents a baby girl and reveals that she has given birth to Athair's child – and that child is Daisy. Before they can escape Edinburgh and travel south, however, Athair confronts them. Unfortunately Rose is compelled to resort to blood magic whenever he is near. Daisy manages to delay him enough for the group to escape again.

Deciding that the only way to keep baby Daisy – and therefore also adult Daisy – safe is to draw Athair away, Rose and Hugo's parents abandon her and Hugo at a petrol station. They are initially upset but eventually understand. They declare their love for each other then return to Edinburgh and leave baby Daisy at a local hospital, knowing that she will soon be adopted into a loving family.

They set a trap for Athair, fight him and reveal the truth about his relationship to Daisy before they are forcibly ejected from 1994 back to 2024.

Rose has been hiding in France for thirty years. Daisy travels there, together with her adoptive parents, Hugo and his parents, for a reunion with her birth mother. She reveals that she is a drug addict and promises to start rehabilitation – but she knows that Athair will continue to pursue her.

CHAPTER

ONE

One month. I heaved myself further up the side of the steep hill, my thigh muscles straining with every step.

One month and three days.

Wiping the clammy sweat from my forehead, I raised my head and eyed Hugo who was a few metres in front of me. He was wearing camouflage trousers; despite the loose fit around his legs, the material was straining across his arse and leaving little to the imagination. If the seam split, I knew I'd see his tighty-whities. I'd watched him put them on this morning from the comfort of my sleeping bag. I would enjoy taking them off him later this evening.

One month, three days and five hours.

Hester, who was nestled against the crook of my neck, gave a contented snore. Otis flitted in the air beside me, his tiny iridescent wings flapping as he fought against the breeze that was gusting down from the summit. He'd declined to sit on my shoulder, announcing that he needed the exercise, but I was certain that he'd been regretting that decision for the last hour. He was determined to keep going, though, as if his display of grit and resilience would somehow transfer to me by osmosis. I shrugged; stranger things had happened.

One month, three days, five hours and thirty-six minutes.

'It's not much further,' Hugo called over his shoulder. 'The gully is just ahead.'

I tightened my jaw and forced a final burst of energy into my aching limbs. It took a second but they finally responded. I caught up with him then scrambled the last few metres on all fours until we reached the rocky outcrop.

Hugo glanced at me, his blue eyes crinkling and his dimple flashing. 'This is it. We've made it. You see the cairn in the bottom corner?'

I nodded and gazed down at the small stone monument nestled below us. It wasn't particularly impressive; no wonder generations of hikers had passed it by without further investigation. But if I concentrated very hard, I could sense the faint throb of old magic pulsating from the ground beneath it. This was definitely the right spot.

Hugo swung his bag off his shoulder and rummaged inside it. 'It's a steep drop,' he said. 'We should use a rope to reach the cairn, just in case.'

Uh-huh. I watched him for a moment or two then I started forward, slipping and sliding down the rocky gully. It wasn't *that* steep.

'Daisy!' he yelled.

'We don't need a rope,' I said. 'I've got this.'

'If you slip and break your ankle, I'll be the one who has to carry you all the way back down. I've told you, we need to be cautious.'

I took another confident step downwards.

Hugo was on a roll. 'Rushing into situations without undue attention is—'

I misjudged the slope and slid on a patch of scree. My arms

flailed in mid-air as I lost my balance and pitched forward. Oops.

Hester, jerking awake from her snooze, shrieked, 'What? What's going on?'

Behind me, Hugo muttered something. As I wobbled, I sensed the surge of magic emanating from his fingertips. In the split second before I started to tumble headfirst towards the sharp rocks beneath me, a powerful blast of air pushed me upright again. Phew.

'Thank you!' I called out cheerfully.

Hugo muttered again. 'If you break your damned neck, Daisy...'

I sucked in a breath and regained my balance. 'Then I'm sure you'll arrange a very nice funeral,' I told him, continuing my descent without a backward glance.

'Where every mourner will agree that you brought your *own* death upon your *own* head because of your *own* foolhardiness.'

'That's as maybe.' I skidded down the last section and reached the cairn before I turned my head to grin at him. 'But they'll also acknowledge that I beat you.' I paused for breath. 'Sucker.'

Hugo scowled, then stuck out his tongue at me. He was a very sore loser. To be fair, so was I.

'I don't want to go to your funeral, Daisy,' Otis said. 'You need to listen to Hugo and take more care.' He looked at Hester, clearly expecting his sister to back him up.

She only sniffed. 'I have a great funeral outfit,' she said. 'Several great funeral outfits, in fact. And I'm sure there'll be an excellent feast afterwards. Nothing beats funeral food.'

That was more like it. I smirked and returned my attention to the cairn. If the old map was correct, the jewelled ceremonial dagger was buried underneath it. I adjusted my footing and knelt to begin the search.

One month, three days, five hours and thirty-eight minutes since I'd last swallowed any spider's silk pills. Not that I was counting.

~

IT TOOK FAR LESS time to climb down the side of the hill than it had to climb up it. The small team of Primes who were waiting at the campsite must have been watching our descent because they had mugs of steaming hot tea ready for us when we returned.

'Well?' Becky asked. 'Did you find it?'

'Do you even have to ask?' Hester enquired.

Hugo produced the dagger and held it up for their perusal. Rizwan beamed. 'Brilliant! Well done, Hugo!'

'Daisy found it,' Hugo said calmly. I raised an eyebrow. 'It's the truth. I can admit it,' He passed the dagger to Rizwan then leaned down and whispered in my ear, 'And that admission proves that I'm the bigger person, Daisy.'

I choked. Hugo grinned serenely, although I was well aware he was still annoyed that I'd not waited for the rope. 'Bigger, sure,' I retorted. 'But not better.' I stepped back so I could look into his eyes. His grin widened.

'This is an incredible specimen of sixteenth-century workmanship.' Rizwan pointed to the dirt-encrusted jewels on the dagger's hilt. 'Look at the way these stones have been cut.'

'I can feel the magic bound into the blade,' Becky breathed. 'It's an extraordinary item.'

Miriam took a sip from her mug of tea then peered over their shoulders. 'The British Museum will be pleased that it's been found after all these years. I suspect the finder's fee will be impressive.'

'Yay!' Otis's fist pumped the air. 'Go, Daisy!'

Hester rolled her eyes, but when Hugo glared at her she cleared her throat. 'Yes. Well done, Daisy. You did a good job.'

I eyed the group. 'You don't have to overdo your enthusiasm on my account.'

Becky jerked and guilt flashed across Rizwan's face; Miriam, however, tilted her mug towards me in a toast. Hugo didn't react at all, which only confirmed my suspicions.

I sighed. 'What's it really worth?'

'It *is* from the sixteenth century, dear,' Miriam said. Her eyes twinkled.

'These gems are real,' Rizwan said.

'It's an important historical item,' Becky added.

I put my hands on my hips and looked at them. 'Don't make me start tapping my toes,' I warned.

Hester gasped in mock horror. 'Oh no! Not toe tapping!' Otis elbowed her sharply.

Hugo grimaced. 'Fine. Its value probably extends to five or six hundred pounds.'

Uh-huh. I was no financial expert, and I didn't oversee the Primes' budget, but I wasn't completely stupid. Between camp-site fees, wages, research hours, petrol and equipment costs, this venture had probably cost several grand. Treasure hunting was supposed to *make* us money, not *cost* us money.

'You can't measure worth solely in monetary terms,' Hugo added quietly. 'Nobody has seen this dagger for hundreds of years. Its historical value is immense.' I waited. He gave me a long look. 'And if it helps distract you and occupy your mind, then it's priceless.'

There we go. I pushed away the surge of frustration. 'You don't have to invent treasure hunts to keep me busy.'

'We didn't invent it, Daisy,' Becky burst out. 'It was a real treasure hunt.' She pointed to the dagger. 'That's real treasure.'

Arguing with this lot was a waste of time. 'I appreciate the thought, truly I do, but you can't walk around me on eggshells. You can't create treasure hunts out of thin air just to please me and keep me busy. I'm doing okay. I'm managing.'

I turned my head and met Hugo's eyes. 'I will tell you if I'm not coping, I promise.' I forced the corners of my mouth into a smile.

'It's not just for you,' Hugo said. 'Even if the dagger isn't very valuable, searching for items like it is a great way to keep up our skills until a larger treasure hunt presents itself. We didn't do this just for you, Daisy.' I gazed at him until a muscle jerked in his jaw. 'But okay,' he admitted. 'It was mostly for you.'

I considered his words and my reaction to them, then pushed myself up on tiptoe and planted a brief kiss on his cheek. 'Thank you,' I said. 'I appreciate your good intentions. But don't do it again, not on my behalf.'

'Alright.'

My smile became genuine. 'Thank you,' I repeated.

Everything was fine. I was managing. Just.

WE WERE LESS than an hour away from Edinburgh on our return journey when Miriam's phone pinged. A moment later Becky and Rizwan's phones also chimed with notifications. I turned around from my coveted spot in the front passenger seat and immediately noted their pale faces as they read the messages. My stomach knotted with dread.

Before I could ask what the problem was, Hugo's phone started to ring. As he was driving, he answered on speaker. I held my breath and waited.

'Pemberville,' he grunted.

'Ah, Hugo old chap.' It was Sir Nigel.

The wealthy older man, who was part of high-elvish society despite being human, usually burbled his way through life with stoical cheeriness; right now, though, his voice was strained and I was certain I could hear panicked shouting in the background. I wasn't the only one; Hester and Otis had bolted upright and even Hugo was looking concerned. 'Are you in the city by any chance?'

'Edinburgh?' Hugo asked. 'I'm about forty minutes away.'

Sir Nigel sucked in a sharp breath. 'And Lady Daisy?'

Normally I suffered a discomfiting shiver when someone used my official title. My elevated status, together with my sobriety, were recent developments that I was still coming to terms with.

Given Sir Nigel's tone, I suddenly had other concerns. 'I'm here,' I said. 'So are three of the Primes – Miriam, Becky and Rizwan.'

'Jolly good.' Sir Nigel didn't sound jolly or good, he sounded anything but. 'We have a slight problem at the Royal Elvish Institute,' he continued. 'I wonder if you could both drop by?' He paused. 'As quickly as possible. I understand that Daisy may not yet be up to large gatherings, but I wouldn't ask if it were not urgent.'

Hugo removed one hand from the Jeep's steering wheel, reached over and squeezed my fingers. As he did so, down the phone line we heard a woman shrieking. Whatever was happening, it wasn't good.

I gripped Hugo's fingers for a second before pulling back my hand so my fingers could stray to my pocket. There was no baggie nestling there with spider's silk pills inside it, only a bit of fluff. 'What's going on, Sir Nigel?' I asked, although I suspected I already knew at least some of the answer.

'It's probably better if you see it for yourself,' he answered.

There was another loud scream. 'I had better go. I will see you soon.' The phone call cut out.

Miriam leaned forward and held up her phone. 'I have a photo,' she said. She suddenly sounded even more off balance than Sir Nigel. 'It's a bit blurry.'

I took her phone from her hand and squinted at the screen. Oh. Bile rose in my mouth. *Oh.*

'Daisy?' Hugo asked.

I didn't immediately answer. I wasn't sure I had any words to offer him.

'What is it? What's happened?' he demanded.

Hester peered over my shoulder. Otis flapped his way closer to the screen and tilted his head. 'Something is, uh, dripping down the front of the Royal Elvish Institute. Some sort of liquid.' His voice quivered. 'It might be paint.'

'That's not paint,' Hester whispered.

'Whatever it is, there's a lot of it,' Becky said. 'It's covering half the building and—' she swallowed '—there's a word.'

Hugo's knuckles tightened. 'Tell me.'

'It says Daisy,' Rizwan said. 'In big dripping red letters.'

Massive letters.

I finally found my voice. 'Hester's right, it's not paint.' I stared at the image. There was only one person who could be responsible for this very deliberate, very pointed act of vandalism: Athair. My fucking birth father.

The fear deep inside me was hardening into rage. 'It's blood.'

CHAPTER

TWO

Not only had the police cordoned off the whole of Charlotte Square, they'd also evacuated all the residents. We had to present ourselves to four different officers and produce identification three separate times to gain access to the area, and even then we couldn't get close to the building. Nobody could. There was an inner cordon that prevented anyone from going near the Royal Elvish Institute. Not that anyone wanted to get close.

From thirty metres away, standing close to a large bronze statue of Prince Albert on a horse, I saw a group of sorcerers that included Gordon Mackenzie and Boonder. Their familiar faces eased my tension slightly. There were also a huddle of witches, a few heavily armed police officers and a sprinkling of highly placed elves. Everyone else must have been ejected from the area long before our arrival.

The building looked considerably worse than it had in the photo. Presumably the police had set up the spotlights to illuminate its façade, but I truly wished they hadn't bothered because they made the wet blood glisten in a sickening fashion. The smell didn't help, either. I'd never had the dubious pleasure of visiting an abattoir and if they smelled anything like this, I'd make sure I never did.

I stared at the huge red letters that spelled out my name. I'd known that sooner or later Athair would come for me but I'd hoped to have more time – and I'd never imagined that his calling card would look anything like this.

Hugo stepped closer to me and wrapped his arm supportively around my waist. The brownies stayed on my shoulder, even though Otis was rigid with fright. Miriam, Rizwan and Becky also remained close. Their proximity meant a great deal and, if I were honest, it stopped me running away to dive under my duvet and pretend none of this was happening.

'Daddy Dearest is a showy bastard,' I muttered in a deliberate display of defiance. I turned to Sir Nigel who was approaching with a woman. She was human, barely five feet tall, with plump cheeks that wouldn't have looked out of place in a bucolic painting of a country farmhouse. Despite her wholesome physical appearance, she exuded authority.

'Thank you for coming so quickly,' Sir Nigel said, as if there had been any real choice in the matter. 'Lady Daisy, Lord Pemberville, this is Detective Inspector O'Hagan. Don't let her humanity fool you. She's tough as nails and highly experienced in dealing with issues involving foul magic.'

O'Hagan dropped into a perfunctory, albeit practiced, curtsey and my eyes narrowed. She was clearly used to dealing with high elves who demanded obvious shows of deference, but I wasn't one of them. Her gesture embarrassed me and made me feel out of place.

'Call me Daisy,' I said. 'The title is more of a surprise to me than it is to anyone else here. And if you curtsey again, I'll think I've time travelled to the Regency period.'

O'Hagan raised an eyebrow. 'Yes, I was told that you'd done

some time travelling. I was also told that I'd like you. I'm beginning to think my informants were correct.'

Hester flicked my earlobe. 'What's wrong with you?' she hissed. 'You should learn to accept curtseys as your due.'

'I'll do that when you start curtseying to me,' I retorted.

'*Me*?' She was aghast. 'Curtsey to *you*?'

Hugo leaned into my other ear. 'I'll curtsey to you whenever you like, Daisy.'

I smiled. Both of them knew exactly how to make me feel better, even if O'Hagan was now looking at us as if we were bonkers. I took advantage of my temporarily improved state of mind and gestured towards the bloodied Royal Elvish Institute. 'Is it human blood?' I asked.

I caught a flicker of relief in O'Hagan's sharp eyes before it was replaced with steely professionalism. She was likely glad that I wasn't collapsing in hysterics – or pleased I wasn't swallowing illegal drugs right in front of her and complicating the situation even further. Given how much she already knew about me, there was little doubt that she was aware of my history as an addict.

I wondered if my hands were about to start shaking; I shoved them in my pockets just in case.

'I'm afraid so,' O'Hagan said. 'We've only conducted preliminary testing with our on-site toolkit, but there appears to be blood from at least six different people.' That was hardly surprising given how much of it was covering the building. I wondered who those people were and if they were now dead; it seemed likely.

'How did the blood get there?' Miriam asked.

'The sorcerers have confirmed that it was through magical means. The perpetrator didn't climb up the side of the building and daub the letters himself.' O'Hagan didn't take her eyes from me. 'If we assume that it's you who is being addressed, do you have any idea who might have done this?'

She knew who'd done it, everyone did, but she wanted to hear it from me and to gauge my reaction at the same time. 'My father,' I bit out. 'The fiend called Athair.' I paused, wondering if she knew what fiends were because most people, even police officers, didn't. When she didn't blink, I knew that she was already privy to that particular unsavoury secret.

'Do you know what he wants?' O'Hagan asked.

I grimaced. 'My attention.'

'Mmm.' She glanced upwards. 'I'd say he's achieved that.' She wasn't wrong. 'Unfortunately,' O'Hagan continued, 'because he is a fiend, I don't have the authority or the ability to bring him to justice. The Royal Elvish Institute holds sway here.'

Rather than dismay, I felt relief. I had no doubt that Detective Inspector O'Hagan was an accomplished, dedicated and experienced officer but subduing fiends was beyond the capability of any human police officer – or police force. And Athair was the most powerful fiend this country had seen for generations.

'If you see Athair,' I told her, 'the best thing you can do is run.'

Her eyes widened a fraction. I wasn't trying to scare her, I was trying to warn her. She nodded and moved away to speak to another group of bystanders.

Sir Nigel fixed Hugo and me with a morose look. 'The Royal Elvish Institute cannot allow this to stand,' he said. His skin was pale and, for perhaps the first time ever, his handlebar moustache appeared faintly askew with several whiskers out of place. 'The board has already convened. They're sending a contingent of witches after Athair to banish the bastard from this realm once and for all.'

I stiffened. 'I'm not convinced that's a good idea. I'm not

sure that any number of witches, no matter how skilled they are, will be able to banish him.'

Hugo nodded grimly. 'Not to mention that the only ace up our sleeve as far as that fiendish wanker is concerned is that he isn't aware that we know he uses Culcreuch Castle as a hideout. If a bunch of witches show up there, try to magic him out of existence and don't succeed...'

Sir Nigel held up his hands, pre-empting our concerns. 'I share your worry. However, the Royal Elvish Institute is nothing if not predictable. They were always going to try something like this at some point. In fact, despite my protests, I suspect they've been preparing the witches to go after Athair for a while. There is a lot to admire about the Institute but, like you, I believe that any attempt to confront your father will end in a bloodbath. I have not mentioned Culcreuch to them for that very reason. Very few people are aware that Athair is living there.'

My brow furrowed. 'If they don't know where Athair is, how will they find him?'

Sir Nigel's expression darkened further. 'There have been reports in the last hour of sightings of him near the Meadows.' He was referring to a large expanse of grassy parkland less than a mile from here. 'The witches are already on their way there.'

I sucked in a sharp breath. Cumbubbling bollocks. Athair would only allow himself to be seen if he wanted to be, so those witches were walking into a very obvious trap. 'I have to go to them. I can't let them face Athair alone.'

Otis piped up from my shoulder. 'You're not strong enough to beat him either, Daisy.'

Gladys, who was sheathed by my side, buzzed in disagreement but Otis was right. 'I know,' I said quietly. 'But he won't hurt me.' Much. 'He wants me to join him. He doesn't want me dead.' Not yet, anyway.

'We're with you,' Becky said bravely. Behind her, Rizwan nodded agreement.

'No,' I said. 'I'll go alone.'

Hugo growled, 'The fuck you will.'

'We don't have time to argue.' The words had barely left my mouth when a faint rumble came through the air, immediately followed by a tremor that shook the ground. Several people shrieked and flocks of nesting birds nearby squawked in alarm then took to the skies to flee. Otis and Hester joined them, rising up and flying at high speed to the edge of the square. Good; I needed them to be safe.

Hugo's blue eyes narrowed. 'It appears we don't have time for anything.'

The rumbling intensified and the earthquake grew stronger. I stumbled forward and fell to the ground; the others were also pulled down with heavy thumps. Above the noise of the groaning sky, I heard glass shattering in the windows around us. And then, amid all those sounds, there was an odd whine that seemed to be coming from higher up.

The earth tremors continued to ripple across the square so trying to get to my feet was pointless – I'd only end up flat on my arse again. Instead, I twisted my head and squinted into the night sky to search for the source of the strange sound. I could see a few twinkling stars, some dusky clouds with a glimmer from the moon behind them – and five dark shapes suspended several hundred feet over my head.

As soon as I saw them they started to drop, as if they'd only been waiting for me to notice them. Each shape plummeted downwards as whatever eerie magic that had held them in place was released and gravity took over. Within a heartbeat, I realised that I was looking at five people, all of whom were heading for a messy landing that would doubtless result in their deaths.

A muted squeak escaped my lips and my right hand flailed towards Hugo, grabbing his arm in warning. I felt his body twist to follow my gaze, but before he'd even spotted what was happening I was already at work.

I conjured up a blast of powerful air magic that I directed towards the falling figures. The magic slid out of me easily these days, unhampered by the effects of spider's silk or any concerns I might have about losing control. But supporting five people would take considerable effort.

My air magic slowed their descent, and it helped that Hugo had joined in and flung up some magic of his own. I felt others nearby also respond, sending up their own power, snagging the bodies to lower them safely to the ground.

Sweat dribbled down my forehead as the figure on the right slipped free of the net of magic and fell faster. As I struggled to pull out more magic to capture him, I heard Miriam grunt and sensed her air magic plume upwards and ensnare his body. I released a breath.

That was when a bright, flickering light caught my eye. It was fire: flames had appeared abruptly on the roof of the blood-soaked Royal Institute of Elves.

'Fiend!' somebody screamed. 'That's a fiend!'

Athair's voice boomed out across the square. 'You thought you could try and banish me? *Me?*'

I didn't dare look directly at him, not until the five people overhead were safely on the ground. I clenched my jaw and tried to remain calm so I could focus on the task in hand. *One problem at a time, Daisy, I told myself. Don't let him throw you off balance.*

'You will pay for your pathetic attack!' Athair yelled.

I'd say this about my birth father – he was certainly a fan of melodrama.

I rolled onto my back to get a better view of the descending figures. None of them appeared to be conscious, which was probably a blessing. I didn't recognise them but everything suggested these were the witches employed by the Royal Institute to banish Athair from earthly existence. I certainly didn't feel vindicated that their attempt had failed so easily, I just prayed for their sakes that they were still alive and we weren't focusing our efforts on saving five corpses.

Something reached for me, gripping my ankle with a sudden, steely grip. I yelped, briefly and lost concentration – and lost my hold on my air magic. I half-expected the poor witches above me to drop like stones despite Hugo and the others' magical efforts, but instead each body continued in a slow, controlled descent.

As I glanced down, I realised that it was Gordon Mackenzie who had grabbed me. 'Boonder has them,' he gasped. 'He's drawn a rune that will bring them safely to the ground.'

Thank fuck. As an elf I could call upon magic faster than any sorcerer or witch, but the runic magic that sorcerers employed, although slower, was often more extensive and powerful. I flashed a grateful smile in Gordon's direction and stopped my energy-sapping flow of air, then scrambled to my feet to gaze at Athair.

He hadn't wasted a moment while I'd been busy; he had taken that precious time to create a scene for himself that wouldn't have looked out of place in Dante's Inferno.

He was standing on top of the Royal Institute between two massive chimney stacks. For some reason he'd dressed for the occasion in a top hat and tails. As if his dress and his precarious position on top of the roof weren't enough, he'd also conjured up a backdrop of twenty-foot flames that were licking upwards into the sky. From the way he casually tossed fire around while ignoring the defensive water magic thrown at him from the elves below, it was clear that his intention was to set the building ablaze. Perhaps he planned to destroy the entire square.

Hugo joined my side. 'Look at that outfit. Do you think he's hoping to be the new Fred Astaire?'

'Well, he's missing one Ginger Rogers, if that's the case.'

As if on cue, Athair's head tilted downwards. 'Daughter!' he bellowed. 'Come join me and watch this city burn!'

'I think he wants you to audition for the part,' Hugo said. 'He wants to see your tap-dance routine.'

I snorted. 'I save that for you.'

'True love is a wondrous thing.'

'You should know,' I replied softly as my eyes travelled across the rooftops. 'We could circle around and come at him from behind.'

'He'll see us coming from a mile off.' Hugo pursed his lips. 'We could add fuel to his fire and throw our own fire magic at him. If that destroys the roof and it collapses, he'll fall with it.'

'That will only compound our problems because he'll end up inside the building. At least at the moment we can see where he is and what he's doing.' I looked around the square. There were still two dozen people or so within its perimeter. Right now they were all in danger; our priority had to be ensuring they got away.

There was a shout from behind us. 'We've got them!' Boonder called. 'The witches are down!'

'Are they alive?' I asked, keeping my eyes trained on Athair.

'Yes. Unconscious but breathing.'

As if he'd heard Boonder, Athair zapped out a bolt of lightning towards the witches. I turned and cried out – and so did Boonder when the lightning struck him in the chest. He stared at me with wide eyes and then collapsed without a sound.

Gordon was by his side in seconds. 'There's no pulse!'

Hugo was already running over to them, stripping off his

jacket and preparing to start CPR. I turned back to Athair as he raised his hands and released another bolt of electricity. This time it hit one of the witches who was lying on the cold ground. 'Stop!' I roared.

Even from a distance I could see Athair's answering grin. 'Make me,' he shouted.

I set my shoulders and gave his silhouetted body a hard look. Very well, then.

CHAPTER

THREE

Ignoring the tattered police cordon, I sprinted for the building. I was no Spiderman – I couldn't scale the stone exterior. A push of carefully directed air magic could help me ascend but I'd be open to Athair's machinations if I tried that. Instead I took the slow – albeit sensible – approach of ducking inside and mounting the stairs.

The Royal Institute was full of smoke. There was a lot of expensive artwork on the walls, not to mention a large library packed with priceless books, so there would be a hefty restoration bill to pay once all this was over – assuming the building didn't end up a complete inferno. I ran up each flight of stairs determined to ensure that didn't happen. Although I didn't owe the Royal Institute of Elves a damned thing, wanton destruction was not on my playlist.

The smoke grew thicker the higher I went. By the time I reached the top floor, my eyes were streaming and I was gasping for oxygen. I didn't waste any time on strategy or stealth because Athair already knew I was on my way; I simply turned left into the nearest room and darted for the windows. I hauled one open and breathed in a blessed gulp of fresh air, then I clambered out and clutched onto the window sill to avoid falling.

From the looks of things, Hugo and the others had pulled Boonder to safety at the side of the square. I saw the sorcerer sit up, his hand clutching his chest; he wasn't dead, then. I exhaled with relief and squinted upwards. There were only two metres from the window to the roof: I could climb that far.

Thanking the long-dead architects for their foresight in creating decorative stonework that provided handy foot and finger holds, I scrambled up until my hands curled around the roof's edge. All that training and exercise I'd done with the Primes had served me well; I now had much more upper body strength at my disposal than I'd ever had in the past.

I conjured up a burst of air magic from below to give me the final push I needed then heaved myself onto the rooftop, scalding my fingers on the hot tiles in the process. Athair's figure materialised in front of me on the flat section of the roof.

There was a wall of flames between us – but that didn't stop him from trying to chat. 'You know, Daisy,' he called, 'if you were a fiend, you'd have managed that far more easily. It took you ages to get up here and now you're covered in soot!'

Whose fault was that? I grimaced at his paternal tone and steeled myself, then I drew on as much of the remaining moisture in the air as I could to bring forth a swell of water magic and douse the nearest flames. They hissed and spat angrily, but at least they subsided enough to leave a clear path between Athair and me. I started forward, moving slowly to avoid slipping down this angled section of roof.

I didn't have a plan, which wasn't like me. This time I'd have to wing it.

Athair stayed where he was, watching me edge towards

him. I kept losing my footing, and I was wary of the remaining fire that was still blazing less than five metres away; its blistering heat slowed my progress even further, but I refrained from producing more water magic to extinguish it. I might be able to use those high flames to my advantage. I liked the thought of burning Athair with his own fire.

Eventually he seemed to tire of my snail-like steps, muttered something under his breath and extinguished the fire with a flick of his wrist. He held out his hand to me. Gladys growled at my side but she needn't have worried; I'd be damned before I'd accept his help.

Athair clicked his tongue as if I were nothing more than a wilful child and withdrew his hand when it became clear I wouldn't take it. 'I could have killed half the city – let alone dispatch all your friends down there – in the time it's taken you to get here,.'

I clambered onto the flat section of roof, came to a shaky halt a few feet in front of him and lifted my chin. 'Then why haven't you?'

'I'm not interested in them. I'm only here for you.' His face loomed towards me. 'But I can end their miserable lives now, if you like.'

It was an obvious taunt. I refused to rise to the bait but I did fix him with a hard glare: if looks could kill, I was on a winner. If only. 'Why are you doing this, Athair? What do you want?'

'Well, for starters you could call me Dad.'

My scowl deepened.

'Daddy?' He tipped his head to one side, his golden skin glittering in the moonlight. 'Papa? Pop?'

My patience was growing thin. I took another step towards him in order to move away from the sloping edge. It was fortunate there wasn't much of a breeze because I had enough to deal with without battling the elements as well as my father. The moment I was sure of my footing, I reached across my body and slid Gladys free. She hummed in delight.

Unfortunately, Athair's red eyes lit with pleasure. 'So, daughter,' he drawled, 'you want to dance.'

I didn't waste my breath answering him as I hefted Gladys in my hands. I'd come a long way with my sword training; practising with Gladys had helped to empty my mind and focus on something other than my desperate craving for spider's silk.

I pushed away the tiny voice of doubt deep in my mind that told me that I'd never be strong enough to beat Athair no matter how skilled I became, and I adjusted my stance. He appeared to be weaponless, which was a big tick in my favour, and I knew I could use his confidence against him. I doubted that Athair had ever faced an opponent who could actually kill him but I could – on paper, at least. Whether I could translate that to reality would soon become clear.

My first strike was important. I swung Gladys towards Athair's chest, pushing as much power behind the movement as I could and yelling loudly, using my voice to add weight to my attack,

Instead of his body, my blade met air. 'You're strong,' Athair said. He'd moved with lightning speed and was now standing a few metres to the side of me. 'But you're very slow.' He reached for his top hat and started to remove it.

Brandishing Gladys again, I roared and ran at him. Before I could get close he threw the hat at me, spinning it through the air like a frisbee. It smacked into my face with such force that I reeled, but I didn't stop moving forward. Blinking hard, I kept going, slicing the sword forward with fast, jabby movements. If it was speed he wanted, it was speed I'd give him. I slashed left then right.

Athair avoided my blows easily. I feinted to my right before attacking to my left but he was prepared for that. He used a surge of water magic to yank Gladys's tip away from his body. 'Careful, daughter,' he murmured. 'I like this suit. I'd hate to see it ruined.'

I responded with a blast of my own water magic, conjuring it with enough force to drench him and make him stagger, then took advantage of his momentary vulnerability to leap at him again. But before Gladys could slice into the exposed golden skin of his throat, he launched a kick at me. The heel of his shoe caught my stomach and I doubled over in pain.

'You snared me with water magic once before,' Athair said. 'You won't manage it again.' He paused. 'Speaking of which, how was your trip back to the past? I'd love to know more about how you managed that.'

I pulled myself upright and jerked Gladys's blade upwards. I intended to slash at his legs but my thrust wasn't strong enough. Athair kicked again, this time aiming his foot at Gladys and knocking her away before she could cut into his flesh. Despite my best efforts, she was wrenched from my grasp and she clattered as she hit the roof.

Athair rolled his eyes and flicked out a burst of air magic that smacked me in the chest and sent me sprawling inches from the roof's angled slope. 'I grow bored with these antics,' I heard him say.

He appeared over me, raised his foot for a third time and pressed it against my chest, forcing the air from my lungs. 'We do not have to fight, Daisy. I didn't come here to provoke an argument, I came to extend an invitation. I can see that you might need a little enticement to listen to me.'

I clenched my jaw and conjured a bolt of electricity that arced upwards and hit him. He barely even blinked; instead, he increased the pressure on my chest, winked and, with a casual smirk, clicked his fingers.

The air sparked and a small fireball appeared. It was less than an inch wide but then it started to grow. While I gasped for air and tried to jerk free from his foot, the fireball became larger and larger. I heard shouts of alarm from below.

The heat was intense. 'How many of your friends do you think I can take out with this?' Athair asked, his casual tone making his threat even more chilling. 'Several at least. I can still see dozens of people down there – they should have run when they had the chance. And I can destroy the surrounding buildings. I wonder if they've all been evacuated. To be honest, I'd quite like to destroy that statue of Prince Albert in the middle of the square, too. That man always annoyed me.'

The fireball rose up until it was hovering above his head and it continued to grow. The fucking thing was immense – and so was its destructive power.

Athair grinned nastily. 'How pretty will that annoying boyfriend of yours be when he has third-degree burns all over his body?'

The fireball started to drop towards the square, growing in size and speed with every inch it travelled. I heard high-pitched screams: people were still down there, though I couldn't tell who was in danger. I couldn't see anything beyond the ball of flames, the night sky and Athair's smug, hateful features. But I could imagine.

'Stop,' I croaked.

Athair continued as if hadn't heard me. 'I'm told that burning to death is one of the most painful ways to go, so at these temperatures it will be agonising. First your skin blisters, then your flesh starts to melt, your own body fat sizzling as you're—'

The fireball dipped out of view. I raised my voice and repeated, 'Stop!'

Athair paused and looked down at me. 'Oh,' he said with

faux innocence, 'you want to watch? You should have said.' He removed his foot from my chest, grabbed the front of my shirt and hauled me to my feet. As he did, I felt a wave of magic surge up from below. Thank goodness.

I glanced down and saw the small collection of assembled elves, plus Hugo, Miriam, Rizwan and Becky and a smattering of others who had joined them. They'd combined their powers to blast the encroaching fireball with water magic of their own.

A wide grin spread across my face as they doused it, extinguishing its might in one fell swoop. Go, team.

Athair looked neither surprised nor annoyed, and my smile vanished. He'd expected that to happen; if he'd wanted to set alight the group below, he could have done it without a slow-moving fireball. The stark truth was that he could kill anyone at any time. This was about putting on a show and proving a point.

My thoughts must have shown on my face because he nodded. 'I don't need to hurt anyone. Being a fiend doesn't mean I'm compelled to murder – the power I possess is about much more than mere life and death. I don't take pleasure in killing anyone unnecessarily.'

I jerked my thumb at the building's façade. 'Oh really?' I asked coolly. 'What about your bloody message? How many unnecessary deaths did it take to create *that*?'

'Perhaps the blood donors were evil. Perhaps they deserved to die. Perhaps it was not me who killed them.' He tilted his head, dark amusement flashing in his scarlet eyes. 'Besides, they served a purpose. Would you be here now if I'd used paint? I wanted to talk to you so I sent you a message and here you are.' He paused. 'Talking. My plan worked.'

'You know, there's a great invention you might have heard about,' I said sarcastically. 'It's called a telephone.'

'Don't be facetious, darling, it doesn't suit you. We both

know you would never answer my call.' He spread his arms wide. 'I want to get to know you. I want you to get to know me. Is that so very much to ask?'

I turned my head and my eyes landed on Gladys; she was only a few metres away but it might as well have been a mile. Even if I held her in my sweaty hands, I couldn't beat Athair. I couldn't even come close – but that didn't mean I had to yield.

'You told me once that I had free will,' I said, surprising myself with how clear and calm my voice was. 'So I'm exercising that free will. I don't want anything to do with you, not now, not ever.'

Athair linked his fingers and gazed at me in a fatherly fashion that made my intestines recoil. 'Your opinion of me has been warped by others. You don't know the real me, Daisy. Is it so much to ask that you get to know me instead of listening to nasty gossip?'

It was considerably more than gossip. 'Get out of my life,' I hissed.

He smiled. 'No.' He released his fingers, leaned to the side and pointed down. 'I'll take that one,' he said.

I didn't know what he meant but I felt a chill through my bones. 'Athair, don't do anything rash,' I said, trying not to allow panic to overtake me. 'Don't—'

'I told you that I'd like you to call me Dad,' he said mildly. His words were followed immediately by a sharp scream.

I looked down and saw Detective Inspector O'Hagan twist upwards as she rose through the air as a result of Athair's magic. The elves tried to counter it but even their combined efforts were no match for Athair.

Sir Nigel leapt upwards, grabbed O'Hagan's ankle and tried to haul her down. Athair gazed at him for a moment then shrugged. 'Two for the price of one,' he said. 'I guess I'll take him too.'

I snarled and threw myself at him. Without even glancing in my direction, he slammed out a powerful burst of magic to hold me back. Sir Nigel and O'Hagan continued to rise in the air as I scrambled to my feet, sparks dancing around my fingertips.

I'd throw everything I had at him. *Everything.* I'd beaten the fiend Baltar by doing that – I hadn't killed him but I'd certainly stopped him in his tracks. I'd do the same to Athair. I sucked in a breath, preparing to act.

'You wouldn't want me to drop your friends in mid-air, would you, Daisy?' he asked.

Hugo and the others would catch them before they hit the ground so I didn't have to worry on that score – but then Athair tossed a third burst of magic. There were more yells on the ground as flames erupted across the square. Hugo – and everyone else – suddenly had their hands full avoiding the fires and trying to extinguish them at the same time. Athair smirked.

I released my breath and my shoulders sagged. 'Please,' I said. 'Stop.'

'Agree to have dinner with me tomorrow night and I will.'

I stared at him. That's what he wanted? All this for a fucking meal?

'It's your choice, Daisy,' he said softly. 'You know I could end the existence of everyone here. I don't want to do that but I will.' He paused. 'Give me your word that you'll have dinner with me tomorrow. Two hours of your company, that's all I'm asking for. Give me that and I'll walk away now.'

O'Hagan was screaming as both she and Sir Nigel hovered in mid-air. They'd risen so high that they'd drawn level with us and I turned my head to look at them. Sir Nigel's lips were moving but I couldn't tell what he was saying. I'd never seen him look so pale.

I knew that you should never negotiate with terrorists but I was on my own and out of options. 'Fine,' I snapped. 'I'll have dinner with you. Once.'

'Fantastic,' Athair said. 'I will send a car for you at six o'clock prompt.'

And then, before I could say another word, there was a sudden, blinding flash of light.

CHAPTER

FOUR

It took several moments for my vision to readjust. Even though my senses told me that Athair had gone, I knew I was still vulnerable. I waved my arms around blindly until first a few lights and then a few dim shapes appeared from the blackness. Only when I was certain that my fucking father wasn't still beside me on the rooftop did some of my tension ease.

Hearing a groan, I spun around and spotted Sir Nigel and O'Hagan lying flat on their backs a few metres away. I knelt beside them. 'Are you alright?' I asked desperately.

Sir Nigel coughed. 'Slightly winded, but I'll live to fight another day.' He strained to sit up while O'Hagan blinked at me.

'You were right,' she said shakily. 'I should have run.' She shook her head. 'I've dealt with a lot of supernatural creatures since I joined the force but I've never felt anything like the cold power that came from that man.'

Although there was no trace of censure in her gaze, I felt guilty. That was my birth father she was talking about, and he'd only come here because of me. Rationally I knew none of this was my fault but emotionally it felt like it was all my responsibility.

As the detective ran a hand through her hair, she glanced over my shoulder and stiffened. A frisson of fear rippled through me until I heard the brownies' voices and realised who had appeared.

'Daisy! Are you okay? Did he hurt you?' Otis cried.

I managed a smile. 'No.'

Hester flung herself at me and I felt her tiny body trembling against my skin. 'I was so worried! What happened?'

'You vanquished him, right?' Otis's eyes were wide. 'You attacked him with Gladys and killed him. That light was when his soul left his body.'

Hester snapped at her brother, 'He's a fiend, you nincompoop! He doesn't have a soul!' But all the same she pulled back and gave me an anxious, questioning glance.

I sighed heavily. 'He left of his own accord when I agreed to have dinner with him tomorrow night.'

Otis's expression changed in an instant. 'You did *what?*' he shrieked.

Hester started to nod vigorously. 'Clever. Now you can take him down when he's least expecting it.'

'I can't take him down.' I stalked across the roof to pick up Gladys. 'I'm not strong enough to come close to hurting him.' And I was beginning to think I never would be.

There was a dull thud from the other side of the roof. I stiffened and spun round, prepared to launch another attack if I had to. Instead a small hatch flipped open and a familiar tawny-haired head appeared. I stared. 'Was that hatch there the whole time?'

Hugo pulled himself onto the roof. 'Of course. Maintenance have to get onto the roof from time to time. They can't clamber around with a death wish like you seem to possess.'

'Believe me,' I muttered, 'if I'd known there was an easier route up here, I'd have taken it.' I stalked towards Hugo, paused in front of him then flung myself into his arms. 'Boonder?' I mumbled the question into his shoulder, terrified of the answer.

'He's on his way to hospital but I think he'll be fine. There are several others with minor burns and cuts. I don't know about the witches who confronted Athair and tried to banish him. They've not regained consciousness.'

I prayed silently that they would be alright, then I burrowed myself deeper against Hugo's body. That was the only moment of the entire night that hadn't sucked complete arse.

IT WAS VERY LATE by the time we got back into the Jeep. Miriam, Rizwan and Becky decided against returning to Pemberville Castle until the next day. Despite my new ownership of a damned castle up north, I still held the lease on my small Edinburgh flat so Hugo and I elected to head there to get some much-needed sleep.

There were still a lot of people on the streets. Naturally the events at Charlotte Square had drawn a number of foolish onlookers who should have known better and who could easily have ended up as charred corpses if Athair had chosen a different path. And they weren't the only people around: a few pubs and restaurants with late licences remained open and there were vehicles on the road and pedestrians on the pavement.

Hugo turned away from Edinburgh Castle and drove up Market Street. A group of university students were clustered on the corner, leaning into each other and grinning with the joyous expressions of the very drunk and the very innocent. I felt a tug of wistful envy, then they were in our rear-view mirror.

I yanked my gaze away and stiffened as we passed the entrance to Fleshmarket Close and the steep, dark steps that led upwards. No doubt Arbuthnot the bogle would be up there somewhere, peddling his illegal wares. I wondered how much spider's silk he had to hand and what the going rate was this month for a dozen pills .

I cleared my throat awkwardly. 'Stop the car, Hugo.'

'Here?'

I nodded. 'Don't wait for me. I'll grab a taxi back afterwards.'

'Don't be stupid,' he muttered. He indicated and pulled into the side of the road. 'The brownies and I will be right here for you when you're done.'

I quashed the guilt and embarrassment and kissed his cheek. Then I got out of the car.

The adrenaline from the encounter with Athair had already faded and there was a strange, empty feeling inside me. The night air felt colder now, although it was probably no different; the only change was the absence of dangerous magical fires flaring up out of nowhere.

I shoved my hands in my pockets and crossed the road, marching up the High Street until I reached the other side of Fleshmarket Close. From its depths, I could hear the faint murmur of voices but they were too low to make out any distinct words.

I didn't hesitate but scurried past, heading for the lights of the small church instead. The rush of warmth as I walked through the doors helped, and I kept my head high as I strolled into the meeting room and took a seat.

Several heads turned towards me, some in recognition. Meetings like this were available at all hours. They had to be.

'Hi,' I said. 'My name is Daisy Carter and I'm a drug addict.'

~

I KNEW I ought to get out of bed; given the events of the previous night – and what was to come later today – there was a lot to think about and even more to do. I'd slept soundly enough and it was clear from the chink of light shining through the gap in the curtains that the sun was already high in the sky, but I couldn't bring myself to move. I was too comfortable where I was, with the duvet wrapped around my legs and Hugo's body pressed against my back, his breath tickling my nape.

'*Busy old fool, unruly sun,*' Hugo whispered into my ear. '*Why dost thou thus, Through windows, and through curtains call on us?*'

I squinted. 'Huh?'

'John Donne. Something about being here with you makes me want to quote poetry.' He laughed softly. 'My old English teacher would be shocked.'

'I could return the favour and recite "Ode to the Penis" to you,' I suggested slyly. I'd come across the poem during our last big treasure hunt when we'd tracked down a golden chess set – and Athair had revealed himself to me.

'Rather than recite,' he said, 'you could show my heavenly penis your appreciation instead. Or,' he nibbled my earlobe, 'you could fetch a bowl of chocolate ice cream and feed it to me for breakfast *then* show your appreciation.'

I snorted. 'You're very demanding for someone who's supposedly in thrall to me.'

'There's no "supposedly" about it.' He dipped his head and planted very small, albeit very tingly kisses along my jawline.

I moaned slightly. 'Chocolate ice cream is not a healthy breakfast.'

Hugo's left hand snaked downwards and cupped my breast

while the base of his thumb brushed against my nipple. His right hand caressed my hip. 'In that case,' he murmured, 'I'll forego the ice cream and have you for breakfast instead.'

'Except I'm not very healthy to be around at the moment either.' I turned over to face him. 'Do you think I did the right thing?'

Hugo's hands halted in their roving quest and his expression grew serious. 'With Athair?' I nodded. 'What else could you have done? He left you with little choice.'

'If I trained harder, maybe I'd be more equipped to beat him in a fight.'

Hugo stiffened. 'And you'd give him even more reason to stop trying to turn you into a fiend like him and strike you dead. You can't let that happen. *I* can't let that happen. I can't do this without you.'

'This?'

His voice was gruff. 'Life.' He took my hand and placed it flat against his chest; I could feel his heartbeat beneath my fingertips. 'You're a part of me now, Daisy. You occupy me, body and soul. And nobody, not even Athair, will take you away from me or change that.' There was a loud clang from the other room followed by a furious yell from Hester. 'Not even those damned brownies,' he muttered.

I smiled slightly. 'I love you.'

Hugo didn't smile back. 'I love you too. You don't know what it does to me when you keep putting yourself in harm's way.'

'You're in greater danger than I am.' We both knew that Athair would happily hurt anyone I loved if he thought it would advance his cause.

'You're the one he wants.'

'You're the one he'll kill when he doesn't get what he wants.'

Hugo was silent for a second, then he said, 'You're right. So really, when it comes down to it, I'm still a bigger hero than you are.'

I rolled my eyes in exasperation but I also grinned. 'Piss off.'

Hugo smirked and planted a kiss on my mouth. 'That's more like it.' He kissed me again. 'I'm going to prove that I'm more of a hero than you tonight. While you're off being wined and dined, I'm going to take advantage of the situation.'

I stared at him. 'And do what?'

'Snoop around Culcreuch Castle. Tonight is the one time when we know Athair won't be there. It's the perfect opportunity to sneak into his lair and learn everything we can about him.'

My breath caught. 'That's incredibly risky, Hugo.'

He grinned. 'I know. That's why I'm the bigger hero.'

This time I didn't respond with a teasing remark. 'I mean it. If something happens to you…' My voice trailed off and I couldn't finish the sentence.

'It'll break you. It'll shatter you into a million pieces.'

I nodded mutely.

'Now you know how I feel every time you put yourself in danger,' he said. 'We'll just have to be very careful.' He pulled me closer. 'We're a team,' he said in my ear. 'Always.'

FIVE

I waited for Athair at Pemberville Castle, Hugo's ancestral home in Perthshire. As the crow flies, it was only thirty or so miles from the old castle that Athair occupied, but my presence at Pemberville was as much a test of Athair's knowledge of my whereabouts as a plan to help Hugo breach Culcreuch Castle. My fiendish father had said he'd send a car for me but he hadn't said *where* he'd send that car. I wanted to know if he was keeping close tabs on me.

When a taxi pulled up in front of Hugo's ancestral home at 5.59pm, I knew that he was.

I hadn't dressed up for the occasion but neither had I dressed down. I didn't want to give any thought to how I looked so I was wearing the same clothes I'd pulled on that morning – although Gladys was sheathed by my side as per usual. I certainly wouldn't give Athair the satisfaction of thinking that I'd been anxiously preparing for this meeting.

In contrast, Hugo was fully equipped. He was wearing tight black clothes so that he could use the dark night to his advantage and not worry about snagging loose material on sharp corners – it was imperative that he left no trace of himself behind. Our only advantage against Athair at that moment was that he was unaware that we knew where he was living, and we desperately wanted to keep it that way. Fortunately, most of the Primes were prepared to provide back-up, although Hugo had forbidden any of them from entering Culcreuch Castle with him.

'Don't let him into your mind,' Hugo cautioned me as we prepared to leave. 'He'll try and manipulate you at every turn. Keep your barriers up at all times.'

'We'll follow you all the way, Daisy,' Miriam said. 'Slim and I will be ready to extract you. If you make the signal, we'll be there.'

Hell would freeze over before I did that; I wouldn't put them in danger, no matter what happened. I'd already argued that they should stay with the others to help Hugo but unfortunately nobody had listened to me. I had work to do on becoming a hoity-toity high elf whose orders were followed without question; that was going to take more than a title and a castle of my own to achieve.

'Don't get caught,' I said to Hugo. 'And don't die.'

'Same to you.' His voice was light but I recognised the trace of fear in his velvet-blue eyes because I shared it. I swallowed then gestured to Hester and Otis. They looked as nervous as I felt, but they flew up and took position on my shoulders. The brownies were under strict instructions to pay attention to everything but to keep their mouths tightly closed. I doubted they'd comply, but their presence would be incredibly useful because there would be less chance that I missed any nuances or misconstrued Athair's words. And they knew not to linger if this all went tits up.

'Let's do this,' I said. I stood tall and walked out.

The taxi driver stayed in his cab and didn't even roll his window down, a smart move on his part because Duchess had emerged from underneath her bridge and was eyeing him with a predatory gleam.

'Stand down,' I told the troll. The last thing any of us needed was her intervention.

She pursed her lips and put her hands on her hips. 'He doesn't look so scary,' she said. 'I reckon I can take him on and solve all your problems, girlie.'

I sighed. 'That's not Athair. That's the taxi driver who will take us to Athair.'

'Oh.' She stared at the poor man, who did his best not to look in her direction, then she shrugged her heavy shoulders. 'Very well then.'

She clapped me on the back making me stagger forwards. 'I'd say it's been nice knowing you but I'd be lying. Enjoy your last few hours. I'll tell Lord Snoot Face not to cry too much once you're gone.' She raised a hairless eyebrow. 'Although between you and me, he's been far too jolly recently. His constant good mood is grating on my nerves – and that's all your fault.'

I'd happily take responsibility for putting a smile on Hugo's face. I curtsied towards her, then spun on my heel and headed for the taxi.

'You can change your mind, Daisy,' Otis urged.

'Yeah,' Hester agreed. 'Stab the driver while you've got the chance. If he can't drive then you can't travel to have dinner with Athair.'

I ignored them and paused at the passenger door to glance at Hugo. Our eyes met for one long moment. I crossed my fingers, got into the back of the cab and prayed that he'd still be in one piece in a few hours' time.

❧

I TRIED to engage the taxi driver in conversation several times during the journey but he was determined not to play ball. I strongly suspected that Athair had instructed him not to talk to me – and he certainly wasn't allowed to tell me where we were going.

I was still nervous that we'd turn into the grounds of Culcreuch Castle and Athair would blow all our plans out of the water by welcoming me with a sly wink, but we drove past the narrow side road that led to it and continued towards Bridge of Allan, a village on the outskirts of Stirling.

I tried not to look relieved as Culcreuch receded in the distance and surreptitiously checked the rear-view mirror. I couldn't see any sign of Slim and Miriam behind us; that was good because if I couldn't see them, neither could anyone else.

Eventually we pulled into the car park of a well-lit restaurant. It was peak time and there were a lot of other vehicles nearby. I could hear chatter and inoffensive pop music drifting out from the restaurant's open windows. My eyes narrowed.

Out of habit I reached for my wallet, but the driver grunted and indicated with his hand that the fare had already been taken care of. Then he cleared his throat and shocked me by delivering not one but two full sentences in a thick Glaswegian accent. 'I am under orders to tell you that I will wait here until your meal is finished. Then I shall drive you back.'

Clearly this was Athair's way of telling me that I would be able to leave the restaurant safely once the meal was over. It wasn't *my* safety that I was worried about, but I smiled and thanked the driver anyway. None of this was his fault.

I climbed out of the taxi and walked slowly towards the restaurant's front door. 'Is it just me,' Hester asked, 'or is this rather disappointing?'

Otis frowned. 'What do you mean, Hes?'

'Athair is the most powerful fiend in the country, he's been around for centuries and the only thing greater than his wealth is his magic.' She pointed. 'And *this* is where he brings his only daughter for their first meal together?'

'First and last meal together,' I corrected grimly.

Otis squinted at the restaurant. 'What's wrong with it?'

'What's wrong with *you*?' Hester demanded. 'This place isn't special, Otis. I don't need to look at the menu to know there won't be an extensive wine list or an exquisite tasting menu. This is the sort of place that does shepherd's pie, fish and chips and chicken in a basket.' She shuddered as if those were the things of nightmares.

Actually this restaurant was exactly where I would have chosen to eat, and that worried me more than almost anything else. 'It's a typical family place,' I said aloud and nodded towards the other cars. 'Normal families come here to eat normal food. Athair is trying to pretend that's what we are – normal. And it's a busy night with plenty of customers, so he's also making sure I won't ruin the evening by stabbing him over the prawn-cocktail starter. Everything Athair does is by design.' My voice hardened. '*Everything.*'

'Cumbubbling bollocks,' Otis whispered.

Indeed.

The atmosphere inside was exactly as I'd expected: warm, inviting and friendly. My spirits sank further while my skin itched from head to toe. I managed a smile at the waiter who greeted us and gave him my name. He pointed at a table where an older man was waiting. As we walked over, I reminded Hester and Otis to stay quiet and out of the way. They nodded solemnly.

The man stood up and spoke to me in Athair's voice. 'Good evening, Daisy.' He dipped his head towards the brownies but didn't remark on their presence then gestured to the free chair. I sat down stiffly and Athair returned to his seat opposite me.

I sighed. This was going to be a long night.

'I apologise for my appearance.' He pointed to his face which was as human as the waiter's. 'I'm sure you understand that I couldn't appear in my natural form as it is now. This body seemed acceptable for tonight.'

I supposed I should have been grateful that he'd not taken on Hugo's body as he had the first time we'd met. It wasn't lost on me that the face Athair was wearing had generous features and kindly laughter lines; it was yet another part of his game.

I shrugged as if I didn't care what he looked like. 'Who does this face belong to?'

'Does it matter?'

I guessed not. I folded my arms to make it very clear that I was here under duress and waited. There was only so much polite conversation I could make and that one question had already used up my quota for the evening.

Athair watched me for a long moment. 'Your antagonism is palpable,' he said eventually.

Hester snorted loudly. When his gaze flicked to her, she immediately squeaked and zipped behind me for cover. Athair didn't bother to hide his amusement.

'I know you've been told that all fiends are hateful creatures wholly imbued with evil,' he said, 'but you shouldn't believe everything that you hear. And you should remember that people always hate and fear what they do not understand.'

He leaned forward. 'Why do you think my existence is kept hidden from most of the population? Places like the Royal Elvish Institute are determined to hide the truth, namely that great power and wisdom can be gained from allowing yourself to become a fiend. They want to keep all the power for themselves.' There was a nugget of truth in Athair's words – but only a nugget.

Otis glared at him. 'What have you ever done that's not been evil?'

Athair didn't take his gaze from me. 'I didn't continue searching for your mother to kill her for keeping you from me. I am capable of restraint, Daisy.'

I was supposed to applaud him for not killing Rose? Unbelievable. 'How many people *have* you killed?' I asked coolly.

Triumph flared in his eyes; he'd succeeded in engaging me in conversation. I clamped down the burst of annoyance I felt at my inability to remain quiet and waited for his answer. 'Too many,' he said. 'And yet not enough.'

Icy fingers clutched at my heart.

'Good evening, folks!' I jumped and turned to the cheerful waiter who'd appeared at the side of our table. If he was aware of any tension he didn't show it, he simply grinned and presented us with two menus. 'Our specials today are on the board behind the bar. I can recommend the hake. It was freshly caught this morning and the chef has created a wonderful cream sauce to go with it. We have a small wine list, if you'd like to see it.'

I shook my head. Alcohol free all the way for me. 'Water is fine,' I said.

Athair tutted. 'I'll have a double Scotch on the rocks. Macallan, if you have it.'

The waiter made a note. 'Do you have any dietary requirements or allergies?'

Hester, who remained in hiding behind my back, piped up. 'No strawberries!'

The waiter took a step back and his eyes swung to me with alarm. When he spotted Otis, he took another step away from us. 'Fucking hell!' Then his cheeks coloured. 'Uh, sorry.' He backed away further. 'Sorry. I've never seen fairies before.'

That was enough to draw Hester out. 'We're brownies!' she protested.

The waiter swallowed hard. 'Okay.' His knuckles tightened on his notepad. 'We don't have a menu for brownies.'

'It's fine,' I reassured him. 'When you bring our drinks, I'm sure we'll be ready to order food. These two will share my meal.'

He swallowed again. A heartbeat later, he was scurrying to the bar and doing his best not to look scared. Brownies were incredibly rare but his reaction was still extreme: they were hardly threatening creatures.

'You see?' Athair said softly. 'People always treat the unknown with trepidation. That young man is terrified of your two pets, even though they couldn't harm him in the slightest.'

'You wanna bet?' Hester snarled.

'And we are not Daisy's pets!' Otis said. 'We're her equals. She has always treated us as equals.'

Athair smirked. I wouldn't let myself be side-tracked. 'What did you mean when you said you've killed too many people but not enough?'

His answer was measured, or perhaps that was just what he wanted me to think. 'I have been alive for a long time. Times were very different when I was your age. They were ... bloodier. Even before I made my transformation, I often had to defend myself. As you have also had to do,' he said, reminding me that I had also killed. But it wasn't the same; it couldn't be.

'However,' Athair continued, 'when I came into this world, the population was less than five hundred million. Now it is close to eight billion. That is not a sustainable number.'

'That's your justification for murder? Over-population?' I sneered.

'No. But it is *a* justification. I will not apologise for the deaths I have caused, Daisy, and I will not promise to refrain from causing more deaths in the future. But given I could click my fingers now and strike every person in this restaurant stone dead, I think I show far more restraint than you give me credit for.'

He was unbelievable. I was finding it harder and harder to keep my temper. 'Just because you can do something doesn't mean you should do it. And you haven't answered my question. How many people have you actually killed?'

He gazed at me impassively. 'I don't keep count because to do that would truly be evil.'

A different waiter appeared. 'Here are your drinks,' he said. He didn't look directly at Hes and Otis but at least he appeared less frightened of them than the last guy had been. 'Are you ready to order?'

I hadn't even glanced at the menu. I flipped it open and picked the first thing I saw. 'The mushroom tagliatelle, please.'

Athair looked down. No doubt he'd choose the rarest, bloodiest steak he could manage. 'I'll have the vegetarian burger,' he said.

I stared at him.

'I hate killing things unnecessarily,' he told the waiter with a brief smile.

My hands curled into fists.

As soon as the waiter had made a note of the order and departed, Athair took a sip of his whisky and smiled at me. 'You have it all wrong, Daisy. Being a fiend isn't about death, it's about life. Very long life. Think of all the good that you could do when you have the experience and the time to create whatever you want. Fiends have the opportunity to be the best at everything.'

He was trying to appeal to my competitive nature but he didn't understand that competition was at its finest when everyone was on a level playing field.

'You care about nothing but yourself and your power,' I said.

'*Au contraire*, my dove.' He raised his glass. 'I care about you.'

'If that were true, you'd leave me in peace.'

'Why would I do that when I could give you so much?' Athair asked. 'When you could become so great if you only allow the scales to fall from your eyes? Together, Daisy, we could become a true force. Our family will be the stuff of legends.'

'Don't listen to him!' Otis hissed in my ear.

He didn't need to worry. I lifted my glass of water and eyed Athair. 'Except I'm already a legend in my own right,' I said simply. 'I don't need you. I'll *never* need you.'

I caught the briefest glimpse of anger in his eyes. 'You will if I kill the other one, the gimp who pretends to be your father but who could never, *ever* compete with me,' he said. I knew from the quiet force behind every word that it wasn't an idle threat: Athair was genuinely considering it.

Horror lit through me. I'd gone too far. I couldn't provoke Athair, couldn't make him any more angry because if I did there was no telling what he would do in return. I tried my best to act casually so he didn't realise how much his words terrified me. To keep my real dad – and the rest of my family – safe, I had to be clever in my response.

'It might have escaped your notice,' I said, 'but I'm now an adult. My adoptive parents are in England – we're not even in the same country any more. I am my own person and I make my own decisions. You can't sway me to your side with violence or bribes.'

'We shall see, daughter. We shall see.' He smiled, which I hoped meant the danger had passed. He looked away from me. 'Ah, I believe our meals are on their way.' He patted his stomach. 'Excellent. I'm starving.'

I didn't say a word. Unsurprisingly, I didn't have an appetite.

46

CHAPTER
SIX

I picked at my food and spent most of my time moving it around my plate. I couldn't finish too quickly because I'd promised Athair two hours – and I had to allow Hugo enough time to sneak around Culcreuch Castle. So I continued to push the pasta from one side of the plate to another and occasionally nibbled on a mushroom. Every second was excruciating.

Athair felt no such compunction about eating his dinner although he did attack his burger with a knife and fork, which baffled the brownies as much as it did me.

'Never trust anyone who eats a burger with cutlery,' Hester said in an overly loud voice.

Fortunately, Athair chose not to take offence. 'It's hard to break a habit that has been formed over several hundred years.'

Otis was growing bolder. 'We lost over a hundred years when we were ensorcelled into a locket. We have adapted.'

'That's probably because you've had the help of my wonderful daughter.' Athair looked at me. 'Despite the old saying, you can actually teach an old dog new tricks. Just think what you could teach me, Daisy. With your influence, I could become a completely different person.'

Adapting your habits in order to hold a burger in your hands was slightly different to learning not to kill anyone who got in your way. 'You are free to eat your food however you desire,' I said icily.

He bared his teeth in a grin, put down his knife and fork and picked up the remainder of his burger with his hands. He took a huge bite, chewed, swallowed and smacked his lips. 'Mmm. Look! I can learn. In fact, to prove it's not a one-off, and because it seems to bother you so much, I will abstain from killing anyone for the next forty days.'

Forty days, I thought sarcastically. Woo-hoo.

'I'll even leave those two elves outside alone,' Athair continued without missing a beat. I looked up, startled. 'You know, the ones who followed you all the way here. The old woman and her male sidekick. I was going to ask my man to take care of them while we had dessert, but your presence has encouraged me towards benevolence.'

'Stab him, Daisy!' Hester hissed. 'Cut off his head and let's get out of here.'

Athair whistled. 'Such violence – and yet you castigate me for far less.'

'If you harm a hair on either Slim or Miriam's head...' I said, unable to stop myself.

'Then you'll do what?' He seemed genuinely curious. 'You know that you can't beat me. Unless you choose to become a fiend yourself, you will never be strong enough to match me.' He raised his index finger. 'Now there's a thought you should consider. Become a fiend and you might have a chance against me.'

I stared at him. 'You're crazy.'

'No, I'm not. I meant it when I said I care about you, Daisy.

I've waited a long time for a child of my own. If your rise means my demise, so be it. I can finally go to my grave knowing that I have created something wonderful. You have so much untapped potential – you can't begin to imagine what you're truly capable of.'

I assumed that he believed that if I became a fiend I would want to join him, not kill him. He was prepared to use any argument to encourage me.

'I dare you,' he said. 'I can teach you a little blood magic, if you like. You can see what it's like.'

'Fuck off.' I shoved a forkful of cold pasta into my mouth. Athair chuckled.

I swallowed the mouthful. I was nearing the end of my tether. 'What did you mean when you said you were going to ask your man? Were you too chicken to come here alone? Did you feel the need to bring back-up?'

'I wondered if you'd pick up on that.' He smiled slyly. 'Despite the current mood, there are some enlightened beings who understand that fiends are not all bad. I can introduce you.'

I scowled. 'There's no need.'

Athair dabbed at his mouth with a napkin. 'No, I insist.' He pushed his chair back and waved through the restaurant window towards the dark car park. 'He'll only be a moment.'

'If you think you can bring a mindless vampire in here...' I began.

Athair pulled a face. 'Please. Vampires have their uses but their scope is limited. Vargas was far fonder of their kind than I've ever been.' He was referring to the fiend I'd killed when I'd time-travelled back to 1994. 'But then you know that already. This ... friend of mine is something quite different. He's not very bright but he's far better at conversation and far more useful than a mere bloodsucker.'

I heard the bell jangle as the restaurant door opened,

followed by several gasps from the diners at the tables around us. Against my better judgment, I yielded to my curiosity and looked around. When I saw who was lumbering towards us, I froze.

Hester and Otis, who'd never had the dubious joy of meeting Arbuthnot, frowned at each other. 'I didn't think this would be the sort of place a bogle would frequent,' Otis said.

Hester eyed my erstwhile drug dealer. 'And he doesn't even look like a *nice* bogle.'

He wasn't *that* bad – at least, that's what I'd thought when I'd needed his services. I wondered if Athair had threatened him, or if Arbuthnot had joined the side of pure evil of his own free will.

Whatever his reason for being there, he certainly wasn't trying to conceal himself. He knocked over several chairs on his way to us and jostled three wide-eyed customers, one of whom choked on her glass of wine. He didn't pay them any attention; his focus was entirely on us.

The second waiter who'd served us might have been relaxed around the brownies but he didn't feel that way about bogles. He stumbled over and twisted his hands together before he fixed his anxious eyes on Athair. 'Uh, is this gentleman joining you?' he asked. It was obvious what he wanted the answer to be.

Athair, still presenting himself as a kindly older gentleman, smiled benevolently. 'Yes.'

The waiter swallowed, his anxiety growing by the second. 'I'm not sure that we have a chair that will accommodate him.'

'Told you,' Otis muttered. 'This is probably the first bogle that's ever walked in here.'

Athair's expression changed dramatically: his gaze hardened and despite his genial features there was now a definite air of menace about him. This was the real Athair, I was certain of it.

'What kind of establishment are you running here?' he snapped at the poor waiter.

It wasn't so much that bogles were large creatures – although they were – but that their bone density was far higher than that of most other beings. I didn't need to see Arbuthnot sit on any of the restaurant's chairs to know that they would collapse under his weight, and I doubted that would go down well with either him or Athair. Neither did the restaurant staff deserve to be killed because their chairs weren't reinforced against bogles.

As much as I wanted the bogle to disappear as quickly as possible, I couldn't afford a confrontation so I sprang up and pointed to an empty table. 'Why don't we move there?' I suggested. 'He can sit on the window seat.' It would be stronger than any of the chairs.

And then, because I didn't want to give Athair the satisfaction of thinking he'd discomfited me by producing my ex-drug dealer, I forced a brilliant smile onto my face. 'It's so wonderful to see you again, Arbuthnot.' I even stood up and kissed his rough cheek, much to everyone's astonishment. When I glanced at Athair, however, instead of disappointment that I remained calm, I saw amused pride at my antics. Damn it.

We shifted over to the new table without too much faff, although everyone in the restaurant held their breath when Arbuthnot sat down on the window seat. It creaked ominously but didn't collapse. Praise be.

He ordered a fruity cocktail, of all things. When the waiter had gone, he reached into his pocket and pulled out a small silver box. He didn't smile but he did waggle his eyebrows suggestively and my stomach sank to my shoes. Oh no. *Oh no.*

'Go ahead,' Athair told him, proving that the bogle was

nothing more than a puppet dangling on his fiendish strings. Arbuthnot grunted and opened the box.

There were no prizes for guessing what was inside. I allowed myself one fleeting glance before I looked away. I didn't need to taste the bitter fizz on my tongue to know that these were high-quality pills. Whichever illegal lab they'd come from, the techs had taken the time to brand each one with a tiny spider and give them a glossy white finish. Only the most expensive and well-made spider's silk looked like that.

My fingers twitched and a gnawing hunger attacked my whole body; it would take a lot more than cold mushroom pasta to satisfy my physical needs now. Wishing that my hand wasn't trembling, I took a sip of water and resolved to pretend that the pills didn't exist.

Neither Otis nor Hester had any such compunction.

Otis hissed and spat at Arbuthnot like an angry cat. 'You don't need spider's silk, Daisy! You're clean now!'

Hester took a different approach. Setting aside her fear of Athair in favour of action, she floated down from my shoulder and grabbed the pill box. She clamped it to her body, even though it was practically the same size as she was, and flew away from the table.

'No!' she screeched. 'No pills! No spiders! No!' She glanced over her shoulder, clearly expecting to be followed, but Athair and Arbuthnot simply watched her.

I tried to remember to keep breathing like a normal person.

Hester extracted a pill and dropped it into a jug of water that was sitting on the bar waiting to be emptied, then she threw in three more. Each one fizzed and slowly dissolved. She took the remaining pills, tossed them onto the floor and zipped down to stomp hard on them, throwing herself at them until nothing remained but specks of white dust.

By now everyone in the restaurant had stopped to watch her; even a couple of the chefs were peering at her from the porthole window in the kitchen door. I knew Hester was aware of her audience when she added a couple of flourishes and mid-air spins. When she'd finally smashed the last few crumbs of spider's silk deliciousness into smithereens, she raised her head and gave a succession of sweeping bows. She turned to me and snapped out the sort of salute of which even a member of the Royal Guard at Buckingham Palace would be proud and returned to the table.

Unfortunately, she was now covered from head to toe in white spider's silk dust. I swallowed hard and dragged my eyes away from her – but my left one was twitching furiously.

'That'll be £1,650.' Arbuthnot spoke aloud for the first time.

'Bill me,' Hester snarled.

'He just did.' Athair regarded her mildly then turned to the bogle and nodded

Arbuthnot appeared to understand the silent request. He reached into a different pocket and pulled out another box. This one was embossed with gold.

'Don't worry.' Athair winked at Hester. 'We have plenty.'

I wanted to be the queen of nonchalant behaviour. I wanted to lean back in my chair, cross my legs and shrug so I could prove to the entire world that I didn't need or want spider's silk. Unfortunately I could only remain very, very still and focus on the breathing techniques that my drug counsellors had taught me.

'You don't look very happy, daughter,' Athair said. 'Are you unwell?'

Fuck. Off.

'You're rather sweaty. Perhaps you have a mild fever?'

As I looked down and ostentatiously checked my watch, my

movement seemed jerky and un-coordinated. There were fifty-two minutes to go. In theory, I could walk away at any time – I hadn't actually given my word that I'd stay for a full two hours – but if I left now, I'd be putting Hugo in danger.

I considered my options while Athair smirked and continued his little drama. He held out his hand, palm upwards. Arbuthnot dropped the small box onto it. 'You can go now,' Athair said to him.

The bogle's heavy brow creased in protest. Athair didn't waste his breath repeating the order; instead, the tiniest flicker of electricity zipped between his fingers, dancing across the tips from pinkie to thumb. The bogle froze then stood up, nodded at me and left.

We all pretended not to notice the collective sigh of relief from the other diners – but they were scared of the wrong person. They should have ignored the large, lumbering bogle and focused their terror on the thin old man with the twinkle in his eyes.

Athair thumbed open the little box. My eyes slid to its contents and away again. A perfect dozen.

'There are many benefits to being a fiend,' he said. He dipped into the box, withdrew a pill and placed it on his tongue. Leaning back in his chair, he closed his mouth and his eyes and gave a small moan of satisfaction.

He swallowed and looked at me again. 'I can enjoy the benefits of all sorts of things without ill effect. I don't worry about high cholesterol. My weight is not an issue. I can imbibe all the caffeine and calories I wish – and I can take all the drugs and alcohol I desire without hangovers, addiction or unpleasant side effects. It's really rather wonderful.'

His lack of subtlety was noticeable but he didn't need to be subtle. Not in this.

Otis tugged at my collar. 'Daisy,' he whispered. 'Ignore him.'

Athair reached for a second pill and I watched him raise it to his lips and swallow it. Then he took a third.

I gazed into his eyes. His glamour was strong enough for there to be no tell-tale ring of silver around his pupils; perhaps the drug didn't even affect him.

'It's quite extraordinary stuff,' he murmured. 'I can feel it coursing through my veins. There's a strange fizz as it hits my heart, and the way it sneaks around the edges of my magic and rubs away at my powers is rather delicious.'

I straightened. Was the spider's silk dampening his magic in the same way it had dampened mine? Was Athair walking into a trap of his own making?

He clearly knew what I was thinking. 'You're welcome to try, sweetheart. Attack me here and let's see if my power has diminished enough for you to beat me. I won't hurt you.' He paused. 'Much.'

I exhaled: so spider's silk *did* affect him, even if only slightly. However, there was no doubt that it wasn't enough to give me the upper hand. I ran my tongue around my mouth, acknowledging my deep-seated jealousy that I was not the person tossing pill after pill into my mouth.

When Athair dipped his finger in for a fourth damned dose, I pushed my chair back and stood up. 'Come on,' I said to the brownies. 'We're leaving.'

Athair also rose to his feet. 'I think not, daughter.'

Thank goodness he was trying to prevent my departure; I'd have been in trouble if he'd let me leave without an argument. I needed Athair to put the drugs away for my own sanity, but I couldn't leave the restaurant if I wanted to ensure Hugo's safety.

I lifted my chin defiantly and eyed my birth father coldly. 'I didn't come here to be goaded back into addiction or mocked because of my past. Not by you. Not by anyone.'

Hester and Otis folded their arms and glared at him as if they were highly trained bodyguards.

'All I wanted to do,' Athair said in a contrite tone that I probably would have believed if it had come from anyone else, 'was to show you what is possible for a fiend. I went too far, and for that I apologise.' He gestured to my chair. 'You promised me dinner. I understand if you want to leave but I would like it if you stayed for dessert.' He spread his palms. 'Please, Daisy. I am *entreating* you to stay.'

I almost snorted. Entreating? As if that would make a difference. The entire charade with Arbuthnot and the drugs had been a test: Athair had wanted to check my limits and probe my weaknesses, and now he thought he had all the answers. But if Athair could put on an act then so could I. Maybe we were alike after all. 'No more drugs,' I said.

'Of course not.'

'No more descriptions of how wonderful it is to be a fiend, and no more waxing lyrical about what I could gain if I was stupid enough to join you.'

'You would gain a great deal,' Athair said.

I took out my wallet, withdrew two crisp notes and dropped them on the table. 'We're done here.' I started walking away.

'Wait!' Athair said. 'I will do as you request for the remainder of this meal.'

I kept walking.

'I hope you know what you're doing, Daisy,' Hester muttered.

'Of course she knows!' Otis whispered, affronted on my behalf.

I didn't have a bloody clue; I was making this up as I went along.

'You can choose the topics of conversation,' Athair called. 'I can tell you about my early life. You can learn more about your true origins. Haven't you ever wondered about your grandparents?'

I allowed myself to stumble as if he'd finally caught my attention. It worked.

Athair took full advantage. 'Or other members of our family? I had several brothers and sisters, you know, and a couple survived to adulthood. Their descendants are probably still alive today.' He paused. 'You can ask me anything you like, Daisy. I will answer truthfully.'

I stopped next to a couple who appeared to be out for a romantic dinner. The man was fiddling with something by the side of the table and when I looked down I spotted a small velvet box. Ah: he'd been planning to propose. Unfortunately, between Arbuthnot's appearance and the melodrama playing out between Athair and me, his thunder had obviously been stolen.

I sent him an apologetic look but he scowled at me. By contrast, his dinner companion blinked at me with what appeared to be relief. Oh dear: she didn't want to have that question popped. That was uncomfortable.

I turned slowly and scanned the room, aware that many of the diners were watching and listening. I stood there for a while, sucking on my bottom lip, then returned to Athair. 'How old are you?' I asked quietly so that I wouldn't be overheard.

Triumph flashed in his expression. 'Six hundred and thirty-two – maybe thirty-three. I'm not sure which year I was born. Birthdays weren't really celebrated when I was young.'

'Where was this?'

'York.' He smiled slightly. 'Back then it wasn't a particularly pleasant place. The Black Death was rife.' He pointed at our abandoned table. 'I can tell you about it over coffee and cake.'

I sniffed then gave a reluctant nod and walked slowly back to my seat. This was turning out better than I could have hoped for; the more I learned about the real Athair, the better my chance of discovering his weaknesses.

And of one day ending his long life for good.

SEVEN

The taxi driver was as taciturn on the return journey as he'd been on our way to the restaurant. Now his silence suited me; I wanted the time to chew over everything I'd learned from Athair, who'd been surprisingly chatty during the second half of the evening. Although it would have been easy to dismiss the information he'd given me as little more than colourful background to his early life, there might be nuggets that could prove useful.

Once we drove onto the long drive that led to Pemberville Castle, my thoughts turned to Hugo. Although I was worried about him, I didn't really believe that his sneaky venture to Athair's lair would result in disaster. Hugo was one of those people who skated through mortal danger with ease; he was far too intelligent and capable to allow anything truly bad to happen. Not that I'd tell him that – his ego managed perfectly well without my intervention.

Fortunately I didn't have to wait long for reassurance because I spotted him as soon as we drew close to the front of his ancestral home. He was chatting casually to Duchess. The taxi driver grunted and parked as far away as possible; he'd clearly seen enough of Duchess already and had no desire to get close to her.

I thanked him and tried to give him a tip, but he declined so forcefully that I guessed Athair had ordered him to refuse my money – and an order from Athair wouldn't be pleasant. I gave up and climbed out of the taxi. The driver took off with such speed that he almost collided with Slim and Miriam who were right behind us.

I watched them for a few seconds until I was sure that Athair had kept his word and left them in peace, then I spun towards Hugo. It had only been a few hours but, damn, I was beyond glad to see him.

I strode up, several burning questions on my lips. 'You're ba—'

Hugo didn't let me finish my sentence before his mouth descended on mine, stifling my words. I felt a flicker of annoy-ance at being prevented from talking but that was quickly superseded by desire when his hands slid around my body and his kiss deepened. Hot fire flared through me, though the sensa-tion started to dissipate when Hugo lifted me and cradled me against his chest. I didn't like being treated as if I were helpless – and Hugo damned well knew it.

Otis coughed in embarrassment and zipped ahead through the massive front door and into the castle where he could save his blushes. Hester stayed beside us watching Hugo's every move. 'Your technique could do with some improvement,' she said to him. 'And can't this wait? Tell us what—'

Duchess's huge, clawed hand snapped out and enclosed Hester's tiny form in her fist. Oh. I wasn't the only one who wasn't allowed to finish their sentences. Suddenly dread trickled down my spine.

Hugo's mouth left mine, dipping in order to trail across my

jawline. 'Stay quiet,' he muttered in my ear, his dark tone at odds with his affection.

I turned my head and tried to scan the dark line of trees beyond the castle without seeming too obvious. It was pointless: I couldn't make out anything. I quickly gave up and leaned against Hugo's chest instead.

Neither Miriam nor Slim spoke but I knew they were behind us from the crunch of their footsteps on the gravel. Hugo kissed me again, nodded at Duchess and carried me across the castle threshold as if I were some sort of ridiculous blushing bride.

My nose wrinkled. A very strange, very unpleasant smell clung to his clothes and hair. Whatever he'd been doing had been interesting – and probably not in a good way – but I held my tongue.

Slim, Miriam and Duchess entered the castle too, the latter with Hester still captured in her fist. When the troll paused to close the huge oak front door and bar it from the inside, my sense of foreboding grew. She was usually more comfortable outside and beneath her bridge, especially at this time of night. I'd never seen her lock that door and hamper her own exit before now.

Hugo didn't put me down immediately so I wriggled to indicate my displeasure. 'Pity,' he murmured, finally allowing me to stand up. 'I was enjoying that.'

Yeah, yeah. I rolled my eyes and suffered his answering grin, then drew in a breath to speak but he shook his head minutely in warning. I raised an eyebrow, stalked across to the nearest shiny suit of armour and lifted up the visor to peer mockingly inside. Nobody was lurking within. Surprise, surprise. I shrugged pointedly at Hugo but he only offered me an uncomfortable smile.

Then Duchess screamed. The sound was like nothing I'd ever heard before, high-pitched and so drawn out that it was a miracle the windows didn't shatter. Within seconds, I'd unsheathed Gladys and adopted a defensive stance. Miriam had pulled out her sword too, and Hugo and Slim were bristling with magic ready to attack any and all comers.

'You bitch!' Duchess roared. 'I'm going to eat you whole!'

'Oh yeah? Come and get me then!'

I looked upwards. Hester was hanging onto the chandelier above our heads and glaring down at Duchess. The troll's hand was open and a dribble of blood was leaking from a small wound in her fleshy palm.

'She bit me!' Duchess gave me a narrow-eyed look that suggested it was my fault. She thumped her chest and pointed at Hester. 'Vengeance is mine by right!'

'You grabbed me in your sweaty, smelly paw and wouldn't let me go,' Hester shouted. 'What else was I supposed to do?'

Duchess snarled and leapt upwards, swiping at Hester. She succeeded in reaching the chandelier, knocked several crystal shards away and made it swing ominously. Hester, who had already darted away, stuck out her tongue.

Duchess jumped again. 'I'm going to roast you alive, brownie!'

Otis zoomed out from the hallway. 'What are you doing to my sister?' he yelled. 'If you hurt her, I will kill you!'

Another crystal shard tumbled from the chandelier and landed on my head. I scowled and threw as much authority into my voice as I could muster. 'Enough! If I could get through dinner with Athair without bloodshed then you lot can stop this now!'

Duchess whirled. 'Oh yeah? Who made *you* queen?'

For fuck's sake.

'She's gotten all uppity since she became a lady,' Hester said. She put on an affected voice. '"*Do this. Do that. Keep yourselves busy while I shag Hugo's brains out.*" It's never-ending.'

My mouth dropped. How had *I* ended up as the bad guy here? Hugo snickered and I glared at him. 'Don't you start.' I folded my arms. 'What's going on? What's with all the secrecy?'

'Bone Zone first,' he said, referring to the large office at the back of the castle that was used for treasure-hunting business. 'Then we'll talk.' He raised an eyebrow at Duchess. 'Some calm would be appreciated.'

'The grumpy goth started it,' she retorted.

Hester opened her mouth to start yelling again. 'No!' I said sharply. Clearly everyone was feeling the tension of the evening far more than I'd appreciated, and there was something sinister underlying the atmosphere that I didn't understand.

I marched towards the Bone Zone as quickly as I could. Tempers were high but nobody was dead. That was important. Things were not that bad. Nobody was badly hurt and, I repeated silently, nobody was dead.

❧

'Oh, he was definitely dead,' Hugo said. 'And he had been for some time.'

I pressed the base of my hands into my temples. With every member of the Primes in attendance, plus Hester, Otis, Duchess and me, the Bone Zone meeting table was crowded. Unsurprisingly, Duchess's large body took up a lot of the space and there was no chair – or even a window seat – that would hold her massive frame. She was at least twice the size of any bogle.

Hugo had altered the door several weeks ago, enlarging it so that she could get into the Bone Zone if need be. He'd reasoned that she sometimes had knowledge and ideas that the rest of us did not, but mostly he'd been trying to keep her quiet and happy; however, as we were frequently reminded, that was an ongoing process. She was currently sitting on the floor on top of several squashed cushions, displeasure emanating from her every pore.

'Take me through it from the beginning,' I said, 'Tell me what happened after I got into that taxi.'

Hugo nodded. 'We noticed them almost as soon as you'd gone,' he said.

Duchess cleared her throat pointedly and shot him an icy glare. 'We?' she demanded.

'Duchess noticed them,' he amended. 'At least half a dozen vampires, all watching the castle. There's no way of telling how long they'd been out there – there's enough tree cover for them to hide out during the day without receiving too much sun damage.'

The troll jerked her yellowing thumb at Hugo. 'He wouldn't let me kill them.' Her eyes flashed. 'He does not want me to enjoy myself. And there is nothing more fun than crushing vampire bones.' She licked her lips.

Becky, the youngest and often most enthusiastic member of the group, looked at Duchess earnestly. 'We've been through this. If they're reporting back to Athair, which seems the most likely scenario, we can use them for our own purposes and feed them misinformation.'

It was a reasonable plan; it wasn't that which was upsetting me. 'So you made sure we didn't say anything when we were outside that might alert them to what you've been doing this evening,' I said. 'I get that. But why were you still concerned once we were inside?'

Several of the Primes twitched uncomfortably and when I looked at Hugo I realised he was barely containing his fury. The tips of his pointed ears had turned bright red and his knuckles were white. The last time I'd seen him look that pissed off was when we'd met for the first time and he'd realised I was a spider's silk user.

'Hugs left for Culcreuch from the rear of the castle to avoid being noticed by the vamps.' Becky was aware of his anger and speaking softly as a result. 'When he did, we discovered signs of an intruder. One of the old store rooms has a smashed window and a small amount of food has been stolen from the kitchen.'

'That was probably Duchess,' Hester said, folding her arms.

The troll bared her teeth. 'It was not! I don't sneak around stealing chocolate brownies like you do. I don't know why you eat them anyway. Isn't it like cannibalism, a brownie eating a brownie?'

I spoke up before anarchy descended again. 'You think someone in Athair's employ might have gained access and be hiding here?'

Hugo growled because he didn't want to believe it, but several of the Primes nodded. I passed a hand in front of my eyes. Cumbubbling bollocks.

'Why can we talk freely in here then?' Otis asked.

'Because with the door closed, no sound will escape these walls and nobody else can possibly have come in here,' Hugo said. 'A while back somebody sneaked into this room and tried to steal a valuable object. Afterwards I had a witch come by and set up a ward to prevent anything like that from happening again.'

I eyed him. 'That was me. I sneaked in and tried to steal the dragon's egg.'

'Yep. Your attempt made it clear that we were more vulnerable than I'd realised. It's not practical to keep the entire castle warded, but one room is manageable. Anyone not in this room at this moment is not keyed into the ward magic and will find it almost impossible to enter.' His jaw tightened. 'And in the unlikely event that someone *is* lurking in the castle, we will find them.'

'We're under siege,' Otis whispered. 'From within and without.'

There were a lot of pale faces around the table. Hugo and his Primes were used to putting their lives on the line but they weren't used to being attacked in their own home. None of us were.

'Okay.' I tried not to look too worried. 'Okay. Tell me about Culcreuch Castle. What happened there?'

Hugo launched into his tale. 'I got to the castle without too much difficulty. There were more vampires, but I was expecting them. They were outside the castle walls and busy feeding, so they were preoccupied and easy enough to avoid.'

Hester squeaked. 'They were feeding?'

'On chickens,' Hugo said. 'Not people. There was a crate of live chickens out front.'

'Athair is keeping his vampires from starvation,' Rizwan muttered. 'But he's not satisfying them enough to prevent them from being useful.'

'Because there's nothing more useful than a hungry vampire.' Hester rolled her eyes.

'Not when you're a fiend,' Otis told her. She shuddered, and she wasn't the only one.

I looked at Hugo. 'Go on,' I said.

'I skirted around the vamps at the back of the building. There were several possible routes into Culcreuch Castle but I didn't want to leave any trace of myself so I didn't want to break through any of the windows or doors. I knew from my previous investigation when we time travelled that there was a tower. I headed there and used air magic to reach the top. A trapdoor led inside.' Hugo smiled tightly, displaying not only a flash of his dimple but also a glimmer of satisfaction. 'It wasn't locked and it wasn't warded.'

'I knew it,' I muttered. 'I *knew* Athair's over-confidence would let him down. You went in?'

'You bet your sweet arse I did, Daisy.' We grinned at each other.

'There wasn't much to find inside,' he continued. 'Some IKEA furniture but not much else of note.'

I blinked. 'IKEA furniture?'

Hugo took out his phone and thumbed through the photos before holding it up.

Rizwan frowned. 'That's a Billy bookcase.' He was right.

I could only assume that Athair had no interest in interior design; as functional and sleek as such furniture was, it was hardly in keeping with a medieval castle. I wondered if he'd assembled the bookcase and the other items himself; it was hard to imagine him with an Allen key in one hand and a set of instructions in the other.

Hugo went on. 'I took care not to touch anything but I've got photos of all the books and papers that were on display. Let's just say that Athair has eclectic tastes.'

I peered at the books: the memoirs of the Marquis de Sade were standing next to what appeared to be a volume of seventeenth -century love poetry. Uh-huh. Eclectic indeed.

'One of the most interesting things was this.' Hugo found another photo. 'It's a pinboard with a map of the British Isles on it. Several locations are marked with numbers. I have no idea what it refers to, but I took several photos.'

'I'll get a larger version printed tomorrow so we can examine it in more detail,' Mark said.

I nodded. 'What about the dead body?' I asked quietly. 'Where was it?'

'In a dungeon at the bottom of the tower.' Hugo passed his phone to Miriam.

She sucked in a breath. 'Not just any dungeon. That's a

bottle dungeon.' She looked up. 'Also known as an oubliette. Essentially, it's a hole in the ground that holds prisoners. There's not enough room inside for them to lie down. Unless they possess incredible skills – or magic – there's no escape.'

Any satisfaction had vanished from Hugo's face. 'There certainly wasn't any escape for this poor man. I'm no pathologist but he must have been down there for a few years at least, judging by the decomposition of the body. There were some deep scratches in the stone walls that he'd probably made when he'd tried to get out. I couldn't lower myself inside in case I became trapped too, but I saw enough from the top. That man didn't have an easy death.'

His voice became quieter. 'There was a lot of dried blood. I couldn't risk disturbing the body too much – Athair mustn't know that I broke into his home – but I took several close-up photos. There wasn't much on the body to help identify him but he had dark hair and he looks human. Definitely Caucasian.'

Miriam squinted at the photos. 'He's wearing a football shirt.'

Becky leaned across. 'Manchester United,' she said. 'It's one of their older strips. If we can date the football shirt, we might pinpoint how long he's been down there. It could help identify him.'

She sounded doubtful but Slim was enthusiastic. 'Good call.'

'What's that?' Becky asked, pointing at the same photo.

Miriam zoomed in on the image. 'Some sort of signet ring. There's a design on it.' She twisted the phone around so we all could see it.

'It's a lion,' Rizwan said. 'Well, three lions to be exact. Lions are one of the national symbols of England.'

'So between that ring and the football shirt, we can assume

he was probably English.' Hester frowned. 'That narrows it down to – what? Thirty million possibilities?'

Hugo grimaced. 'Far fewer if we focus on missing persons, but there's still not a lot to go on.'

'The ring might help,' Rizwan argued.

Miriam nodded. 'The least we can do is to try and find out who he was and discreetly let his family know what happened to him.'

I stared at the ring and wondered what its owner had done. What had made Athair throw him into an oubliette and leave him to die? Whoever that poor man was, he'd deserved better than that. Everyone did.

'His family deserves closure,' I said and glanced at Hugo. 'We've learned a lot tonight. Between what Athair told me at dinner and what you found at the castle, we know a lot more about him than we did a few hours ago.' None of it was good news but there was a lot to work with. 'As long as we don't rush into anything and we're careful, we—'

I was interrupted by an almighty crash. We all stiffened in alarm.

'Is anyone else in the castle?' Slim asked urgently.

'Everyone who should be here is in this room,' Hugo said grimly. 'I think we can agree that our intruder is still here.'

I stood up, determination coursing through my veins. 'Well, it's fortunate that we're all hunters. Let's go hunting and take care of them before they cause any real problems.'

The dark gleam in Hugo's blue eyes was reflected in everyone else's eyes, too. A moment later, we were all heading for the door.

EIGHT

We each went in a different direction. This was familiar turf, even for me, and that meant we had the advantage. We knew where the best hiding places were, we understood the various creaks and their causes and, perhaps most importantly, we were determined to safeguard our home.

I wasn't sure whether I'd feel the same about the Assigney mansion a few miles down the road, which technically was mine. I was only a guest here at Pemberville but I felt more at home here. Maybe it was because of Hugo, or maybe it was because this was where I'd shivered and vomited and hallucinated my way through my withdrawal from spider's silk. In the end the reason didn't particularly matter: what was important was my determination to track down whoever was threatening the safety of Pemberville Castle.

It didn't take long to work out what had caused the loud crash. A suit of armour – the same suit of armour I'd pretended to check for intruders only an hour earlier – had fallen to the ground and its shiny pieces were strewn across the marble-tiled floor. Whatever – whoever – had knocked it over was nowhere to be seen. Just to be sure, I double-checked the other four suits standing to attention around the vast hallway but, alas, nobody was hiding inside.

I walked into every single room and looked around; given the size of Pemberville and the vast number of rooms that was no mean feat, but no matter how many curtains I pulled back or tables I ducked under, I couldn't find anyone.

There was only one place where I thought I might be on the intruder's trail. When I popped my head into the small cupboard where Otis and Hester kept their clothes and occasionally slept, Gladys buzzed. It was only a brief note, and the sentient sword sounded more surprised than vicious or angry, but there was nothing to see inside the cupboard beyond what I'd expected. Despite my repeated requests, Gladys remained silent throughout the remainder of my search.

After almost an hour, I returned to the main hall. Miriam had collected the pieces from the fallen suit of armour and was putting them back together, although that appeared to be more complicated than we'd expected. I was certain that she had the feet the wrong way around. Given her frustrated expression, I decided against telling her to swap the right and left boots. It wasn't as if the hollow knight would be going into battle any time soon.

'I've checked every room and I couldn't find anything,' I said. 'Not even a whisper of an intruder.'

Becky nodded. 'Rizwan and I searched the basement and the attic. There was nothing there.'

'I have been through the ground floor,' Duchess agreed solemnly. 'I cannot sense anyone.'

Hugo paused halfway down the stairs. 'Anything?' he asked. We shook our heads.

Otis buzzed in from the right and Hester from the left, their faces blank.

'Maybe it's a ghost,' Mark suggested.

Uh-oh. Hester immediately stiffened and started whipping her head from side to side in alarm. 'Or maybe,' I said quickly, before she descended into hysteria, 'whoever knocked the suit of armour over escaped before we left the Bone Zone.'

Hugo's expression was grim. 'The doors are bolted and the windows are locked tight. The pane of glass that was smashed earlier was covered with plywood hours ago. I checked and it's not been touched.' He looked at me. 'Is there a chance that Athair's magic extends to this? Could he use his powers to reach inside a building? Or could he somehow transport himself here?'

I swallowed. 'I don't know,' I whispered. 'But if he can do that, I think we might be fucked.'

Miriam cursed and gave up on her attempt to rebuild the suit of armour. She'd reached his chest, but his shoulders and arms appeared to be a step too far for this time of night. She dropped the helmet to the floor and turned to face us.

'If it was Athair, he's not here now,' she said in a brisk tone that suggested she wouldn't accept any nonsense even from the most terrifying fiend the country had ever seen, 'We should bed down for the night in the Bone Zone where we have a degree of safety. In the morning, we will complete another thorough search then engage the services of more witches to draw wards around the building, not just one room. It means no more visitors for the time being, but I think we all agree it is necessary.'

We all nodded. Even if her suggestion hadn't been eminently sensible, I doubted anyone would have dared to argue with her.

Duchess jutted out her bottom lip. 'I'm not staying inside. I'll return to my bridge. Whoever sneaked in here only managed it because I wasn't at my post.' She pulled back her heavy, rounded shoulders. 'It will not happen again.'

'It's not your fault, Duchess,' Otis said.

'It probably *is* your fault,' Hester muttered, although this time she spoke quietly enough for the troll not to hear her. It was just as well; I had the beginnings of a very nasty headache pushing at the back of my eyes. I desperately needed some peace and quiet and, from their pale, exhausted expressions, everyone else did too.

It DIDN'T TAKE LONG to transform the Bone Zone into sleeping quarters; our camping gear was still at the front door after our last excursion, so we simply had to pull out our sleeping bags and haul them through the castle before we bedded down for the night. But we were all uncomfortable and we had a fitful night. We didn't know who had breached Pemberville Castle or where they were now.

Nobody voiced their worries aloud but we were all thinking the same thing: if it was Athair who was lurking around the castle, he was strong enough to break through the ward surrounding the Bone Zone and attack us when we were at our most vulnerable. The fact that Hugo wrapped his arms tightly around me and refused to let go even when he fell asleep, indicated his state of mind just as my inability to sleep indicated mine. It was a rare night indeed when sleep eluded me.

Dawn still came relatively early to Scotland, even though the summer solstice was weeks behind us. The Bone Zone was a windowless room but my body clock had adjusted sufficiently for me to know when the sun was rising without needing to see any glowing rays of sunshine or to look at my watch.

I extricated myself from Hugo, stood up and stretched before I walked to the long table and located his phone. Something about the photos he'd shown us last night was niggling at me; there was something I'd seen that felt peculiar. Unfortunately I wasn't sure what it was.

I was as familiar with the password to Hugo's phone as I was with his body, from the faint silvery scar on his hip where he'd fallen during his first official treasure hunt to the perfect curve of his impressively tanned arse. Even so, I turned and held it up with a questioning look. He nodded from the cocoon of the sleeping bag where he was watching me. I inputted the password, unlocked the phone and located the photos.

I paused at the map of the British Isles, zoomed in to peer more closely and then zoomed out to get a view of the whole thing. Thirty-two places around the country had been numbered neatly in black ink. Had Athair done that? And if so, why? I nibbled my bottom lip and squinted harder. Hmm.

'What is it, Daisy?' Slim asked softly.

I jumped, surprised to hear his voice. When I looked around, I realised that everybody was awake and watching me; clearly I wasn't the only person who had struggled to sleep.

'I don't know. Maybe nothing.' I turned the phone around. 'Rizwan, you said you were getting this printed out and enlarged?'

Rizwan was already wriggling out of his sleeping bag. 'I'll do it now.'

'I didn't mean do it *right* now. It's still early. After breakfast is fine.'

'It's no problem. I'll do it now.'

Now I felt guilty that I'd hauled him out of bed. 'In that case,' I said, 'I'll nip to the kitchen and get coffee on for everyone.'

'And bacon rolls?' Becky asked hopefully.

I looked at the group and grinned at their expressions. It might have been a difficult night but if everyone had an appetite then things weren't that bad.

'I'll help,' Hugo said, finally sitting up.

Becky groaned. 'What?' he frowned at her. 'You don't like my cooking?'

'It's not that.'

'What then? I can't leave Daisy to go to the kitchen alone,' he protested. 'Our intruder might still be out there.'

Nothing had attempted to breach the ward surrounding the Bone Zone, and there had been no more sounds of anyone lurking inside the castle. I was beginning to think there was nobody out there; I was certainly hoping that was the case.

Becky mumbled something inaudible so Hester translated. 'Hugo, if you go with Daisy, it'll be hours before we get so much as a crumb for breakfast. The two of you will get distracted and start canoodling over the bacon...' Otis pulled a face '...and we'll be lucky if we get any food before noon.'

I felt my cheeks start to warm but Hugo only winked. Miriam stood up. 'I'll go with them,' she said.

'We don't need a chaperone,' Hugo told her.

I looked at the raised eyebrows; apparently we did. I blushed harder, suddenly remembering the previous week when Hugo and I had wandered off ostensibly to make tea for them all and returned three hours later without a single hot beverage in our hands.

'You'd never catch me acting like that,' Hester proclaimed loudly.

'Give me a hot young man and I would,' Miriam said with a wink.

'Me too,' Becky agreed.

Slim nodded. 'Me three.'

Hester rolled her eyes. 'You lot have no sense of decorum.'

'Come on,' I nodded at Hugo and Miriam. 'Let's get breakfast sorted and make sure the castle is intruder free along the way.' I injected a firm note into my voice. 'We'll be no longer than twenty minutes. As you're all so wide awake, let's see what the rest of you can accomplish in that time.'

'Trying to cover up your embarrassment with authority?' Hugo enquired.

'Yep.'

'And failing miserably?'

'Yep.'

Everyone grinned. I fanned air at my cheeks and scooped up Gladys. At least my trusty sword wasn't laughing at me.

She hummed loudly. Unbelievable.

With Miriam's eagle eye watching us, we made it back with almost two whole minutes to spare carrying a vast tray filled with rolls, crispy bacon and enough coffee and tea to satisfy the caffeine needs of a small army.

Rizwan had finished pinning up an enlarged version of the map that Hugo had found in Culcreuch Castle. I gulped down a mug of steaming coffee and gazed at it. There were indeed thirty-two places marked in total and I examined each one: twelve points in Scotland, seven in Wales and the remainder in England.

Each one was neatly numbered, although three of the spots had been scribbled over and different numbers inscribed. It looked to my untrained eye as if they'd been written in old-fashioned ink.

I could easily imagine Athair using a quill to write; the numbers had an antiquated appearance, with little curls and flourishes that wouldn't have looked out of place on an ancient manuscript. What I couldn't imagine was what they represented because there didn't appear to be any order to the numbered areas.

Number one was in the Midlands, not far from Birmingham; its closest marker, which was in the countryside less than seventy miles away, was number twenty-nine, while number two was located on the northern fringes of the Scottish coastline. There didn't appear to be any logic to the system and there was no suggestion as to what each marker represented.

I chewed on my bottom lip as I considered the map, then I drained the dregs of my mug, massaged my neck and wandered to the Bone Zone door.

'Where are you going?' Hugo asked.

'Call of nature,' I said. The nearest bathroom was only a few metres away; although we'd not yet managed to scour the whole castle a second time to find the intruder, I was doubtful that anyone was still out there. 'I'd like some privacy for my morning ablutions,' I added primly. 'I will shout if anyone is hiding behind the cistern.'

Hugo smiled but his eyes remained serious. 'Make sure you do.'

I skirted around three of the Primes, who were still in their sleeping bags and munching on their rolls, and headed out.

I checked for any signs of life but unsurprisingly the small bathroom was empty: there were no fiends, bogles, trolls or even spiders lurking inside. I locked the door, emptied my bladder then bent over the sink to wash my hands. I brushed my teeth, splashed my face with water and removed the crusty gunk from my eyes. Given my lack of sleep, I needed all the help I could get to stay alert and sensible.

I dried my skin with a towel and stared at my pale face in the mirror. Before I could start to agonise over the dark shadows under my eyes, I caught sight of a tiny flapping wing in my peripheral vision. For goodness' sake. Otis wouldn't have dared to sneak in, so doubtless it was Hester who had slipped underneath the crack in the door.

I groaned slightly. 'Is it too much to ask for a few minutes' peace?' She didn't answer. 'Hes?' Again, she didn't say anything but I heard the familiar buzz of wings from behind the cabinet that stood against the far wall. 'Yeah,' I grumbled. 'You *should* hide.'

I expected a sarcastic rejoinder but none was forthcoming. I unlocked the bathroom door and nudged it open with my foot – and then I blinked.

'See?' Otis nudged his sister as they hovered in mid-air in the hallway. 'I told you she wouldn't be long.'

I stared at them then, without a word, I slowly turned back towards the bathroom and fixed my gaze on the cabinet.

'Daisy?' Otis flitted to my shoulder. 'What's wrong?'

I licked my lips. 'Get Hugo,' I whispered.

Hester was by my other shoulder in an instant. 'Something's there? The intruder? I can't see anyone.' Her voice started to rise. 'It's a ghost, isn't it? It's definitely a ghost! Oh my God, oh my God, oh my God!'

I raised a hand to hush her; she subsided but I could feel her quivering. 'Otis, get Hugo, please,' I repeated.

He took off instantly, rising into the air and darting towards the Bone Zone. I took a step into the bathroom. 'I know you're in here,' I said aloud. 'You might as well show yourself.' There was a faint thud from behind the cabinet and Hester squeaked. I hardened my voice. 'I can use magic and force you out. It'll be easier if you do this voluntarily.'

I heard hurried footsteps as Hugo appeared beside me looking ready to do battle with any number of evil forces. I put my hand on his forearm and quickly squeezed it, shaking my head to tell him to stay back.

A heartbeat later there was another flicker of movement.

When the miniscule figure appeared, all three of us gasped. I'd been right on one account: it was definitely a brownie who had sneaked into the bathroom. It just wasn't Hester or Otis.

She was the same size as my trusty companions – barely a few inches high – and her wings matched Hester's translucent iridescence, but any resemblance stopped there. While Otis looked like a thumbnail version of a jaunty factory worker from the nineteenth century, and Hester dressed exclusively in funereal black as if she fashioned herself on Queen Victoria with some elements of more up-to-date Goth-Girl chic thrown in, this brownie looked like an honest-to-goodness princess. In fact, I wouldn't have been surprised if she'd told us that she'd stepped out of the pages of a fairy tale.

She had long blonde hair that curled down her back yet somehow avoided getting tangled up with her wings; her features were delicate and her nose was cute and upturned. She was wearing a sky-blue hoop dress with a lace trim. I reckoned Disney would licence her in a heartbeat if they knew she existed.

'Good morrow,' she said nervously in a musical voice then flew down to the sink and perched on the edge of the white porcelain.

Hugo and I gaped at her; Otis, however, had already sprung into action. 'My lady!' He darted forward, took her hand, bent over and kissed it. 'You are a true vision.' He smiled and I realised that his cheeks were flaming red. His blush wasn't holding him back – far from it. He straightened up, took off his cap and smoothed down his hair. 'I am Otis.'

The blonde brownie was also blushing, although the colour on her cheeks was more like a blooming rose than a fire engine. 'It is a pleasure to make your acquaintance. My name is Eloise.'

Hester snorted. 'Of course she's called Eloise,' she muttered.

'She wouldn't be Bertha or Drusilla or Prudence, would she?' I wasn't sure anyone was called by those names nowadays, but I took her point: everything about this unexpected brownie was pretty, even her name.

'I am so sorry for breaking into your home,' she said. She lifted her chin and addressed Hugo, suggesting that she was aware of whose home she was in. 'It is a truly stunning castle.'

'How long have you been here?' Hugo asked. His voice was low and gentle but I sensed the steel behind it. Eloise was tiny, beautiful and wholly unthreatening – and that made us very suspicious indeed.

A trace of guilt crossed her face. 'Since last night.'

'You smashed the window to get in?'

Her head drooped. 'Yes.'

Otis looked horrified. 'You did that? Are you alright? Did you cut yourself on the glass?'

Hester crossed her arms and glared at her brother. 'Unbelievable. She's the intruder, Otis! She's probably a thief. She's *definitely* evil.'

Eloise shrank visibly but she didn't try to deny it, which was curious in itself. 'I am a thief,' she admitted. 'I stole some of your food.'

'I knew it!' Hester said. She scowled at Eloise as if she deserved to be hung, drawn and quartered for her actions.

'You were hungry?' Otis asked.

'Starving,' Eloise mumbled.

I felt my heart go out to her, and I wasn't the only one. Otis reached out and offered her a hug. She edged away, shaking her head; she didn't want his touch.

'I'm also afraid that it was me who knocked down the suit of armour,' she said quietly. 'The visor was open and I needed somewhere to hide, so I flew inside but my foot caught and the visor dropped. I was somewhat over-zealous when I tried to find a way out. I panicked and made the suit fall.'

Otis gasped sympathetically. Hugo took a step back and gestured to Miriam, who was standing just behind us. I knew that he was asking her to close the door to the Bone Zone before Eloise glimpsed what was inside.

'So she's not just evil,' Hester said loudly. 'She's clumsy too.'

'That's enough, Hester,' I said.

My little sidekick stuck out her tongue. Then, because pulling faces wasn't enough, she aimed a kick at my jawline. 'Hey!' I protested. 'That hurt!'

'It was supposed to hurt,' she sniped.

Otis wasn't paying us any attention; he was focused entirely on Eloise. 'What is it?' he asked her. 'What's wrong?'

The blonde brownie was cowering as she stared at me with wide, terrified eyes. It appeared she was expecting something from me, but for the life of me I couldn't work out what. 'Are you alright?' I asked.

'She's shaking like a leaf,' Hugo murmured.

'Don't hurt her too much,' Eloise pleaded. 'I'm sure she didn't mean it.'

I tilted my head, baffled. 'Hurt who? Hester?'

Hester kicked me again. 'I did mean it,' she said. 'And I meant that kick too.' She eyed Eloise. 'If you don't believe me, I'll kick you as well and you can feel for yourself how much I meant it.'

I ground my teeth. 'Hester...' Shaking my head, I addressed Eloise again. 'I'm not going to hurt anyone,' I said. 'Although I might hide all the chocolate brownies as punishment.'

'Don't you bloody dare, Daisy.'

I ignored Hester's hiss. 'That's not how we do things around here,' I said. I watched Eloise carefully. She was still trembling; it was next to impossible to fake that sort of physical reaction.

'Why are you here, Eloise?' Hugo asked. 'Why did you break in?'

'He told me to,' she said in a small voice.

Cumbubbling bollocks. I already knew the answer but I asked the question anyway. 'Who?'

'His name is Athair.'

'I knew it!' Hester crowed. 'I knew she was evil the moment I saw her!'

Eloise flinched while Otis gazed at her in horror. 'You work for *him*?'

'I'm bound to him,' she whispered. 'He is my master.'

'The vampires outside aren't enough for him? He has to send you to spy on us too?' I asked sourly.

It was Eloise's turn to be surprised. 'Oh,' she said, her eyes widening. 'I'm not a spy, I'm a messenger. I would have given you the message last night but I was afraid that you'd be angry when you realised I'd broken in, so I thought I'd wait until everyone calmed down. But then you disappeared into that room over there, and I couldn't follow you. I didn't want to call out in case the troll heard me. I only broke the window at the back so I could stay away from her.' She shuddered. 'Trolls are scary and my master told me to avoid her if I could.'

Probably because Duchess would squash the likes of Eloise in a heartbeat without thinking to ask any questions first. I curled my hands into fists and felt the bite of my fingernails in the fleshy part of my palms. 'What message?' I growled. 'What message did Athair give you?'

Eloise drew in a breath. 'He said that there's a lot more he can show you besides magic.' She closed her eyes. '*Surge Domine et dissipentur inimici tui et fugiant qui oderunt te a facie tua.*'

Huh?

Hugo translated for us. '"Rise up, Lord, and let thine

enemies be scattered; and let them that hate thee flee before thee".'

'More violence,' I said flatly. Surely Athair had realised by now that such threats of blood loss and war were of no use?

'It's a biblical quote,' Hugo explained.

I shrugged; that didn't make any difference to me.

'Not all the gold was found,' Eloise said softly. Her eyes remained closed. '"*They let the ground keep that ancestral treasure, gold under gravel, gone to earth, as useless to men now as it ever was*".' Then she repeated, 'Not all the gold was found because some of it had already been taken and moved elsewhere.'

Hugo's body stiffened beside me and I suddenly knew that he understood what she was talking about even though it remained complete gobbledegook to me. But then I'd been a treasure hunter for less than a year and my knowledge of ancestral treasures was considerably less than his.

Hester's knowledge was apparently even less than mine. 'So, Eloise,' she said, ticking off her fingers. 'You're evil, you're clumsy, you're a spy and you're crazy.' She sniffed. 'Not bad going.'

Otis rounded on his sister. 'That's enough!' he yelled. 'Stop being so mean! She needs our help, Hes, and you can't stop being a bitch! You need to leave poor Eloise alone. She can't help who she has to serve – we might have ended up with Athair if Daisy hadn't found us first. We might have been in her position. You can't blame her for what's happened.'

'She's bewitched you,' Hester sneered. 'That didn't take long. One pretty face is all it takes to fool you, Otis. I thought you were better than that.'

'Fuck off!' I'd never seen Otis so furious with his sister before.

From his expression, he was ready to smack her down but

Hester wasn't prepared to back off. 'She's with Athair, you nincompoop! Doesn't that mean *anything* to you?'

'But she's not a fiend, Hester! She's a brownie, she's one of us!'

I suddenly knew that this scene was exactly what Athair had been hoping for. He'd known for thirty years that Hester and Otis were my loyal companions. I wondered how long it had taken him to find a brownie to bind to his side. I also wondered how he'd achieved it and how deep that binding went. Hester and Otis had been forced into a similar bond with me when I'd opened the locket into which they'd been ensorcelled decades before, and they had told me that brownies lived to serve. Of course I'd released them almost immediately – but they had stuck around regardless. I didn't know if that was through choice or obligation, though they promised me it was the former. However, in my darker moments I suspected the latter.

I looked at Eloise again; she was still huddled on the side of the sink, pure misery etched onto her face and the tips of her little wings drooping as if with shame. Hugo nudged me and we exchanged glances. I nodded and he cleared his throat. 'Stay with us,' he said to her. 'You're safe here. We'll keep Athair away from you.'

If anything, the little brownie looked even more miserable. 'I can't stay,' she whispered. 'I have to return to him.'

'We've got magic,' I told her.

'And plenty of magical friends,' Hugo added. 'We can find a way to break whatever binding he has in place.'

'I am not tied to him through magical means,' Eloise said quietly. 'I must return to him now. I have delivered his message and he will not be pleased that I have delayed this long. I was supposed to speak to you as soon as you returned from the restaurant.' She lifted her head and for an instant, I glimpsed a flash of iron will. 'Please,' she said distinctly, 'do not force me to stay here.'

My shoulders sagged. 'We wouldn't do that.' We would *never* do that. I dreaded to think what means Athair was employing to keep Eloise tied to him.

Otis looked at her helplessly. 'Stay with us,' he pleaded.

She only shook her head. 'I cannot.'

And that, it appeared, was the end of the argument.

'Athair deliberately sent her here when you were meeting him. He could have easily given you the message himself, but he ordered that brownie to come here so she could snoop around.' Hugo looked furious, as if her incursion were his own fault. His spine was rigid as he paced the length of the Bone Zone. 'I should have expected something like this – I should have been prepared.'

'You weren't here, dear,' Miriam murmured. 'If anyone should have been better prepared, it's the people who stayed behind in the castle.'

Several of the Primes looked put out at her words. 'She's the size of my fucking thumb,' Mark growled. 'She's hardly easy to detect.'

'Exactly,' Miriam said, realising her mistake when she saw Mark's expression. 'That's why Athair sent her, and why she managed to stay hidden when we searched for hours last night.'

They were blaming each other, but there was only one reason Athair had forced Eloise to break into Pemberville Castle and that reason was me. Hunger for a soothing dose of spider's silk scratched at my insides but I pushed it away as best as I could. 'This is my fault,' I said. 'None of this would be happening if it weren't for me. I'll get my things and head over to the Assigney mansion. Athair will stop bothering you if I stay away.'

Hugo stopped pacing and swung towards me. 'No.' The force behind the single syllable was enough to make me shiver.

I tried to ignore my churning nausea. 'The lives of everyone in this room are at risk because of your association with me.'

He glared at me. 'In that case we both leave here,' he said. 'We are in this together.'

'This is your home, Hugo.'

'My home is wherever you are,' he returned instantly. 'We belong together.' He folded his arms across his chest. 'Nobody – not even your birth father – will change that. I don't care what he does.'

'You're not going anywhere without me,' Otis said, the anger in his expression almost matching Hugo's.

'I was going to say that!' Hester snapped.

'Well, I said it first. So there.'

She opened her mouth to yell at him but Miriam cleared her throat and interrupted. 'You're forgetting the most important point.' She sounded genuinely irritated.

I turned to her in surprise. She wasn't the only Prime who was looking pissed off.

Slim moved next to her. 'Do you really think that this is the first time our lives have been in danger?' he asked.

Becky nodded vigorously. 'We risk our lives every time we go out on a treasure hunt.'

'We *choose* to take that risk,' Rizwan said.

Miriam smiled. 'We *enjoy* taking that risk.'

'And we are family,' Mark added, giving me a hard look. 'We are *all* family.' Suddenly there was a very large and very painful lump in my throat.

'Besides,' Rizwan said, 'don't you think that Athair wants you to leave? He wants to separate you from us so you'll be more vulnerable. He's manipulating everything.'

I realised that he might have a point. I reached for Hugo's hand, needing his warm, reassuring touch. 'If any of you get hurt...'

'We know what we're doing,' Becky said. 'And we don't need you to make our choices for us.'

I pressed my lips together until I'd composed myself. 'I love you guys,' I whispered.

There was an array of warm smiles in response. 'We love you too, Daisy,' Becky responded.

The more logical part of my brain started to take over. Fight, not flight, I told myself. That was what I needed to do. Then I corrected myself: that was what *we* needed to do.

'I doubt Athair sent Eloise here to snoop,' I said shakily. 'He didn't need to do that. He sent her here to do what you said, to separate me from you and to sow dissent between us.'

I extended my hand towards the group, acknowledging what had just happened between us, then nodded at the brownies who had resolutely turned their backs on each other. 'He also wanted to prove that he could get to us whenever he wants. Perhaps he was hedging his bets in case I cut dinner short last night. Everything Athair does is about power and control.'

There were several nods of agreement.

'Whether she's under his control unwillingly or not, that brownie will describe everything she saw here to him,' Rizwan pointed out.

Becky twisted a length of her hair in her fingertips. 'There was nothing lying around that Eloise had access to. She won't have learned any state secrets.' She pointed to the enlarged photographs on display around the room. 'She won't have seen any of these. The ward surrounding this room was in place long before Rizwan printed those out.'

'But she can tell Athair that this room is warded,' Hugo muttered. 'He'll assume we have something to hide.'

'And that means he'll try to get inside the castle again,' Mark said. 'Either with that damned brownie or with some other poor creature he's enslaved.'

I cleared my throat. 'So we let him.'

Everyone turned to me. Hugo raised a questioning eyebrow. 'Let him?'

'We don't secure the castle – after all, the vampires will immediately report anything we do. Wasting time by creating a ward to cover the entire castle will only confirm Athair's suspicion that we have something to hide.' I was warming to my subject. 'We get rid of the ward around this room as well. Once we've removed all evidence of Hugo's visit to Culcreuch, of course.'

Hugo's anger was diminishing. He winked and gave a self-congratulatory bow.

My smile widened. 'If Athair wants to come here, we let him. We don't allow him to feed off our fear, not even for a second. And we wrongfoot him whenever we can while working on ways to undermine his power.'

'That's easier said than done, my dear,' Miriam said mildly.

I nodded, but I wasn't finished. 'The message,' I said to Hugo. 'You understood it, or at least part of it?'

'I think so,' he admitted. 'Eloise said "*They let the ground keep that ancestral treasure, gold under gravel, gone to earth, as useless to men now as it ever was*". It's from *Beowulf*.'

'The old poem?' I asked.

'A modern-day translation of it,' he said. 'It was written over a thousand years ago.'

'Okay. Does anyone know what treasure it refers to? That's obviously what Athair wants us to focus on.'

Every single Prime nodded; clearly it was only Hester, Otis and me who didn't know.

'The Staffordshire Hoard,' Hugo explained. 'It was dug up around fifteen years ago. It's the largest hoard of Anglo-Saxon gold and silver metal work ever discovered. The items were mostly military with very little magic attached, but even so it was an incredibly significant find.'

There was a faint fizz in my veins. 'Staffordshire?' I asked.

'Yes.'

I glanced at the photo of the enlarged map. 'Parts of Birmingham are in Staffordshire. Where exactly was this hoard found?'

'In a small village near Lichfield,' Slim said. His eyes also travelled to the map.

I pointed at the marker that had been labelled number one. 'There?'

'There.' He inhaled. 'Right there. I should have made the connection earlier.'

'Eloise said not all the gold was found.' Hugo scratched his jaw. 'She said it twice.'

Miriam frowned. 'Once the hoard was uncovered, the area was scoured for signs of more. There's no chance anything was missed.'

'She also said,' Hugo added, 'that some of it had already been found and moved elsewhere.'

'There's never been any suggestion that was the case,' Mark said. Hugo only shrugged.

'What about the biblical quote she mentioned?' I tried to remember it. '*Surge Domine...*' My voice trailed off. 'Something about the Lord rising up and enemies scattering?'

Hester filled it in. '*Surge Domine et dissipentur inimici tui et fugiant qui oderunt te a facie tua.*'

I blinked at her in surprise. 'I know my Latin. So what?' she said sourly.

Mark flipped open the nearest laptop, tapped the keys then sucked in a breath. 'One of the items found at the Staffordshire hoard was inscribed with that very quotation.'

The fizz in my blood intensified. Everyone else simply looked confused.

'Athair wants you to go and look more closely at the Staffordshire Hoard because there are some items that haven't been located yet,' Becky said.

'Seems that way,' I answered.

Hugo eyed me. 'He knows you like hunting for treasure so he's providing you with a hunt.' He glanced at the map. 'Thirty-two treasure hunts, in fact.'

I smiled broadly. 'Yep.'

Miriam nodded. 'He wants to please you, to deepen your relationship and prove that you'll benefit from a continued association with him. Complete the first treasure hunt and he'll provide details for the second, and so on. He's mapped it all out.'

'Literally,' Hugo murmured.

'We should ignore him, right?' Slim asked. 'His end game is to make Daisy a fiend. We don't want to do anything that might play into that.'

'Definitely,' Otis agreed. 'And Daisy doesn't want to make him think he's controlling her, not even for a second. There's plenty more treasure to be found. We don't have to go searching for the stuff that Athair shows us.'

'That's where you're all wrong,' I said.

Rizwan wrinkled his nose. 'You want to go looking for Athair's treasure? Really?'

I felt Hugo's eyes on me, watchful and intense. 'What is it, Daisy?' he asked. 'What are you thinking?'

'Take a step back and look at the map again,' I said. 'There are thirty-two spots all over Britain. Presumably each one will lead us to treasure of some sort. Athair's been around long enough – he's bound to know where a lot of stuff is buried. Maybe he even buried some of it himself.'

'So?'

'Every corner of the British Isles is covered by Athair's marks apart from one.' It had taken me a long time to work out what was peculiar about the map but it seemed glaringly obvious once I'd seen it. We weren't looking for what was on the map, we were looking for what *wasn't* on it.

The others squinted at the map until, one by one, they saw the same as me. 'There's nothing marked in either Lincolnshire or North Norfolk,' Rizwan said. 'Nothing at all.'

'And yet,' Mark murmured, 'those areas are amongst the most popular for metal detectorists because they often contain the most treasure.'

'There's a reason why lots of treasure is found there,' Hugo said. 'The Vikings, the Romans, the Normans, the English Civil War – those places are steeped in history.' He glanced at the Primes. 'How many times have we been to Lincolnshire?'

'Half a dozen at least,' Slim said.

Hester flitted up to the map. 'It might be a coincidence.'

I nodded. 'That's always possible. But if this map is what we think it is, then Athair wants to send me – to send *us* – all over the country. It's not that long since we found that bejewelled dagger and you set up that hunt because you wanted to keep me busy.' I pointed at the map. 'I reckon this is the same. Athair is providing us with work that he thinks will endear me to him, but he also wants to control what that work is and where we go. And he doesn't want us to go to Lincolnshire.'

Otis frowned. 'Why not?'

'I don't know.'

'Could there be treasure there that he doesn't want us to find?' Becky mused.

'I don't know that either.' I paused. 'But it's worth investigating.'

Otis still looked doubtful.

'I'd say so.' Hugo flashed his dimple. 'We can be in Lincolnshire by nightfall.'

Mark folded his arms. 'I hate to be the ghost at this party, but we don't know where to go or what to look for. That's a vast area to cover – it'd be like looking for a needle in a haystack when we don't know what a needle looks like.'

I grinned. 'That's why we don't go there. We do what Athair wants. Hugo, the brownies and I will investigate the Staffordshire Hoard and he'll believe he has us under his thumb. We'll go on our own because then we're deliberately separating ourselves from the rest of you to keep you safe. You lot stay here under the watchful eye of those bastard vampires outside. In the meantime, you find what we should really be looking for.' I stepped up to the map and waved my hand. 'It will be in the one place where Athair doesn't want us to go.'

ELEVEN

It wasn't a perfect plan but it was the best we had; in this scenario there was no such thing as a perfect plan. Until something else presented itself to us, we agreed that this was the best option.

We made a big show of it, taking our time to load our gear into Hugo's jeep before performing a set of elaborate farewells in front of Pemberville Castle for the benefit of any vampires who might be passing on information to my bastard birth father.

Despite my trepidation, I couldn't deny that the upcoming journey felt good. We were taking action. We might not be successful but we weren't puppets on Athair's string, and we weren't going to yield to his fiendish desires. Whatever he did, whatever tricks he pulled, I would never be his. I'd be dead before I'd be a fiend.

It was early evening by the time we arrived in Hammerwich, the village close to where the Staffordshire Hoard had been found in 2009. It was a pretty place overlooked by a large white windmill. There was a parish church, a small shop that sold the usual daily necessities from newspapers to milk to bars of chocolate, and two well-kept parks. In the dappled sunshine of the dying day, the village exuded a quiet appeal though it was not a hive of activity. Fewer than five thousand people lived here – and it showed.

Hugo parked by the side of the main street while Hester stared out of the window and huffed a bored sigh. 'It's not a terribly exciting place, is it?'

'Perhaps, Hes, you'd rather be enslaved by a fiend,' Otis said sniffily. 'Perhaps that would provide the sort of excitement you're after.'

Oh dear: this was the longest I'd ever seen the siblings argue. I'd hoped that the journey, not to mention the hunt, would be enough to settle their differences. It appeared that I'd been wrong.

Hester flew to my shoulder and said in an extraordinarily loud voice, 'Tell Otis that I would not be stupid enough to get myself caught by a fiend in the first place.'

Hugo and I exchanged looks.

Otis replied equally loudly, 'Tell Hester that if she did get caught by a fiend, nobody would want to rescue her.'

This was becoming ridiculous. 'Enough already,' I said. 'You're arguing over nothing.'

'Are not,' Otis sniped.

'Are too,' Hester yelled.

I pinched off a headache. 'You know what? The two of you should stay here until you sort yourselves out. We have far bigger problems to worry about and we don't need this.' I unclipped my seatbelt and stepped out of the Jeep.

A second later, Hugo joined me. 'Are you sure that leaving them alone together is a good idea?' he asked.

'They'll work things out between them.' I gave him an arch look. 'After all, we did.'

He pursed his lips. 'Yes, but that's because I'm irresistible.' He pointed to his face. 'How could you possibly say no?'

'It's one of the great mysteries of life,' I replied.

Hugo smirked and draped an arm around my waist. 'You love me really.'

'Yeah,' I said. 'I do.' I pushed myself up and gave him a lingering kiss. 'They love each other, too. They'll sort it out.'

He brushed a curl away from my cheek. 'You're a wise woman, Lady Daisy.'

'Make sure you remember that.' I grinned. 'Come on, let's see if we can find any locals to talk to. We could try the church up the road.'

Hugo shook his head. 'Nah, that shop is our best bet. Betcha.'

I raised an eyebrow. 'Winner buys dinner?'

'Done.'

Under any other circumstances, we might have split up to seek out information with as much speed and efficiency as possible, but we weren't in any rush. Regardless of what treasure Athair was leading us towards, I didn't care whether we located it or not. This operation was about smoke and mirrors; as long as Athair believed that we were following his lead and didn't realise that our ultimate goal was to locate whatever might be hiding in Lincolnshire, nothing else mattered.

With that in mind, Hugo and I strolled casually towards the little shop which would soon be closing for the day. It felt almost as if we were on holiday.

A few cards posted on the front door advertised the services of a dog walker, a person who was hoping to sell some garden furniture and a request from a family who needed a cleaner. So far so normal.

I entered with Hugo on my heels. A bell above the door tinkled to announce our entrance and the man behind the counter glanced up and smiled warmly. From his expression, he was not used to strangers wandering in. 'Good afternoon,' he said, in an accent that suggested he'd spent most of his life in Birmingham rather than in this rural locality.

I smiled back, assessing him rapidly as wholly human. There was no suggestion of anything remotely sorcerer- or witch-like about him, and I certainly didn't receive any whiff of magic.

'Hello.' I scanned the nearest shelves, reasoning that he'd be more amenable to chatter and questions if I actually bought something. Hugo raised a hand in greeting, wandered towards a carousel of postcards and started to examine them.

I grabbed a couple of bags of crisps and some forlorn-looking sandwiches and dropped them onto the counter. The man rang them up on his till and I paid, while Hugo's attention remained on the postcards. I glanced over my shoulder and grinned ruefully, as if to suggest that this was a regular occurrence and I'd have to wait until he'd made his selection. Then I engaged the shopkeeper in supposedly idle chat.

'We're not from around here,' I said. 'That's probably obvious.'

He gestured to my pointed elven ears. 'Oh, I know most of the locals and I certainly know all the elves who live nearby. Frankly, there's not many of your kind around here. What brings you to Hammerwich?'

Delighted that he was happy to talk – and therefore more likely to help us with information about the Staffordshire Hoard – I told him the truth. Or at least a version of it. 'We're treasure hunters,' I said. 'We couldn't resist coming to the place where some of the greatest treasure has been found in recent times.'

'I thought that might be the reason,' the man told me. 'There's not much cause for visitors to come to Hammerwich otherwise.' He leaned forward as if confiding a secret. 'That's why I like it here.'

He wasn't being rude, simply stating a fact that he liked his life quiet and his customers regular. I could understand that. 'It looks like a lovely place to live,' I said.

'It is.' He templed his fingers together. 'But I'm afraid you won't get much satisfaction in terms of the hoard. All the treasure is in museums in Birmingham and Stoke-on-Trent, and the site is just a field. There's nothing to see there.'

'It seems an unusual spot for buried treasure.'

He nodded. 'That it does. Those archaeologists and specialists think it was passers-by who wanted to hide the stash somewhere random and return for it later. It was likely pure chance that it was buried here and not elsewhere. Thirteen hundred years that gold lay in the ground. It's crazy when you think about it.'

It certainly was. And if Athair had been telling me the truth about his age, the Staffordshire Hoard had been hidden five hundred years before he was even born. That begged the question as to how he knew there was more of it to be found. I was beginning to think he'd sent us here on a wild-goose chase and there was nothing more to uncover. Busy work indeed.

Hugo came over with three postcards in his hand, each displaying an item from the hoard: a gold sword hilt with a red cloisonne decoration; a shiny panel with a cross emblem, and an image of a display from one of the city museums that included several gold objects. 'Do you think there's more out there waiting to be discovered?' he asked, dropping the postcards onto the counter.

The shopkeeper snorted. 'It's been fifteen years since the Staffordshire Hoard was found,' he said. 'Every hobbyist detectorist within a two-hundred-mile radius has been here thinking that they'll find something new that nobody else has dug up.

There's nothing else to be found out there, I can promise you that.'

Hugo and I exchanged unsurprised looks. Before either of us could say anything else, the bell above the door jangled again and a young woman in her late teens with unkempt frizzy hair and a harassed air dashed into the shop. She was a low elf, I was sure of it.

Despite our vague ethnic kinship, she ignored us; her focus was on the shopkeeper. 'You took my card down!' She waved her hand accusingly at the glass door and its three adverts. 'That's not fair, Alan!'

He gave her a long-suffering look. 'You know the terms, Amy. If you want to put a card in the door, it's ten pounds for the month.'

'I told you that I'll pay you next week!'

'And when you pay me I'll put the card back up again. But the others have paid first and it's only fair that you do the same.'

She looked irritated. 'Who gives a fuck about some old garden chairs?' she asked. 'And why would you get a dog if you can't be bothered to walk it yourself? My advert is important, Alan! I need to get my necklace back!' She leaned towards him; for a moment, I thought she was going to grab his shirt and threaten him. Or worse.

The shopkeeper – Alan – didn't appear at all perturbed; he just sighed and gestured towards Hugo and me. 'You are not helping your cause, Amy. Besides, I have other customers to deal with.'

She turned her head, as if noticing our presence for the first time. 'Whatever,' she muttered. 'They're not local. Who cares about them?'

I grinned. I decided that I liked Amy.

She drew in a breath. 'All I'm asking, Alan, is that—' She

stopped and she looked at us again, or rather she looked at Hugo. Her jaw dropped. 'You're Lord Hugo Pemberville,' she said.

It didn't matter where we went, sooner or later somebody always recognised Hugo.

'And I'm Lady Daisy Assigney,' I said brightly, to be perverse rather than because I wanted attention. 'Daughter of a lost high elf!'

'Nice,' she said without looking at me; her attention remained on Hugo.

Alan, who appeared fascinated that she'd recognised us, spoke up. 'They're here for the Staffordshire Hoard.'

A faint flash of disgust crossed Amy's face. 'It's not here, not any more. There's not even a hole in the ground to look at.' Her lip curled. 'I thought someone like you would be too smart to bother coming here for that.'

Hugo didn't miss a beat. 'You'd be surprised what you can learn from old sites. Sometimes you have to visit a place to truly understand it. The Staffordshire Hoard has been found but that's not what interests me. What is truly fascinating is the history of a place.'

Amy's eyes narrowed and she examined him carefully. 'Hmm.' She sniffed. 'To be honest, I thought you'd be taller.'

I couldn't prevent a laugh escaping. That apparently made me worthy of Amy's attention because she glanced at me with a knowing grin. 'So,' she said to Hugo, 'how do you feel about arachnids?'

Alan let out an exasperated hiss. 'Amy...'

'This is nothing to do with you, Alan, as you've already made very clear by refusing to display my advert.' She raised an eyebrow at him. 'You ought to be careful when you head home. There is a pair of brownies out there who look pretty tough.

They're at least three inches high and they're definitely cruising for a bruising.'

Only with each other, I thought, although I was impressed that Amy referred to Hester and Otis as brownies and not fairies. There weren't many people, not even elves, who recognised them as such.

Then she caught me off guard. She looked at me and raised her eyebrows. 'Is Lady Rose really dead?' she asked. 'Or is she only pretending to be dead?'

I hadn't mentioned my birth mother by name. Not only did Amy know far more about our world than first impressions had suggested, but she was also far cannier given that Rose was indeed pretending to be dead. Suddenly I liked her even more, despite her brusque, antagonistic edge.

I smiled vaguely. Sensing she wouldn't get any more from me than that, she returned to Hugo. 'Well?' she demanded.

Hugo and I gazed at her. 'What?' he asked finally.

'How do you feel about arachnids?' she asked impatiently, as if he possessed limited intelligence.

Hugo looked perplexed but nevertheless he answered. 'I have no strong feelings about them,' he said.

'Good.' Amy smacked her lips and shot Alan a triumphant look. 'Come on, Lord Pemberville,' she trilled, taking Hugo's arm. 'Let's head outside and talk business.'

She dragged him out of the shop, leaving lucky old me to pay a very bemused shopkeeper for Hugo's postcards.

CHAPTER

TWELVE

I caught up with them in the nearest park. Amy and Hugo were sitting on a bench with Hester and Otis hovering nearby. From the brownies' expressions, their curiosity about Amy had supplanted their mutual antagonism – at least for the time being. I couldn't blame them; she was fascinating.

She tilted her head. 'So here's the thing,' she said. 'I have a problem and I think you can help me. I'm flat broke and I can't pay you for your services, but I don't think you need the money.' She looked up at me and nodded knowingly. 'Neither do you. But you're here for a reason and I know this village like the back of my hand. If you help me with my problem, I reckon I can help you with yours. Sound fair?'

'What makes you think we've got a problem?' Hugo asked.

'Duh.' She rolled her eyes. 'You're not here for the Staffordshire Hoard because it's not here, so you're here for something else.' She pointed at me. 'You look like you've not slept for a month.'

One night. I hadn't slept for one night.

She pointed at Hugo. 'And you look scared.'

Did he?

'I have an affinity for such things,' Amy said airily. 'I can sense feelings in the same way other people can smell farts.'

Otis coughed at her words and Hester nodded knowingly. 'Sure,' she said. 'That might be true. But this affinity of yours has probably got more to do with you overhearing our conversation.'

Otis agreed. 'I told Hester that we had to stop arguing because it wasn't fair on you, Daisy, especially when you were so tired after getting no sleep last night.'

Hester chipped in. 'And I said we should stop arguing because Hugo was already scared enough by everything that was going on and Otis was frightening him even more.'

Hugo blinked. I looked at Amy. 'Yeah.' She shrugged. 'Alright, I did overhear them.' She grinned. 'But that doesn't mean I'm wrong.' The bolshy teenager had a point.

'For the record,' Hugo said, 'I am not scared of Otis.'

'Nobody's scared of *Otis*,' Hester retorted. 'But you're scared when he shouts and argues because of what it might mean for his state of mind and the effect that Athair is having on him.'

More likely Hugo was scared of the effect that Athair was having on us all. Not that I said that; instead I frowned at Hester, silently telling her to stop blabbing everything about us in front of a complete stranger.

Hugo also gave her an exasperated look though he didn't actually disagree with what she'd said. 'Go on, then,' he said to Amy. 'What's your problem? And how can we help?'

'Simple,' she said. 'I lost my favourite necklace in some woods near here a couple of weeks ago. I need someone to find it for me. That's what I wanted to advertise in Alan's shop.'

'Why don't you go and find your necklace yourself?' I asked, puzzled.

'There's a spider or two in the woods and I've got a touch of arachnophobia. They freak me out and every time I try to enter the woods, I get a bad case of the willies. I start to sweat, my hands shake.' She shuddered. 'Even the thought of spiders is too much for me. The day I lost my necklace, I saw one of them – in fact, that's how I lost my necklace. I was going for a wander, saw a huge spider, freaked out and ran out at high speed. My necklace must have fallen off when I was running away.'

I felt a wave of empathy for her; small, dark spaces made me feel the same way.

Amy regarded Hugo implacably. 'Anyhow,' she said, 'it's obviously fate that I bumped into you because you're a treasure hunter. In fact, you're the best treasure hunter in the country. You'll be able to find my necklace for me.'

'Perhaps,' he said, but his eyes gleamed with typical confidence.

I scowled. 'He's not the best treasure hunter.'

'I *am*,' Hugo said without missing a beat.

'I will find your necklace, Amy,' I declared. 'Spiders don't bother me.'

She smiled innocently and I suddenly realised she'd manipulated me; I'd all but promised I'd do what she wanted. She really was smart – or I was very stupid. 'As long as one of you finds it, I'll be happy.' Amy clasped her hands together. 'So tell me, what do you need from me in return?'

I grimaced. Unfortunately we didn't have a great deal of information to pass on. 'There is a rumour that some of the treasure from the Staffordshire Hoard is yet to be discovered,' I said, hedging my words.

Amy stared at me. 'I thought we'd already been through this. It's gone. It's in a museum. There's nothing left here.'

'But maybe 2009 wasn't the first time it was discovered,' Hugo said. 'Maybe somebody else found it first and dug part of it up.'

'That's stupid. Why wouldn't they dig it *all* up?' she asked.

Good question. 'We don't know,' I answered. 'It might not have happened recently. In fact, the part of the hoard which is missing might have been removed up to eight hundred years ago. Maybe there are some old local tales that might be relevant.'

'Or someone who's eight hundred years old and remembers it being dug up the first time,' Amy said sarcastically.

I managed to avoid looking at Hugo. 'Yeah,' I replied. 'Or that.'

She folded her arms. 'On reflection, I think that you've got the easier gig,' she muttered. 'I'll do my best. But I'm not promising anything.'

'That's all we can ask,' Hugo told her.

I nodded fervently. There was next to no chance that she'd find out anything, but a deal was a deal; we'd look for her necklace.

'It'll be dark soon,' she said. 'You should wait until tomorrow to look for the necklace. It'll be too hard to find it in the woods once the sun goes down.'

That was fair. 'Alright. We'll hunt for it first thing in the morning,' I told her. 'Let's meet back here at midday to exchange what we've found.' Or not found, I added silently, thinking of Athair's supposed secret gold.

Amy pursed her lips and nodded, then she grinned, stood up and started to jog away. 'Watch your backs!' she called out.

We watched her go. 'Interesting girl,' Hugo said. 'Strange but nice.'

'Yep,' Hester said. 'She's not as strange as Otis though.'

'But she's a lot nicer than Hester,' Otis snapped.

I groaned. 'I thought you were past this.'

'We are! We're all friends now.' Hester gave her brother a tight hug and he winced in response. 'See?'

I sighed. 'Come on,' I said. 'Let's find somewhere to camp.'

Hugo quickly agreed. 'And before anarchy descends again.'

I tried my best not to think of the spiders we'd meet the next day. I wasn't particularly bothered about the eight-legged variety that so terrified Amy, it was the ones that came in pill form that caused my heart to thud with fear. If I was going to struggle every time I saw a real spider because it reminded me of my fizzy pills, I would be in serious trouble. Maybe this would be a good test of my will power and I'd come out stronger in the end.

Then Hugo gave me a soft smile and I realised that his little dimple would be distraction enough. Screw spiders. Real or otherwise.

THERE WAS a lot to be said for having purpose, even if that purpose was only searching around a few old trees for a lost necklace. Purpose provided motivation, it gave meaning – and it improved my mood no end.

The next morning, as we walked through the quiet streets of Hammerwich towards the woods where Amy's prized possession was located, I found myself breaking into a happy hum. Within a few beats Hugo had joined in, drumming a beat on his thighs that matched my tune. If we hadn't been dedicated to the art of treasure hunting, we could have formed a duo.

Otis performed several spirals in the air, dancing in time to our acapella music, and even Hester yielded and started to tap her foot on my shoulder. This was all I needed out of life: good company, good fun and a reason to get up in the morning. Athair would never understand that.

There had been no update from the research team back at Pemberville Castle but I reasoned that no news was good news. The lack of information meant that they were safe and hadn't been troubled by the vamps; they were simply too busy tracking down leads related to Lincolnshire to get in touch. Yep, something to do with the fresh air and the morning sunshine was definitely making my mood buoyantly optimistic.

That sensation continued all the way to the woods, but as soon as we crossed the tree line my positive feelings vanished.

From a distance the woods looked pleasant; the variety of trees suggested this was ancient woodland that had been here for centuries. As we entered it, I expected pretty plants, tangled undergrowth and an atmosphere imbued with the best that nature had to offer; what I got were dark shadows, a smell of rotting meat and a sense of foreboding so strong that my footsteps faltered barely a few steps in.

Hugo's expression was tense, and Hester and Otis looked wide-eyed and fearful. 'I'm not the only one who feels that, am I?' I said darkly.

Hester swallowed hard. 'There's something wrong here. We should leave. We're not supposed to be here.'

She was right. It was as if something was clinging to the air, warning us off: the woods *wanted* us to leave. It put me in mind of a mosquito alarm that emitted a high-frequency tone that could be heard only by people under the age of twenty-five and was designed to discourage teenagers from loitering in certain areas, or an ultrasonic cat deterrent.

Beads of sweat broke out across my forehead. It was difficult to resist the urge to turn tail and run out of the woods but I held my ground and Hugo reached for my hand. 'Amy wandered into these woods of her own free will,' I muttered,

'I can't imagine why,' Hugo said. 'Do you want to give up? We can leave now and tell her we can't find her necklace.'

I glanced at him. I knew he'd abandon the woodland in an instant if I asked him to, but I also knew he wanted to go further inside for the same reason that I was determined to stay: something desperately wanted us to leave this area and that made me desperately want to know why. 'Not a chance,' I murmured. He grinned.

'You two are crazy,' Hester said, burrowing under the collar of my jacket. 'I'm staying out of the way. Tell me when it's safe to came out again – preferably when we're back out in the open.'

Otis watched his sister disappear into the folds of fabric; usually he'd follow her, but this time his jaw set hard. Their recent argument was obviously still lingering in his mind and he wanted to prove he was different to her; he wanted to act independently, even when his instincts told him otherwise.

He dragged his eyes away from Hes and looked at me. 'I'm perfectly fine,' he said. 'Let's start searching for the necklace.' He pulled back his shoulders and flicked his wings defiantly. 'I bet I find it first.'

'Probably.' I tried to sound cheerful. 'But stay close so we've got a chance to spot it too.' I didn't add that I needed to keep sight of him at all times in case something untoward happened.

Otis tried to disguise his relief at the order. 'Sure.' He pointed to his left. 'Let's go that way first.'

We picked our way carefully through the trees. The pressure to leave the woods didn't diminish but thankfully it didn't get stronger. We kept moving, pushing against the invisible force that seemed determined to expel us as we scanned the ground for Amy's necklace. I kept my eyes on the left-hand side while Hugo searched the right and Otis scanned the area in front of us.

'There are some fresh molehills behind that bush over there,' Hugo said. I paused to look. He was right.

Otis buzzed, 'And I think that's a badger's den in front of us.'

Interesting: whatever was trying to push us out wasn't malevolent enough to scare away the animals. That thought lightened my spirits somewhat. 'Maybe it's a strange sort of ward,' I said. 'Something environmentally friendly designed to preserve the woods but keep out the destructive force of humans and elves.'

'Brownies aren't destructive,' Hugo said. Otis flashed him a grateful smile.

'No, but their DNA is closer to ours than to a badger's. It could be something a local witch has conjured up to keep the likes of us out.'

'Possibly,' Hugo said. 'Although—' He stopped in mid-sentence. A slow grin spread across his face, causing his dimple to appear and my heart to skip a beat. 'There. I caught a glint of silver. That's a chain. I think we've found it.'

His sharp eyes galvanised us into action. We spun round and dashed towards the spot. Otis zipped through the air, letting out a crow of delight as he got close, while Hugo and I followed on foot.

'It's definitely a necklace!' Otis called.

Hester popped her head up to observe the proceedings. 'Well, whaddya know?' she said. 'There really is a necklace and this isn't just some sort of weird trap.'

I grinned and knelt down to scoop it up, but before I could Hugo put a hand on my arm. 'Wait,' he advised. 'It might yet be a weird trap.' He circled around the silver chain. 'Let me check it first.'

The necklace was nestled on a bed of verdant green moss; I could see its broken clasp even without kneeling down. There was nothing that suggested a trap; there were a few twigs nearby and a brown leaf caught in one of the silver links, but the placement was messy rather than artful. There wasn't a scrap of evidence to suggest that Amy had sent us here with a nefarious purpose.

'I can't sense any magic, Hugo. This isn't the source of that repelling force. We'd know if it were.'

'I'm only double checking. It pays to be prudent.' He sent me an arch look. 'As you should have already learned when you took a tumble down that gully before finding the dagger. One day, when you're as experienced as I am, you'll understand the value of being extra careful.'

Yeah, yeah. I rolled my eyes; this situation was not remotely similar to that one. 'Look,' I pointed down. 'There's a teeny spider. Who knows? That might be the one that freaked out Amy. There's no danger here, no trap.'

Otis flitted closer to the tiny creature. 'It's very small,' he said doubtfully. 'I mean, *I'm* small and even I think that spider is small. Is that really what scared her so much?'

We watched the small black arachnid scuttle across the moss. It paused for a moment, as if thinking then jumped, twisted around and darted out of sight. It was definitely far more afraid of us than we were of it, and it was far too small and far too real to cause my cravings for spider's silk to rear up.

I glanced again at Hugo then bent down and scooped up the necklace. Nothing changed and no traps were triggered.

'It doesn't mean I wasn't still right, Daisy,' Hugo admonished. 'Look before you leap.'

'He who hesitates is lost,' I returned.

I caught his flash of amusement and smiled. I picked up the necklace to give it a cursory examination. It was a pretty thing and the silver was real, although it didn't appear particularly valuable in monetary terms. Given Amy's determination to get it back, I suspected its sentimental value was high.

I put it carefully in my pocket to make sure it wouldn't go astray again. 'Mission accomplished,' I said. 'But not every question has been answered.'

Hugo's eyes gleamed. 'Do we leave this godforsaken place as fast as we can?' he asked. 'Or do some more investigating to find out why it feels as if we shouldn't be here?'

'Do you even have to ask?' I asked.

Hester, who was still buried amongst the folds of my coat, hissed in irritation. 'Yes! Yes, we do have to ask. And you know what the answer is? It's no. Hell, no. Let's get the fuck out of here as quickly as possible.' Nobody responded and she muttered under her breath, 'Why do I even bother?'

Suddenly Gladys, who'd remained sheathed by my side during our search, hummed loudly. It wasn't a light-hearted sound; I knew that tone, and it wasn't an attempt at banter with Hester. That sound was a warning.

I stiffened, immediately withdrew her blade and tightened my hand around her grip. My gaze swung nervously from side to side as Hugo stepped forward, squinting at the undergrowth. 'Something's in there,' he said.

No sooner had he finished speaking than there was a rustle. Hester squeaked and her head disappeared back under my collar. Otis bravely remained where he was but his wings were quivering as he scanned the area.

There was another rustle. I licked my lips. It was coming from somewhere low, close to the ground. 'It's probably just a small animal,' I whispered. 'One of those moles. Or the badger who lives nearby.'

Hugo grimaced. 'They're nocturnal animals, Daisy. It's ten o'clock in the morning.'

'There will be other creatures here. Plus it's pretty dark and gloomy. Maybe they think it's night time.'

As if in response, there was a scratching sound somewhere to my left. I turned just in time to see a large fern-like leaf tremble as something brushed it from underneath. Definitely an animal, then.

I held my breath – and that was when the first leg appeared. Cumbubbling bollocks.

CHAPTER

THIRTEEN

The leg was long, spindly and covered in wiry black hairs. Its narrow, tapered tip tapped the ground three times before a matching version of the same leg appeared. And another. And another.

Although the creature's body hadn't emerged, I knew exactly what I was looking at. This was a spider. It wasn't like the teeny-tiny spider we'd already spotted; if the legs on this version were anything to go by, this was the size of one of the wheels on Hugo's Jeep. At least.

'Bloody Amy,' Hugo muttered. 'She told us. She told us there was a huge spider. It turns out that she wasn't exaggerating.'

More of the creature slid out from underneath the fern. I gazed at its rounded, furry belly, which grew more russet in colour as it was revealed. I clenched my jaw, banking down the temptation to blast the thing was as much fire magic as I could muster. It wasn't doing anything wrong. Not yet, anyway.

It tapped its foreleg again then slipped forward another inch. As I lifted my eyes, I realised I could see the spider's face. There were two large pincer-type appendages close to its mouth and several furry stripes across its head, which gave it something of a punk-like appearance. But it wasn't that which caught my attention; once I'd caught a glimpse of the spider's eight glittering eyes, it was impossible to look away.

My mouth was dry and my palms were sweaty. I'd never understood arachnophobia before now but suddenly, confronted by a spider that was the size of a spaniel, I got it. My hand shot out and I grabbed Hugo's arm. It was a truly dumb thing to do because that movement was more than enough to catch the spider's attention.

All eight eyes swivelled towards us, then the spider hissed and reared up. I expected it to attack us but instead it jumped away, disappearing from view with a speed that took my breath away. I swallowed with relief; we'd been far luckier than we deserved.

'Perhaps it's time to leave after all,' Hugo said.

There was no perhaps about it. I nodded and hastily re-sheathed Gladys. 'Let's go. Now.'

'Thank fuck,' Hester's muffled voice said.

And with that, we sprinted away in the opposite direction. At first we kept pace with each other but it didn't take long for Otis to pull away, his small body and his ability to fly making him far faster than Hugo and me. He scooted forward, zipping between tree trunks and leafy bushes. By the time I called out, he was already out of sight.

'Otis!' I shouted. 'Stay close!'

If he'd heard me, he didn't answer. I tried to speed up but the ground was getting boggier and with every squelching foot-step it was harder and harder to run with any speed. I gritted my teeth and looked helplessly at Hugo. 'Can you see him?' I asked. 'Can you see Otis?'

'No,' he answered abruptly.

That was when we heard the scream. I'd never heard a

sound like that from Otis before but it was definitely him – and it was definitely a shriek imbued with pure terror.

Hester rocketed upwards, yanking herself out of her burrow in my jacket. Her face was white with fear and her hands were bunched into fists. 'Otis!' she cried. 'Where are you?'

Again there was no answer and Hester's body quivered. I snapped my hand out to grab her before she also took off. 'We can't lose you too, Hes. Stay with us and don't go flying off. We'll find Otis, I promise.'

She struggled for a moment then relaxed. I released my hold on her. Her bottom lip was trembling but she was calm.

'Come on,' Hugo said. 'I think he went this way.'

I called out again, shouting Otis's name at the top of my voice as we ran in the direction he'd disappeared. There still wasn't any answer and his silence was more chilling than his scream.

We finally escaped the squishy ground for a firmer section that made it easier to run. Hugo sent out a blast of carefully directed air magic to push aside the low-hanging branches and thick foliage that lay in our way.

I could feel my heart pumping hard in my chest then, when we veered around the thick trunk of a large oak tree, it seemed to stop altogether. Oh. *Oh.*

We were in a small clearing. Weak sunlight was filtering in from a gap in the foliage overhead. Strung from one tree to another was a glistening, silvery web that stretched horizontally for at least twelve metres and vertically for even more. Drops of water from a recent rain shower clung to it, sparkling in the dim light.

Under any other circumstances I'd have been awestruck by the web's beauty, but I couldn't admire it now because in front of the web – and blocking much of our view – was another spider. This arachnid wasn't the size of the first one we'd seen, nor was it the size of the second monstrous version.

This spider was the size of a car.

I'd withdrawn Gladys again without even thinking about it. Doubtless a creature such as this was covered under the country-wide law that protected magical species in their own habitat. I couldn't attack the spider, not under any circumstances, but I could certainly use Gladys to hack away at the web. And if Otis was in danger, I'd do whatever I could to protect him.

Standing beside me, Hugo gulped in a sharp breath, his eyes flicking from side to side as he assessed the situation. Hester had no such compunction. She was already flying over and yelling at the top of her voice, 'Where is my brother, you eight-legged freak?'

The giant spider jumped; apparently it had been unaware of our approach. It executed a perfect half-turn and I caught a brief glimpse of Otis trapped in the sticky folds of the glittering web before his body was obscured again. My stomach lurched with fear. I wouldn't allow him to become a spider's lunch. I couldn't.

'You and me, buster!' Hester shouted, her voice cracking on the last word. 'You and me! Put 'em up! Come on!'

The spider, an immense creature of monstrous, cold beauty, gazed at her with its eight glistening black eyes. I could see images of Hester reflected on the shiny surface of each eyeball. Compared to the arachnid, she was minute – she had no chance.

Panic clawed at my throat, then my limbs acted almost of their own accord and I lurched forward with Gladys raised. I barely managed three steps before Hugo grabbed my collar and hauled me back. I hissed at him angrily but he shook his head, his expression far calmer than mine. Wait, he seemed to be telling me. Just wait.

The spider chittered at Hester as it rubbed its pincers together. I heard a whoosh as it exhaled a blast of air, then its vast mouth opened revealing a gaping black hole. Terror for Hester and Otis rocked me to my core.

'Good morning,' it said.

I blinked. So did Hester. Even Hugo, who had acted with far more sense than the rest of us, appeared stunned. The spider spoke in a deep male voice – and he had an accent. In fact, he sounded almost exactly like Alan the shopkeeper. A Brummie monster spider with good manners? I shook my head. What on earth was going on?

Hester recovered first. 'Free my brother,' she shouted, 'or prepare to die!'

'That is exactly what I am trying to do,' the spider huffed. He reared up and rubbed two of his legs together in front of Hester. 'However, it is not easy with these limbs. Perhaps you can help. Your fingers appear dainty enough to extract him safely.'

Hester didn't relax; she was squinting at the giant creature with undisguised suspicion. 'This is a clever trap, right? Encourage me to help free Otis and trap me in the process!'

Her concern was reasonable until you considered all the facts. 'It's not a trap, Hester,' I said softly. 'The spider speaks the truth.'

'You don't know that!' she protested.

Hugo gave her a crooked, gentle smile. 'Yes, she does.' He glanced at me then at the spider. 'The smell,' he said. 'That deep scent that pervades these woods, and the magic that accompanies it, are designed to repel curious passers-by. That came from you, didn't it?' he asked the spider.

The creature stared at Hugo. It was impossible to tell what he was thinking; it could have been disgust, admiration or even love. The facial features of enormous spiders were not designed to give much away, not to my eyes anyway. 'It is clearly not as effective as it used to be,' he said finally. 'After all, you are here.'

'Oh, it's effective,' I told him. 'It was so strong that it ramped up our curiosity. Most other people would have turned and walked away but I'm afraid we like to investigate places that others would avoid.'

The spider tapped another of his long legs on the ground. 'Hmm. You are not the first to enter these woods in recent days.'

He was talking about Amy. 'Did she see you?' I asked. 'The other person who was here?'

'No, but she saw one of my children.' He raised his body an inch before lowering it again: I supposed that was the arachnid version of a shrug. 'Elves have always been more resistant to my spells than other creatures. That makes you ... more annoying than the others who walk on two legs.'

I wouldn't disagree with him on that point. Hell, I wouldn't disagree with him on any point. I wouldn't dare.

Hester had no such qualms. 'Why are you all standing around talking?' she shrieked. She flung herself at one of the spider's massive legs as if she were trying to knock him off balance. Unsurprisingly, he didn't move an inch. 'Otis is still trapped! Help him!'

'Sorry, Hester,' Hugo said.

I nodded. 'Sorry.'

She glared at us. 'Don't apologise to me! Apologise to Otis!'

The spider shuffled to the side and exposed the full scale of his vast web – and Otis's tiny, trapped figure. 'I *am* sorry,' the spider murmured. 'It was never my intention to trap your kind. We do not eat two legs – only six legs is food for us.'

Six legs? Insects, then: flies, beetles, those sorts of creatures. But it would take a vast amount of normal-sized insects to fill this spider's belly. Horrified, I wondered if there were bluebottles flies zipping around these woods who were similarly gargantuan but I shook off the thought before it took hold. Hester was right: our priority had to be Otis.

He'd been silent since his scream for good reason. As far as I could tell, he'd flown headfirst into the web and instinctively started to struggle. The more he'd thrashed around, the more he'd been trapped as the silvery web silk had reacted and wrapped more tightly around his body. Several strands around his head had forced his mouth closed, and his poor wings were similarly bound. No wonder the spider had told us he couldn't free Otis from his own trap; disentangling the little brownie was not going to be an easy feat for anyone.

'Don't worry, Otis,' I told him. 'We'll get you out of there.' Somehow. Unable to speak, his body twitched in silent response. Unfortunately that only embedded him further in the tricksy web.

'Try not to move,' Hugo advised. Otis glared at him to indicate that was easier said than done.

Hester sniffed wetly and reached forward to touch him. 'Don't,' I advised her. We had enough problems; if Hester brushed against the web silk, she'd probably be trapped as well.

She withdrew her hand but sent me a mournful, pleading look. 'Please help him,' she whispered. 'Please hurry.'

The giant spider chittered again. 'Your sword will be best. I can guide you where to make the best cuts.'

I'd all but forgotten Glady was in my hand. She hummed quietly as if to indicate that she was aware of the need for delicate movements. I nodded and carefully twisted her blade while the spider raised one leg and gestured to a section of the intricate web. I licked my lips, raised Gladys and carefully sliced through several strands of silk.

Otis was trembling so much that the whole web was shaking; one slip and I could inadvertently hurt him – or worse. I held my breath and felt sweat break out on my forehead.

I glanced again at the spider. He moved his leg, pointed to another section and I directed Gladys to follow. In the end it took eight separate cuts in specific areas before Hugo could reach in and pull Otis free from the web, although the little brownie body was still bound up by several loose strands.

I reached into Hugo's cupped hands where Otis now lay and gently brushed one of them, then drew back abruptly. No wonder he'd been so effectively bound up: the web silk was like super glue.

There was a flicker of movement in my peripheral vision. I turned and spotted several smaller spiders waiting by the side of the clearing, six of them, each with a small pile of newly harvested leaves beside them. I felt a brief chill as I wondered how many of these creatures were lurking inside the woods before reminding myself that they were friendly. I should have learned my lesson from Athair: appearances were often deceptive.

'Nettle juice,' the giant spider explained. 'It will dissolve the silk.'

Hugo placed Otis gently on the ground and scooped up the piles of nettle leaves that the smaller spiders must have collected for this very purpose. With nothing more than a grimace as the plants stung him, he squeezed the leaves until dribbles of green juice slipped out and fell onto Otis's body. 'That must hurt,' I said.

'It does,' Hugo replied through gritted teeth. 'But I'm being a tough man so you'll look kindly on me later.'

I considered a snarky response, then I leaned in and kissed his cheek. His grimace gave way to a brief smile. 'You can kiss the rest better later,' he said.

'I will,' I promised while Hester tutted with annoyance.

We waited for the nettle juice to do its work. The giant

spider had told us the truth; although it took several minutes, the green liquid worked and Otis was eventually freed.

It took him a while to speak. First he flexed his wings to make sure each one was in working order before he attempted to flap them and rise up in the air. Next, he brushed himself down, his face blank as he wiped away the remaining droplets left by the nettles. His exposed skin now had a definite green tinge to it but I decided telling him that probably wouldn't help his mood.

Eventually Otis straightened his shoulders and looked at Hester. His bottom lip trembled – and a second later he threw himself at her. 'You were prepared to take on that monster for me. You'd never have won but you didn't care. You are a true warrior, Hester.'

The spider watched them. I hoped he wasn't upset at being called a monster. 'The tiny two legs speaks the truth,' he said.

Hester hugged Otis back, her emotions equally choked. 'I thought you were going to die. The last things we said to each other were angry and I thought I'd never get the chance to say anything else. I'm so sorry I argued with you. I won't do it again.'

Otis smiled. 'You will, Hester,' he said. 'But that's okay. I'd be disappointed if you didn't. I love you, no matter what you do.'

'I love you, too.' She started to cry.

I looked away; it felt like we were intruding on their close sibling relationship by watching them. I bent down and carefully picked up a few more nettle leaves to clean Gladys's blade.

As I did so, Hugo spoke to the spider. 'I apologise sincerely for intruding into your habitat. We should have heeded your scent warning and left the area immediately.'

'The fault is mine,' the spider told him. 'I know my appearance is frightening for your kind, and that my web holds particular dangers for certain creatures. I should have done more to ensure the safety of any two legs who ignored the warnings.'

'This is on us, not you,' I said firmly. 'We made the mistake.'

The spider's eight glittering eyes fixed on me. 'I used to do more to keep your kind away, so I must take responsibility for my actions. To do otherwise is to be powerless.'

I suspected that the spider was trying to teach his assembled children a lesson, but I was adamant that we were the ones at fault, not him.

'I have grown complacent in my old age,' he continued. 'In the past this did not happen to me. It has been many hundreds of years since I mistakenly caught a creature I did not want to trap, but I cannot forget the power I possess. Spider's silk is wonderful. It is strong and it is beautiful.' He sighed. 'But it can be deadly if due care is not taken.'

I stiffened immediately. I knew that he did not mean drugs – it was doubtful he even knew that the drug spider's silk existed – but suddenly it was all I could think about.

Only Hugo seemed to sense the direction my thoughts had taken. His hand reached for mine, his thumb brushing against my palm in an attempt to reassure me.

Blood roared through my ears and my heart rate ratcheted up. I could almost taste the spider's silk on my tongue, the way it tingled and teased before I swallowed it down, the way the chemicals translated to my brain and my magic and the very core of my being.

Otis coughed. 'Don't worry about it,' he said. 'We're engaged in a mortal battle with a fiend. This was a mere stumble by comparison.'

I thought about the way the drugs would fly through my veins at supersonic speed, electrifying my body with a delicious thrill that was like no other.

'Shh,' Hester hissed, nudging her brother. 'Don't say things like that. You could have died, Otis. The spider might give us compensation for our suffering.'

'*Our* suffering, Hes?' he asked.

Hugo's hand increased its pressure on mine but I was lost in my imagination as I remembered how spider's silk would rub up against my magical powers and ... and ... and...

'Did you say fiend?' the spider asked. 'Those who have been corrupted by magic of the blood?'

'I'm afraid so,' Hugo replied.

The spider hissed. 'That is unfortunate. I thought they had all been destroyed generations ago, but I suppose that evil always finds a way.'

I was brought back to reality with a bump. I shook my head free of my traitorous, self-defeating thoughts and gazed at him. 'Why would you think that?' A sudden new tension filled my body. 'Why would you think they'd all been destroyed?'

'I often heard whispers from the villagers who lived near this place. When I was small, I often ventured into their dwellings and watched them. I heard this whisper from several of them a long time ago. But it was many, many moons ago,' he admitted.

The spider's eyes swivelled around, watching each of us in turn as he expressed his confusion. 'I heard that one of your kind possessed the means to rid this world of every fiend, so I assumed they had already done so. Why would you not destroy them if you had the means to do so? Fiends are indeed devilish and dangerous. They should not exist.'

All four of us were staring at him in shock.

'What means?' I asked, my voice little more than a desperate whisper. 'What means would rid us of every fiend?'

'I do not know,' he answered. 'I did not hear the details.'

'How long ago was this?' Hugo demanded.

'As I said,' the spider told us. 'Many moons.'

Hugo persisted, anxiety colouring his words. 'How many moons exactly?'

'I do not keep track of time in the way that you do,' the spider said mildly. 'Your lives are fleeting but I have been in these woods for a very long time. And it has been a very long time since I have been to the village below.'

He lifted his enormous head and seemed to gaze off into the distance. A ball of frustration tightened my stomach, but then he spoke again. 'I heard of it after these woods were first coppiced but before the *magna pestiliencia* took hold.'

Hester buzzed in my ear, 'Huh? Is he still speaking English?'

I checked Hugo's expression; neither the brownies nor I understood the spider's words but, from the look on Hugo's face, he did.

'You said one of our kind possessed these ... means,' Otis said. 'Do you mean a brownie? Or an elf?'

The spider tapped one of his legs, then another. 'I mean one of you,' he said. 'All of you. Your kind with two legs.'

That didn't exactly narrow it down. It felt like we were being handed the keys to the kingdom – but before we could grasp them, they were falling into a bottomless drain in front of our eyes. 'Can you remember anything else about these whispers?' I asked.

'I cannot. It was a very long time ago.' The spider regarded us solemnly. 'I sense a change in you,' he said. 'In all of you.' He wasn't wrong. A new sense of possibility seemed to cling to us all even though my frustration at the lack of hard facts and answers was almost painful.

'We should go,' I told him. 'Thank you so very much for your help.'

He nodded. 'You are welcome.' He turned his glittering eyes on Otis. 'My sincere apologies again, Tiny Two Legs. My children will help you find your way out of these woods.'

'Thank you,' Otis whispered. 'I am glad we met you.'

I was too. 'What's your name?' I asked.

The spider chittered for a final time, as if he were chuckling. 'My kind have no need for such labels,' he said.

He turned away and bent towards the ragged gap in his web that I'd created with Gladys's help. He clearly had some work to do in order to repair it. 'Fare thee well,' he told us and then, in a quieter voice, 'If you truly are locked in battle with a fiend, you have my deepest condolences.'

CHAPTER

FOURTEEN

None of us said much as we traversed the woods on our way back to open land and empty skies. It might have been the presence of the spiders, which herded us through the trees as if we were errant sheep who had to be shown the way, or it might have been their father's revelations that kept us silent. We were all chewing over what we had learned and what it could mean for our future.

Despite my preoccupation, I couldn't avoid the blast of relief when we finally stepped out of the woods and gazed upon Hammerwich. Enjoying the moment, I breathed in the fresh cold air then turned back to thank the spiders for their help but all six of them had already gone, their duty complete.

I scanned the trees for a long moment and shrugged. They were in the right place; the woods were clearly protected and the spider family as safe as they ever could be. Those trees had stood for many hundreds of years and hopefully would remain for hundreds more.

Hugo pulled out a water bottle and took several long swallows. Hester tilted her head up to the sun and Otis rubbed at the greenish skin on his bare arms with a faint frown. It appeared that nobody wanted to be the first to speak. I nibbled on my bottom lip and watched a lazy pigeon flap past us.

But we had to talk about it sooner or later. I cleared my throat. 'It might mean nothing,' I said. 'Even if what he said is true and somebody possessed the means to rid the world of fiends – and actually did so – they couldn't be eradicated forever. Blood magic still exists therefore fiends still exist.'

Hugo screwed the lid back onto his water bottle and looked at me. Usually, his blue eyes reminded me of smooth velvet but now their colour put me in mind of a gathering storm. 'Fiends have *always* existed in some form or other. We can trace their history back to the turn of the first millennium. There are fiends embroidered onto the Bayeux Tapestry and that's been in existence since the eleventh century. They are described in the Domesday Book.'

He was referring to the survey of swathes of the country that had been completed at the behest of William the Conqueror in 1086. 'And there are records in a temperature-controlled vault in the Royal Elvish Institute that reference all known fiends throughout the centuries. You've seen them, Daisy.'

He was right: I'd managed to gain access to that information not long after Athair had first revealed himself to be my father. 'Records can be altered,' I said, playing devil's advocate. 'Especially historical ones. A lot of those records have been kept hidden from the general public. The less people know about them, the easier they are to change.'

Hugo shook his head. 'But even when those historical records are hidden from public view, there are still too many of them to give credence to such a radical event. It never happened, Daisy. There has never been a purging of every fiend. Whatever rumours the spider heard, nobody has ever rid the world of them all.'

He paused. 'But just because it didn't happen then, doesn't mean it couldn't happen now,' he added softly. 'It doesn't mean those rumours were false, it simply means that the final event has never taken place.'

'Yet,' Otis whispered.

A broad grin spread across Hester's face. 'Yet!' she shouted.

I was a long way from sharing her excitement. 'Do you think it might have something to do with the map you found at Culcreuch Castle? Could it be related to Lincolnshire? Could that be the reason why Athair doesn't want us to go there?'

'It's certainly possible.' Hugo gazed at me. 'But we don't have any concrete information. All we have is vague guesswork and ancient rumours.'

I nodded and bit my lip. 'What the spider said about coppicing the wood and the magna pesti-something? What did that mean?'

'The *magna pestiliencia* is one of the names for the Black Death,' Hugo explained.

I stiffened. Athair had told me he'd been alive during that time. 'Mid-fourteenth century,' I said. 'Right?'

He nodded. 'And coppicing woodland is an ancient woodland management technique that dates back to the Stone Age.'

'Three million years ago?' Otis asked in disbelief.

'Yep. Give or take.' Hugo pointed behind us. 'But although these woods are ancient, they're not wild. They've not been here since the dawn of time. The people of Hammerwich are probably responsible for coppicing them in more recent times. If we can find out roughly when the coppicing started here, we'll get a more accurate idea of when the spider might have heard that rumour.' He eyed us. 'It's not much. Like Lincolnshire, it's not much more than another shot in the dark.'

He wasn't wrong, but desperate times called for desperate measures. 'We have to take what we can get.'

He grinned suddenly. 'That we do.'

WE MEANDERED BACK to the little park and perched on the bench where we'd chatted to Amy the day before. It was pleasing to see that we were no longer the only visitors: the small children's area, complete with swings, slide and a climbing frame, was occupied by two or three families enjoying the midday sun. There were also a few cars and pedestrians on the streets. Hammerwich was still a quiet place but at least today it wasn't entirely devoid of life.

Hugo looked around, double-checking that nobody was near enough to overhear our conversation, then took out his phone. He put it onto speaker and placed it on the bench as he called the team of Primes back at Pemberville Castle.

Becky answered on the second ring: she'd clearly been waiting for our call. 'Hey! How are you guys?' Her bubbly voice was like a balm. 'Have you had any joy locating that extra missing gold?'

To be honest, I'd forgotten the reason we'd come to Hammerwich. Athair's wild goose chase seemed even less important now than it had before.

'We're still investigating,' Hugo replied, in a tone that suggested the same lack of interest.

Becky got the message instantly. 'Fair enough,' she said cheerfully. 'Hang on. I'm putting you on speaker. The others are here. Mark is ready to give you an update on our Lincolnshire progress.'

There was a fuzzy noise before Mark's familiar voice filled the line. 'We've got a long list of locations in Lincolnshire that might be of interest,' he said. 'There are plenty of vanished items and mysterious places that haven't been fully explored.

For example, there are the remains of an old Templar church at a place called Bruer. Some stories suggest that the Templars kept an idol there that was of great importance – there's a chance that idol was John the Baptist's decapitated head.'

I recoiled. Eugh.

'Then there's something called the Brass Wellie from Boston,' he told us. 'There's a lot of debate about what it actually is, but it's a lost object of some significance and definitely has some magical power, although it appears to be agricultural in nature.'

He paused for breath. 'And in more rural Lincolnshire there's a decorative grave marker. Four hundred skeletons were recently uncovered nearby. I'm waiting to hear back from one of the archaeologists on that particular project, so I can't tell you much more at the moment. However, I should also mention the items that have already been discovered but whose existence remains unexplained, such as the Corieltauvi Bull Rider. That's a small figurine, two thousand years old, that was dug up by a metal detectorist. Or the Witham Shield from the Iron Age, which possesses mystic elements. And if it's not objects we're searching for but actual creatures, there is the supposed river god, Old Muddyface.'

I heard Rizwan in the background. 'Not a god, obviously. Probably another damned troll.'

Duchess's voice boomed, 'Another *what*?'

'Another wonderful troll, Duchess. What did you think I said?' He was lucky she was often hard of hearing.

Mark continued. 'There's a selkie called Jenny Hearn, who's been hanging around the Trent for decades.' He sighed with exasperation. 'We've tried to contact her but she's not known for either her enthusiasm or friendliness. To be honest, so far we probably have more than a hundred places, people and objects of interest in Lincolnshire. I don't see how we can narrow them down without further information. And there are probably hundreds of other things out there that we don't know about.'

Rizwan's muffled voice spoke again. 'Tell them about the dead guy.'

Mark sighed. 'There is a chance that we've identified the corpse you found in Culcreuch Castle. A metal detectorist called William Hausman vanished several years ago. The timing of his disappearance matches the decomposition.'

'Where did Hausman disappear from?' Hugo asked.

'King's Lynn,' Mark replied. 'It's in Norfolk, but it's only a stone's throw from the border with Lincolnshire.'

My fingers twisted together. The geographical coincidence couldn't be ignored: perhaps poor Mr Hausman had gotten too close to whatever the spider had alluded to – and whatever Athair was trying to hide.

Hugo raised his eyebrows at me in question. I knew what he was asking and I nodded. What other choice was there? We had to add the spider's information into the mix. 'It's possible that we have something else which might help. Or,' he demurred, 'it might not.'

'Why do I suspect it will be the latter?' Mark asked drily.

Hugo smiled slightly. 'There are some woods to the north of Hammerwich,' he said. 'Find out what date coppicing started there and narrow your search to items and people from between that date and the outbreak of the Black Death.'

For a long moment there was silence on the other end of the phone until eventually Miriam responded. 'Hugo, dear,' she said with infinite patience. 'Hammerwich is in Staffordshire. It's nowhere near Lincolnshire.'

'I'm aware of that, Miriam.' Hugo hesitated. 'We met a very old creature who'd heard a rumour about someone who lived during that period of time and who possessed the means to expel all fiends in one go.'

Hester leaned into my ear. 'You know, when he says it like that, it sounds completely ridiculous,' she muttered.

I grimaced. Yeah. It did.

'Exactly how many wild goose chases do you want us to go on?' Mark asked.

Hugo winced so I answered for him. 'Just these two.' I tried to sound cheerful. 'They might be linked.'

'Uh-huh.'

'Call it gut instinct,' I said.

This time it was Duchess whose voice I heard in the background. 'My gut instinct is telling me very loudly that it's time for lunch,' she declared. There was a chorus of groans. I suspected this was not the first time today that Duchess had mentioned her stomach.

Becky spoke up. 'Are you both sure about this?'

'We're not sure about anything, Becky,' I told her, trying to be honest. 'But it's got to be worth a shot.'

'Then we'll do our best,' she said, but even she sounded doubtful.

'Thanks.'

Hugo picked up the phone. 'Email the list of places and things you've already found,' he said. 'It'll be helpful to look over it.'

'No problem.'

There was a chorus of goodbyes before Hugo ended the call. 'Don't worry,' he said, when he saw my expression. 'The Primes have been here before. We've had lots of treasure hunts that began with smoky whispers and eventually led to great success. This hunt will be even more successful.'

I raised an eyebrow. 'What makes you think that?'

'Because this time the two of us are working together. We won't fail – we are the greatest hunters Britain has ever seen.'

I grinned. 'Even when we don't have the foggiest idea what we're hunting for.'

Otis pumped the air. 'Go, team!'

A slim figure caught my eye and I looked up in time to see Amy push open the park gate and head towards us. I waved at her. 'We found her necklace,' I said. 'That's not nothing, either.'

Hugo grunted in response then leaned back against the bench and draped an arm around my shoulders as we watched the teenager approach. 'Top o' the morning to ye!' she called in a mock Irish accent.

I glanced at my watch: it was past noon but I wasn't so old that I didn't recall what it was like to be a teenager: any time before 3pm had felt like morning when I was seventeen years old.

I smiled at her but Hugo was less welcoming. 'You should have told us about the spider, Amy,' he chided.

Her eyes widened. 'What do you mean? I did tell you. You said spiders didn't bother you. In fact,' she said, 'I believe I specifically said the words *huge* and *spider*. I didn't lie, not even by omission.'

Hester spiralled a metre into the air and closed the gap between them. While her wings beat behind her, she thrust out her hand towards Amy. 'I like your style,' she proclaimed gravely. 'I like it a lot. Shake my hand.'

If Amy was taken aback by Hester's actions, she didn't show it; she simply inclined her head like a queen and extended her pinkie to the little brownie. Hester smacked her lips in satisfaction and, with some awkwardness, managed to grab hold of the tip of Amy's fingers and shake it.

Hugo muttered something inaudible under his breath. 'Stop that,' I told him. 'Amy reminds me of you.'

He snorted. 'Rubbish. She's far more like you than me.'

Amy glanced at us and we snapped our mouths closed like two guilty school kids. She pulled her hand back from Hester. 'Can I assume from your complaint about spiders that you didn't manage to find my necklace?' She sounded resigned to our failure.

'Don't worry, we found it.' I reached into my pocket and carefully withdrew the necklace, stood up and handed it over. 'Here you go.'

To my astonishment, Amy's eyes filled with tears. She bit her lip, obviously trying desperately to hold them back then she gave up and let them trickle down her cheeks. 'Thank you,' she gulped. 'Thank you so much.'

'The clasp is broken,' I told her. 'You should get it fixed before you wear it again.'

She sniffed loudly. 'I will.' Her fingers tightened around it and she gave an embarrassed laugh. 'I know it's silly to react like this over such a simple object but it belonged to my gran. It was a present from her before she died.'

I offered her a gentle smile. 'There's nothing wrong with being attached to objects, especially when they remind us of the people we love.'

'Thank you.' She sniffed again and rubbed her eyes. 'For a high elf, I guess you're not so bad.'

'See?' Hugo said. 'I'd never say anything like that. She's definitely more like you than like me.'

My smile grew. 'I'll take that as a compliment.'

Amy dropped her gaze and her smile vanished as quickly as it had appeared. 'Unfortunately, I'm not sure that I managed to keep my side of the bargain,' she said, guiltily. 'I spoke to everyone I could think of about the Staffordshire Hoard but even the old biddies who've lived here all their lives had nothing to offer. I tried the church – the vicar likes to yap about the parish records and how wonderful they are. Apparently they date back to the sixteenth century, but he wouldn't let me look at them and he said they only list births, deaths and marriages.'

I was impressed. Given the vague information we'd given her and the limited time she'd had, Amy had put considerable effort into the search. 'Thanks for trying,' I said. 'It was always a long shot.' My desire to find Athair's supposed treasure had never been strong and it was diminishing by the second; we had far more important matters to deal with.

Amy wasn't finished. 'The only real lead I could come up with is the old witch's cottage. You might find something there.'

I paused, genuinely surprised. 'Go on.'

She looked awkward. 'There's not much to tell. It's about half a mile that way,' she waved a hand vaguely. 'It's been falling down for years but nobody's done anything about it. Some people say it's cursed and anyone who demolishes it will receive seven generations of bad luck. I don't think that's true, but nobody is willing to test the theory.'

I couldn't suppress my interest and clearly Hugo felt the same. 'Why do you think there might be something there?' he asked.

'I don't,' she said. 'You're the ones who seem to think there's more gold to be found. Not me.' We both waited. 'But,' she added reluctantly, 'there are some interesting stories about the witch who lived there. You know how we didn't treat witches very well back in the day?'

That was something of an understatement.

'Well,' Amy continued, 'the old story goes that there was an old woman who lived there a few hundred years ago. Whether she was an actual witch or not, she was poor for most of her life and always struggled to make ends meet – until all of a sudden she started flashing the cash. She bought a bunch of stuff at the local market and started wearing nicer clothes. Nobody could work out where she got her money from. Her neighbours got jealous and started pointing fingers, saying that the devil had paid her to do bad things.' Amy rolled her eyes. 'The woman was tried as a witch and burned at the stake.'

'There was never an explanation for where she got the money?' I guessed.

'Nope. She could just have nicked it from somewhere.'

'Or she could have somehow found the Staffordshire Hoard and dug part of it up,' Hugo said. 'And she didn't dig it all up because she was executed before that could happen.'

'It's a theory.' Amy sounded doubtful. 'But it could just be an old story that's not remotely true. Sorry I couldn't come up with anything better.'

I glanced at Hugo. 'It's plausible.'

'It is.' He looked closely at Amy. 'You're an elf.'

'A low elf,' she said quickly. 'I'm not like you.' That was exactly the sort of thing I used to say.

Hugo persisted. 'But you've got some magic?'

She shuffled her feet. 'A bit.'

I understood where he was going with this. 'How's your earth magic, Amy?'

She wrinkled her nose. 'What do you mean?'

'There's a nifty trick that I can show you with earth magic,' I told her. 'It might help you when you go to the cottage to hunt for the hidden gold.'

'Me?' She stared at us. 'Why would I do that?'

Hugo and I exchanged glances. 'You're smart and you can think on your feet,' he said. 'You also seem to have a talent for searching.' He smiled faintly. 'As long as there are no spiders to worry about.'

I nodded. 'And we've got other places to be. You could take up the search for us. Anything you find will be yours.'

Amy crossed her arms and nibbled on her bottom lip before

eventually shrugging. 'Alright,' she said. 'Tell me what I need to know.'

FIFTEEN

The only person who was displeased by the turn of events was Hester. As soon as we waved goodbye to Amy and got into the Jeep, she started to complain. Loudly. 'You absolute bunch of bloody idiotic nincompoops!'

I clicked my seatbelt into place. 'What's wrong now?'

'We have a decent lead on some real treasure and you handed it over to a teenager! When she gets rich and you've got bills that you can't pay, don't come crying to me!'

Otis sprang to our defence. 'Hes, they're already rich,' he said patiently. 'They can pay their bills – even Daisy can pay her bills. She's not a hard-up delivery driver any longer. She's a lady. With a mansion.'

'That's no reason not to guard against a rainy day! Or to grow those existing riches!'

'You know there's much more to what we do than money, Hes,' I said. Being rich was not anywhere near my to-do list. Besides, as Otis had said, thanks to Lady Rose I was already more than wealthy enough for all of us. 'Amy has done most of the heavy lifting. She's the one who pinpointed the old witch's cottage. If there's any treasure to be found there, she deserves it.'

'Plus,' Hugo added, 'we're less concerned with the treasure that Athair wants us to find and more interested in·what he *doesn't* want us to find.'

'Based on what?' Hester asked sarcastically. 'An old map with a blank space on it and the ramblings of an ancient giant spider? We don't have any real information to go on. We don't even know where to find information.' She folded her arms, affected a pout and turned away. 'It's ridiculousness.'

'Well, I think they've done a wonderful thing,' Otis said. 'Even without the immediate concerns about Athair, they're inspiring the next generation of treasure hunters. They're creating a wonderful legacy.'

'Yeah, yeah,' Hester grumbled. 'At the very least, you should have negotiated a percentage.' She looked out of the window at Amy's departing back and her voice dropped. 'I hope she'll be alright. Treasure hunting is dangerous and I like her. I don't want her to get hurt.'

I smiled softly. I suspected that was at the root of Hester's complaint but, regardless of her youth, I reckoned Amy would be fine. More than fine, in fact.

Hugo's phone pinged and he picked it up and glanced at the screen. A slow smile spread across his face. 'The Primes have come through. They've found information that the woods near Hammerwich were not coppiced until just after the turn of the thirteenth century. That helps narrow down the time frame. Now we're looking for something that could remove all fiends in one go that existed between the years of 1200 and 1345.' In other words, long before Athair had been born.

Otis smiled brightly. 'That's only 145 years to worry about. Easy. We could get the golden skull back from Sir Nigel and time travel back. That'd be really interesting.'

'Sure,' Hester said. 'I, for one, am incredibly eager to spend more than a century living in a world without antibiotics, sanitation and Google.'

Hugo intervened. 'Unfortunately, even if we were allowed to use it again, the skull doesn't work like that.'

'But that doesn't mean we're out of options.' I grinned.

Hester sighed. 'You're talking about books, aren't you? Dusty, boring research. If there was anything to find in books, wouldn't somebody have already found it?'

'You have to know which questions to ask before you can find the answers. With enough time, I'm sure I can inspire an army of bookworms to help us,' Hugo said. 'We know more about what we're looking for now, so we can hit every library and museum in the country that houses old books. It will take time but we're bound to find something sooner or later.'

'Or we can speed things up, narrow down our search and try something else,' I suggested.

He raised his eyebrows. 'Go on.'

'Athair is hundreds of years old,' I said. 'That spider is hundreds of years old. It's their *lived* history that has given them the knowledge we lack.'

'Uh-huh.' Hugo scratched his chin.

I grinned widely. 'My old friend the Fachan is hundreds of years old, too.'

SMOO CAVE WAS the last place in Britain I'd ever thought I'd return to. I wouldn't have described my first visit there as a pleasant experience, even though without it I wouldn't have had Gladys. But when we finally arrived at the familiar campsite after hour upon hour of relentless driving north, I couldn't deny the warm fuzziness I felt upon seeing the familiar signs and the open campsite.

With no other tents and no sign of any camper vans, we had our pick of the spots. It took less than fifteen minutes to erect our tent, lay out our sleeping bags and get our equipment ready for the next day's excursion into the cave. I was trying not to think too hard about that; the less mental space my claustrophobia could occupy, the less it would bother me when we entered Smoo Cave. If I could beat drug addiction, I could certainly overcome my fear of small dark spaces.

Hugo tidied up the loose items in the back of the Jeep then strode towards the centre of the campsite. He glanced around, side-stepped three metres to his left and planted his feet firmly on a particular spot, then put his hands in his pockets, turned around and eyed me with a knowing glint. Something tugged at my mind and an old memory rose to the surface; before I could stop it, a flush rose to my cheeks.

'It's as if we were here only yesterday,' Hugo murmured. 'You know, I was standing right on this very spot when you told me that you wanted a threesome.' His gaze travelled up and down my body with a hot, possessive look. 'The trouble is, Daisy, I'm not prepared to share you with anyone.'

I licked my lips. My flush was deepening. 'I was hallucinating at the time, as you well know. The threesome I envisaged was me, and,' I held up two fingers to emphasise my point, 'two of you.'

'One of me isn't enough?' he teased.

'There's always room for improvement.'

A low guttural rumble sounded in his chest. 'You can't improve upon perfection.'

I laughed aloud as Hugo continued to smoulder.

I was vaguely aware of Otis and Hester looking at us,

looking at each other and muttering about re-visiting the local pub before they hastily flapped away. If the bar staff were the same as last year, the brownies would be welcomed with open arms. I didn't pay them much attention; it was nigh on impossible to drag my gaze away from Hugo.

'Do you practise that look in the mirror?' I asked him. 'That "come hither so I can ravish you immediately" look?'

'I don't need to practise it. All I need to do is look at you and think of how good you feel in my arms.'

My attempts at humour vanished, replaced by a tightening in my belly with several delicious, anticipatory butterflies thrown in for good measure.

Hugo continued, 'I remember the exact words you said to me.'

'Oh, yes?' I asked, with an expression of innocent curiosity.

'You said "I want your hot skin against mine and your arms wrapped around me".'

I ran my tongue across my lips. 'Did I?'

'You don't remember?'

'I don't remember it like that,' I said. 'In fact, I'm certain I said more than that.'

Hugo's blue eyes danced. 'What else did you say?'

I took a step towards him. 'Well,' I drawled, 'as I recall I also said quite distinctly that I want to feel you inside me.'

'Inside you?'

'Mmmhmm.'

'Me?'

'Mmmm.'

He closed the distance between us, stopping only when we were toe to toe. He didn't touch me but I could feel his hot breath on my skin. There were goosebumps all over my body even though it wasn't a cold afternoon .

'I like it when you blush like that,' Hugo said roughly.

'I like it when you flash your dimple like that,' I replied.

His mouth curved into a deeper smile and his dimple became even more noticeable. My heart beat harder. 'I think,' I whispered, 'in fact, I *know*, that I'm one hundred percent completely and utterly addicted to you. Who needs drugs when Lord Hugo Pemberville is around? The more time I spend with you, the more I want you. You're already inside me, Hugo.' I tapped my temple. 'You're in here.' I touched the centre of my chest. 'And you're in here.'

His eyes darkened with satisfaction. 'There's no escape from me, Daisy.'

I leaned in until nothing was separating us beyond a sliver of air. 'Why would I ever want to escape?'

Hugo groaned. A heartbeat later, his mouth claimed mine. 'I'll follow you to the ends of the earth.' He kissed me again and his hands tangled in my hair before moving down my body. He pulled me against him so tightly that it felt as if we were fused together.

'I want to grow old with you. I want to spend the next decades of our lives together. I don't care if we're hunting for the world's greatest treasures or staying at home watching *Bargain Hunt*. As long as I'm with you, I know I'll be happy.'

And with that, we stumbled towards the tent.

THE FOLLOWING morning I was bending awkwardly over the outdoor tap and brushing my teeth when Hester approached. I didn't want anything to dispel the warm buzz of contentment that I'd woken up with, not yet. There were plenty of hours left in the day for doom-laden dejection.

I managed a vague nod in her direction, hoping she'd give

me a sunny good morning then wander away again. Unfortunately, she simply hovered beside me with an expression that suggested she had something to say and that she wouldn't let me escape until she'd said it. I briefly debated running away but instead I rinsed out my mouth and straightened up to face her.

'Can I talk to you for a minute?' she asked, twisting her hands together in an uncharacteristically nervous movement.

'Of course, Hes.'

She nodded gratefully but she didn't say anything. I waited for several beats then I tried to fill in the blanks for her. 'You're worried about going into Smoo Cave after what happened last time,' I guessed. 'It won't be like that. I know it must have been scary for you when I fell into that hole, and I know you thought I was dead, but everything turned out fine in the end. This time it'll be even better.'

'I'm not scared about the cave. And if you die, it'll be all your own fault anyway,' Hester said, a bit too loudly.

I looked at her and she pulled a face. 'Alright.' She sniffed and dropped her head. 'Maybe I'm a bit scared about the cave. In fact, maybe I'm terrified. Maybe the moment you let go and dropped into that black hole was the worst moment of my life.' Her wings twitched. 'But that's not why I want to talk to you.'

I gazed at her. 'Okay.'

She licked her lips and again she didn't say a word. I was still supposed to guess what we were talking about then. 'You're still annoyed about what happened with Amy?' She shook her head. 'Uh, you think I should stop trying to find a way to defeat Athair and hide from him instead, like Lady Rose did?'

This time she scowled. 'No. Daisy Carter does not hide from anyone,' Hester said icily.

I grinned. True. 'Then are you here because you want me to buy some more chocolate brownies before we head to the cave?'

She huffed with obvious irritation. Not that, then; definitely not that. I squinted at her more carefully. There was real misery etched on her face and I felt a blast of cold fear. 'What is it, Hester? What's wrong? Are you ill?' She shook her head. 'Is Otis ill?'

'No.'

I crouched down and tried to meet her eyes. 'Then what is it,' I asked as softly as I could.

She flew towards the tap, settled on top of it then wrapped her arms and then her wings around her body as if she were trying to cocoon herself from the world. My alarm grew tenfold; this was not like Hester at all.

'You and Hugo are really happy together, aren't you?' Her voice was small and I had to strain to hear her words. 'Even though you lurch from problem to problem, you truly love each other. I see the way you look at each other. It's not just the sex stuff, it's nothing to do with that. It's the light you both get in your eyes. You smile at him in a different way to the way you smile at everyone else.'

I blinked. The last topic of conversation I'd expected was my relationship with Hugo. 'I'm in love with him,' I said.

Hester exhaled. 'I know. That's obvious to anyone with eyes.' She pulled her wings even more tightly around herself. 'That other brownie we met, the one who works for Athair. The pretty one.'

'Eloise? What about her?'

Hester bit her lip. 'Otis really likes her.'

I was starting to get a sense of where Hester was leading with this, but I realised I'd have to wait for her to say it. 'He seems to,' I said cautiously.

'Oh, he definitely does.' Her mouth turned down. 'He doesn't know anything about her, except that she works for the most evil creature in the entire country, but he still really likes her.'

'It didn't sound as if she had much choice in her employer,' I said.

Hester sent me a baleful glance. 'Otis found her attractive, Daisy. He wanted to help her – in fact he still wants to help her. When we were in the pub last night, he was talking about how he could storm Culcreuch Castle on his own and try to rescue her.'

My eyes widened with alarm. 'That would definitely not be a good idea.'

'I know that. He knows that too.' She allowed the tips of her wings to unfurl and flicked them upwards in a shrug. 'It was only talk. Even Otis realises that would be stupid.' She sighed. 'But if he meets her again and he's still attracted to her and they end up falling in love...'

She didn't finish her sentence. She lifted her head to reveal a miniscule glassy tear rolling down her cheek. 'What will happen to me?' she whispered.

My heart went out to her. 'Hester—'

'You're in love,' she burst out. 'He'll be in love. And I'll be all alone. I'll never meet any other brownies who I might fall in love with – there are hardly any brownies around, for one thing. For another, even if I did meet a handsome brownie, he wouldn't like me back. I'm not kind like Otis. I'm bitchy and opinionated and mean and...'

'Brave and clever and absolutely wonderful,' I said, meaning every word. 'We love you, Hester. I love you. Otis loves you. I'm pretty sure Hugo loves you. All of the Primes love you. Why wouldn't this mysterious brownie love you, too?'

'It's not the same, Daisy, and you know it' Hester said. 'I don't even know why I said all that. I'm never going to meet a brownie I could like in that way. I'm going to be alone.' Another tear fell. 'Forever.'

She didn't want platitudes; she didn't want me to tell her that Mr Right was around the corner and that he'd sweep her off her feet at any moment. She didn't want me to make up stories, she wanted me to speak to her truthfully. It was probably the first time I'd seen this sort of vulnerability from Hester and it might be the last. She deserved the sort of honesty she'd always given me.

'Okay,' I said. 'First of all, Otis has only met Eloise once and it was a short meeting, so let's not get ahead of ourselves. Second of all, it's true that you aren't for everyone – you're more special than that. You know who you are. You're not afraid to say exactly what you think. It will take a special brownie to appreciate your inimitable fabulousness.'

I gazed at her. 'Don't ever think that you don't deserve love and happiness, Hester, because you do. You absolutely do. The right boy might show up out of the blue when you least expect it. Or,' I added seriously, 'he might not. If he doesn't, we will always be here for you. You will always have a place with us and we will always love you because we're your family. However, if you want to go searching for someone to share romance with, I'll be thrilled to be your wing woman. As soon as this business is over, we can go on the hunt for other brownies.' I smiled slightly. 'You know I enjoy a good hunt.'

Hester unfurled her wings, wiped away her tears and dropped her arms. 'As soon as this business is over?' she asked with a familiar edge of arch sniffiness. 'When will this business ever be over? When will you ever finish Athair for good?'

I answered as honestly as I could. 'I don't know, Hes, but I have to believe that it will happen. And if you want to fall in love with someone, you should believe that will happen too.'

She inhaled a ragged gulp of air and nodded. 'Thank you, Daisy.'

'You're welcome.'

'If you ever tell anyone about any about this – even Hugo – I swear I will—'

I held up my hands. 'I won't breathe a word to anyone. I've got your back, Hester. Always. I love you.'

This time Hester's smile lit up her entire face. 'I love you too, Daisy.'

CHAPTER

SIXTEEN

Whether it was an act or Hester really did feel better, she was acting her usual self by the time Gordon Mackenzie appeared. The sorcerer looked tired – doubtless he'd had to leave Edinburgh in the wee hours to get here – and Hester wasted no time commenting on his lack of fizzing energy.

Despite his yawns and her typically impolite commentary, there was a glint of steely determination in his eye. Gordon might not know the details but he understood that our venture into Smoo Cave was of the utmost importance. He'd been at the Royal Elvish Institute; he'd seen the danger Athair presented with his own eyes.

I gave him a quick hug and, to my surprise, Hugo did the same. Once upon a time he could barely look directly at Gordon; now, with the matter of Lady Rose resolved and their past differences smoothed over, he was genuinely happy to see him. I knew that Hugo felt tremendous guilt about his past actions, and he'd discussed them at length with Gordon and me, but if we didn't make mistakes we'd never learn.

'It's a good thing you checked with me first before you tried to get into the hidden caves again,' Gordon said. 'The rune was re-sealed after your last visit.'

He gave a sombre nod; he was well aware of what had happened last time. Hugo had found the key that was part of Sir Nigel's treasure hunt for the Loch Arkaig gold and I'd fallen into a dark chasm where I'd met the Fachan. The ancient one-eyed man had challenged me to a fight. When I'd not lived up to his expectations as an opponent, he'd taken pity on me, granted me Gladys to aid my future endeavours and shown me another way out of the caves. I had been very, very lucky.

'Are you truly ready to return?' Gordon asked.

Hugo didn't answer; instead he looked at me. I didn't have any spider's silk to help me this time.

I curled my hands into fists, allowing myself to enjoy the flare of momentary pain as my fingernails dug into the soft flesh of my palms and nodded, mentally girding my loins for what was to come. I'd been into the dark bowels of this cave before; I could do it again.

'Alright,' Gordon said. 'In that case, let's get this show on the road.'

We walked in single file along the well-worn path until the small beach with its softly lapping waves and the mouth of Smoo Cave were visible. There was nothing scary about the first section of the cave and I could easily keep my claustrophobia at bay. There was plenty of space in the large cavern and, as it was a popular tourist attraction, there was even a helpful wooden walkway to guide us inside.

'It's fine,' I said. 'It's all fine.'

Hugo shot me a quick glance and checked my expression before smiling. 'Yes,' he said. 'It is.'

From his position on my right shoulder, Otis gave me a reassuring pat. From her position on my left, Hester snorted. 'For goodness sake. Keep yourself together!' Then she leaned more closely into my ear and lowered her voice. 'All you're doing is visiting an old friend. Nothing more, nothing less.'

I breathed out. We kept on walking.

Within minutes we'd reached the end of the first network of caves and were gazing down at the murky pool of black water. Hidden from view beneath its surface was an old rune that was locked to protect the way ahead.

I eyed the water for several seconds, then turned away to prepare myself. To get to the deeper caves – and closer to the Fachan – we would have to swim.

Hester and Otis secured themselves in my waterproof bag, where Gladys was already waiting, and I stripped down to my underwear. I stepped to the edge of the dark water. Hugo and I had already discussed this: when you were nervous, there was nothing worse than having to wait. Anticipation was not always your friend. To that end, he'd agreed that I should take the lead and be the first to plunge in.

I gripped an underwater torch, double-checked that the bag was secure on my shoulders and allowed my toes to dip in the icy water. Cumbubbling bollocks: it was freezing.

Gordon was already working on the rune, drawing one of his own in the air beside us. As soon as it was complete, he nodded. The underwater rune glowed green and there was a faint rumble followed by ripples across the surface of the water. The passageway was open. It was time to go.

'I'll see you on the other side,' Hugo told me. 'Wait for me.'

Of course I'd wait – I wasn't going anywhere in that cave without him. I simply smiled and then I jumped in.

The rush of cold water, not to mention the darkness, was more disorientating than I remembered. I could feel my heart pounding hard in my chest, and for a moment panic overtook me and I had no idea which way was up. Then the glow of my torch highlighted the rising bubbles and I caught the green light emanating from the open rune. There: the passageway was right there.

I twisted in the icy water and swam as fast as I could, thrusting my head through the narrow gap and then the rest of my body. I kicked hard as my lungs started to burn. Before panic overcame me, I was out of the tunnel and swimming upwards. My head broke the water's surface and I gasped for air.

That hadn't been so bad.

I quickly swam to the side and hauled myself out. I was shivering violently so I didn't waste any time. I dropped my bag onto the rocky cave floor, opened it up and took out another torch to illuminate the area for Hugo.

Hester and Otis flew out while I grabbed a towel to rub myself down and I muttered at them to move behind me before I conjured up two small fireballs. Their magical light outshone both battery-powered torches.

I glanced around the cavern and double-checked that nothing had changed since my first visit. By the time I was satisfied, Hugo was emerging from the water. I offered him my hand and helped him out.

'I'd say it's good to be back,' he drawled, shaking off most of the water before opening his own bag to take out a towel and some clothes. 'But I'd definitely be lying.'

I grimaced in agreement. 'Let's hope that the Fachan is currently in residence and we're not here for too long,' I said, also pulling on a set of warm, dry clothes.

Otis held up crossed fingers 'And that he has the answers we need.'

I glanced at Hester. She didn't argue, just bowed her head and said, 'Amen.'

I pushed my feet into my shoes then eyed the dark tunnel that led into a far larger cavern. The first time I'd squeezed through that tunnel I'd suffered a debilitating panic attack but I vowed that wouldn't happen this time.

I took three big gulps of air, steadied myself and checked on Hugo. He reached for my hand. 'I'm ready,' he said.

I squeezed his fingers. I'd have to let go to wriggle through the narrow space but I held his hand a second longer before I plunged ahead. The faster we did this, the better.

The first few metres were easy but the tunnel rapidly narrowed. When I was forced to crouch Otis and Hester took the lead, staying a short distance behind the bobbing fireballs to the rear, Hugo kept up a commentary even when we ended up wriggling on our bellies.

'You know,' he said, 'Despite my earlier comment, I'm looking forward to this. I'd like a chance to speak at length with the Fachan. He must have seen some glorious things in his time. I wonder how old he is. And look at the walls of this tunnel! There are seams of metals – you can tell by the glinting cracks. It might be tin, or something more precious.'

His words were mostly nonsense but they reassured me. When I finally pushed myself onto the floor of the larger cavern, I was breathing normally and there was no fearful tightness in my chest.

I grinned at my three companions. I had this; I was doing fine. 'Nothing to fear but fear itself!' I declared loudly.

'You go, girl,' Hester said while Otis pumped the air and performed a somersault. Hugo mostly looked relieved.

'Onwards?' I asked. He nodded.

We turned left, away from the gaping chasm that Hugo had once traversed with the aid of the Primes and some cunning ropework, and walked into the passage that led to a much narrower chasm. I'd fallen into that one when the ground had collapsed beneath me on my previous visit and I'd expected to feel a tremor of forgotten trauma. When we reached the dark hole, however, I realised I felt nothing other than an eagerness to find the Fachan and learn about ways to destroy all fiends.

'You've got the rope?' I asked Hugo.

'Yes – but you promised that climbing down there was only a last resort.'

'Don't worry, I'm not in any rush to throw myself in.' Taking care not to get too close to the edge, I crouched down and cupped my hands to amplify my voice. 'Hello? It's Daisy! Are you there?'

Unsurprisingly, there was no answer. I called again and then, because good things often came in threes, gave a third yell. Hugo handed me a small stone around which I'd wrapped a written message; I'd assumed the Fachan was literate though I couldn't be sure.

I carefully dropped the stone and tilted my head to listen for the thud as it hit rock bottom. There was nothing: I couldn't hear a damned thing.

'Now what?' Otis asked nervously.

'I guess we wait,' I replied.

TO AVOID A NASTY ACCIDENT, we moved several metres away from the hole. Hugo rummaged in his bag and eventually found some food. When he handed Hester a small chocolate brownie carefully wrapped in tin foil, she shot me a look as if to ask if I'd put him up to it. I shook my head. Hugo hadn't required any encouragement from me, he'd packed it of his own volition and for her enjoyment alone. Her answering smile was bright enough to compete with the hovering fireballs above our heads.

One hour passed, then two. When time stretched into the third hour, I started to twitch. I looked at Hugo's bag, wondering how much rope he was carrying; probably not enough, but I could try using air magic to soften my descent without worrying about its adverse impact on this environment. In the worst-case scenario, I could repeat what I'd done the first time and simply fall into the dark hole because the Fachan would catch me if he was down there. Hopefully.

I checked the time again. Once we hit the four-hour mark, I'd make a move.

Another five minutes ticked by. I shuffled closer to Hugo, dropped my head on his shoulders and yawned – then suddenly there was a thud.

Otis jolted upwards with such speed and shock that he hit the tunnel roof. He groaned and rubbed his head as Hester checked him over.

Hugo and I got to our feet and gazed towards the source of the sound. 'That came from behind us, right?' I asked. 'The larger cavern?'

'Yes. Do you think it's him?'

I certainly hoped so; if another creature was living down here, we could be in real trouble. We exchanged glances then started walking back down the tunnel. Gladys stayed in my bag but I could feel her vibrating. Was she nervous about being back in the place where she'd been trapped for so many years? I gently touched her hilt, doing what I could to reassure her, and she buzzed in quiet acknowledgment before falling silent again.

We stepped out of the tunnel into the cavern. 'The Fachan?' I called tentatively. 'Are you there?'

Bless him, he didn't keep me waiting. From the impenetrable darkness of the far end of the cavern, his voice boomed, 'Daisy Carter! I knew this day would come. Finally you are here to challenge me.'

I'd been expecting this. 'No,' I said quickly. 'I'm still not ready to fight you.' I would *never* be ready to fight him. 'I'm here with my friends because we need your help.'

He strode out of the darkness with a long, lolloping gait and fixed his one bulbous eye on me. His expression gave nothing away; he didn't even blink.

'This is Hugo,' I said. 'And Hester and Otis. You've met them before.' Briefly: they'd been with me the second time I'd bumped into the Fachan, although they'd left very quickly when some fiends had shown up.

'You called Daisy pathetic,' Hester said helpfully.

The Fachan rumbled, 'She *is* pathetic.'

Hester held up her hands. 'I'm not disagreeing.'

Hugo stepped forward and stretched out his hand. 'It's nice to meet you properly.'

The Fachan pursed his lips. 'Ah, good. A new challenger. Bring out your sword.'

'No,' Hugo said. 'I—'

The Fachan's head whipped towards me. 'The boy smells of you.'

'Uh—' I didn't know what to say and I floundered for the right words. 'Uh, he is mine. That's why.'

'He belongs to you?'

I hesitated. 'Um, yes, I guess he does.'

Hugo raised his eyebrows but thankfully didn't argue. It wasn't really the time.

'I see.' The Fachan sniffed, reached for the sheath at his back and slid out a massive gleaming sword. He pointed it at Hugo. 'He is definitely not here to fight?'

'Definitely,' I said.

'And neither are you?' he enquired.

'Nope.'

The Fachan pondered this for a moment then broke into a huge, unexpected smile. 'I did not think so, Daisy Carter.' He bowed his head. 'It is good to see you again.'

Relief washed over me: he wasn't going to demand a battle

to the death after all. I smiled back and my shoulders relaxed. 'You were injured last time we met,' I said. Baltar had wounded him badly before I'd shocked all of us and killed the fiend outright. 'Have you recovered?'

His eye twinkled. 'I have.' He gestured to his long, sinewy body. 'And without any scars to show for it. You also appear to have recovered from your injuries.'

For a moment, I had no idea what he was referring to and then I realised: he must have spotted the tell-tale silver circles around the pupils of my eyes from the spider's silk. Those thin lines no longer existed; within two weeks of stopping using the drug, they had faded away.

I inclined my head. 'I have.'

'I am pleased.' He thrust his sword towards me and its tip reflected the gleam of the fireballs. Hugo stiffened protectively at my side but I nudged him with my elbow. He didn't need to worry.

'And where is Gladius Acutissimus Gloriae et Sanguinis?' the Fachan asked.

Otis squinted. 'Huh?'

'He means Gladys,' I explained. I fumbled in my waterproof bag and pulled her out. As soon as she was fully exposed, she gave a high-pitched whine. I blinked: I'd never heard my sword make that sound before and I had no idea what it meant.

The Fachan grinned broadly. 'It is good to see you again,' he said.

I knew instantly that he wasn't talking to me. I twisted Gladys and offered her hilt towards him.

'No,' he replied immediately. 'She is not for me to touch. She belongs to you now.' And then, scolding me, he added, 'You should not permit anyone else to touch her, not even me.' He glanced at her blade. 'You have been taking good care of her but she remains thirsty for blood.' He rolled his massive shoulders in a shrug. 'Such is the way of swords.'

I didn't really have a response for that so I smiled awkwardly and let her drop back by my side. 'Thank you for coming to greet us,' I said.

The Fachan inclined his head. 'You have come here because you want to know the truth,' he said. 'You want to know whether you are the child of a fiend.'

'Uh, no.' I grimaced. It was somewhat galling that the Fachan had already worked that part out, probably because I'd finished off Baltar when even he couldn't have ended the fiend for good. 'I already know that I am.'

If he was surprised, he didn't show it. 'I see. Then why are you here, Daisy Carter?'

I cleared my throat. 'We have heard rumours that a very long time ago some people possessed the means to rid the world of fiends for ever.'

Hugo added, 'Around eight hundred years ago. Before the Black Death, which was itself created by a fiend.'

The Fachan didn't miss a beat. 'Yes, I remember the Black Death. It was a difficult time for your kind.'

That was something of an understatement but I wasn't there to discuss the horrors of a fourteenth-century plague. 'You know a great deal,' I told him. 'You've witnessed so much. Do you have any idea what these rumours might allude to?'

He regarded me implacably but didn't reply.

Hester couldn't contain herself. 'If you know anything,' she burst out, 'you have to tell us!'

Otis added his voice to hers. 'Was there ever a way to destroy all the fiends?'

The Fachan's expression didn't change. 'Yes,' he said finally. 'There was.'

CHAPTER

SEVENTEEN

There was a moment's silence before all four of us started peppering the Fachan with questions.

'What was it?'

'What did it do?'

'How is that possible?'

And, of course, 'Can we find it and use it now?'

The Fachan sighed heavily. 'You are searching for a truth that can no longer be found.'

I felt a churn of nausea. 'Please,' I whispered. 'Can you elaborate?'

The Fachan stroked the edge of his sword absent-mindedly. 'Fiendish blood runs in your veins, Daisy Carter. Even if the sceptrum could be found, it might destroy you as well as those who are true fiends.'

That was a risk I was more than willing to take, but Hugo stiffened in alarm. 'It's fine,' I murmured to him and turned back to the Fachan. 'Tell us more. What is this ... sceptrum?'

'For generations, many of your kind have been concerned about the existence of fiends – and with good reason. One of your kings commissioned the greatest minds of his time to create an object that would banish them from this land forever, together with several other items of vast power. He was a particularly pathetic ruler,' the Fachan said with a distinct edge of distaste. 'Your people do not often choose their leaders well.'

My skin was prickling with anticipation despite his dark tone. Finally we were getting somewhere. 'Which king?'

Something flickered in his single yellow eye. 'That information will not help you.'

I clasped my hands. 'Please.'

The Fachan sighed again. 'I do not know his name, such details are unimportant to me. I am aware that he was violent and he did not treat those weaker than himself with respect. He possessed no honour.'

I glanced at Hugo but he only shrugged. 'That could have been any number of monarchs in our history,' he said. Unhelpful.

The Fachan rumbled with amusement. 'Your boy speaks the truth.'

'He couldn't have been that bad if he was trying to destroy all the fiends,' Otis interjected.

The Fachan's eyeball swivelled towards him and the brownie flinched. 'I would imagine – although I do not know for certain – that this king simply wanted his power to be the greatest. There was a crown, a sword, a chalice, a helmet, an orb and a sceptre, each possessing its own magic. It was said that whoever wore the crown would never lose his head, and whoever wielded the sword would fell armies. Whoever drank from the chalice would control the skies, and whoever wore the helmet would communicate with the natural world. Whoever held the orb would gain riches beyond all comprehension, and whoever wielded the sceptre could defeat all foes.' Then he added, 'Be they fiend or otherwise.'

'I've never heard of anything like this,' I breathed. 'How could such objects exist and nobody know about them?'

A sad smile curled around the Fachan's mouth. 'Hubris. It took many lives to create these objects. Power does not come from nowhere and much blood was spilled in the jewels' creation. Anyone who understood how they had been created was killed on the king's orders. He wanted none but himself to wield that sort of power.'

'What happened?' Hester asked.

The Fachan gave her a long look. 'What always happens. The king died.'

'What happened to the objects? What happened to the sceptre?'

'Everything was swallowed by the sea only months after they had been created.'

I felt the sting of bitter disappointment. 'They were on a ship that sank?' If that were true, we were screwed; we couldn't scour the oceans, not with any reasonable chance of success.

'There was no sailing vessel involved,' the Fachan said somewhat cryptically.

My brow creased. 'Then wh—?'

I didn't come close to completing my sentence before a strange low rumble interrupted me, quietly at first but quickly growing in intensity and volume. The cave floor started to shake with such violence that I was thrown off my feet. Rocks fell from the cave walls, some small ones that bounced towards us, others the size of boulders with black jagged edges that crashed around us.

It was happening: the cave was collapsing and we were going to be buried alive.

I cried out. I couldn't help myself; the one true terror that I'd always possessed was coming true. Fortunately, Hugo's presence of mind was far greater than mine and within seconds he'd covered me with his body to shield me from the cascade of falling rocks. He grabbed Hester, pushing her tiny body into a nook underneath my shoulder, and motioned to Otis to follow. While the brownie hastily complied, Hugo yelled at the Fachan.

I felt a bubble of magic erupting from Hugo's fingertips. He conjured up a blast of air that pushed away the worst of the debris as if he were creating an invisible umbrella to protect us.

I struggled to grasp my own tendrils of power, desperately hoping that logic would reassert itself over blind panic and I could join my strength to his, but Hugo squeezed my hand in warning. He was telling me not to draw on my magic, not yet.

With a further lurch of terror, I realised why: he could only maintain the magicked air bubble for so long and I needed to take over from him when he no longer had the energy. But if the cave was collapsing, it was doubtful that we could sustain the magic for long enough to be rescued even with our combined efforts.

I squeezed Hugo's hand in return to show that I understood, although I was already certain that we wouldn't get out of this. There was no chance of escape. The strange, detached thought that Smoo Cave was taking back the life that I owed it from my first trip there flashed through my mind, then a dull explosion reverberated around us with such force that I stopped thinking altogether. I simply closed my eyes, tensed my body and prepared for the worst.

Unfortunately, when it happened it was even more disastrous than I'd envisaged.

'I gave you everything!' Somehow Athair's irate voice penetrated the thunderous noise. Smoo Cave wasn't collapsing as a result of a natural calamity, this was Athair's doing. He'd followed me here and I was the reason why everyone inside this cave would die. This was all my fault.

I could hear shards of rock breaking off from the walls of the cavern and falling around us but Athair's voice was louder. 'I have gone to untold effort, all for you! And this! *This! This* is how you repay me?'

I tried to get up but it was difficult to move with Hugo on top of me. I gave his fingers another tight squeeze, indicating that I had to deal with this. He hesitated, then moved so I could get to my feet.

The Fachan didn't appear to have moved an inch. He was standing in exactly the same place he'd been in when the rumbling had started, although he was now covered in at least an inch of rock dust. His massive yellow eyeball swivelled upwards and I tilted my head to follow his gaze. As more of the dust beyond Hugo's magicked air bubble cleared, I saw what the Fachan was looking at.

Far above our heads there was a gap in the rock and beyond it I glimpsed a flicker of weak sunshine: it appeared that Athair had punched a hole through the earth itself. My mouth dried. The power imbued in that one magic spell was beyond anything I could ever do.

My fiendish father called down to me; I couldn't see him but it was definitely his voice. 'I wouldn't move if I were you,' he shouted.

'Do we try to run?' Hugo asked in a low voice.

I shook my head. 'We can't,' I said grimly. 'We have to deal with this.' I turned to the Fachan. 'You should get out of here. This is our fight, not yours. You should get away.'

The Fachan didn't move. Before I could press him to act, a large shape dropped into the hole above: Athair was on his way down. He plummeted towards us at high speed, dislodging another cascade of small rocks, and he only slowed down when he reached Hugo's air bubble. But where that magic would have prevented stones of any shape and size from getting near us, it did nothing to stop Athair.

He dropped through the bubble and landed with effortless ease and precision less than a metre in front of us.

He was wearing his own face. Although the magic sustaining my little fireballs had been extinguished as soon as I'd felt the first tremors, the glow from the two torches and the faint light seeping in from above was more than enough to illuminate his taut, shimmering golden skin. He was barefoot and bare chested with only a jet-black kilt slung around his hips; perhaps he wanted me to think that he was some sort of Highland hero.

Then I glimpsed the rage in his scarlet eyes and I knew he had finally realised the truth: I would never ever think of him as a hero. The penny had finally dropped.

Hugo started forward, raising his hands in preparation for a magical attack, but I thrust my arm out to stop him. Athair smirked. 'I did wonder if the boy put you up to this,' he said. 'It occurred to me that you might be weak enough to let him control your actions but I can see that is not true. You command him, not the other way around.'

Hugo and I worked together. Sometimes Hugo erred on the side of caution, and sometimes it was me, but we were a team and neither of us dominated the other. I doubted Athair could conceive of a relationship that involved such mutual respect, but I wasn't going to try to persuade him that such equality existed. If he believed that Hugo only did what I told him, it would keep him safer. And I knew that Hugo was too intelligent to let Athair's words goad him into any futile attack.

'What's your problem?' Hugo asked in a deceptively casual tone that confirmed my thoughts. 'Why would you care that we're here?'

Athair's red eyes flashed. 'Why would I care?' he growled. 'Why would I fucking *care*?' He took a threatening step towards him and my stomach lurched. 'I have spent thirty years preparing for my daughter. She wanted you, so I let you live. She wanted to be a treasure hunter, so I found treasure for her to hunt.' He looked at me. 'And yet all she has done is thrown my hard work in my face.'

Athair's ego was astonishing, but I was starting to understand what had pre-empted this showdown – and that there might be a way out of this situation.

'There is no reason for you to be upset,' I said in a far calmer voice than the situation warranted. 'We went looking for your treasure – we went to Hammerwich. Our investigations there are ongoing.' I waved what I hoped looked like an airy hand. 'This is merely a side venture unrelated to the Staffordshire Hoard.' Essentially, that was true.

'Except the remaining Staffordshire treasure has now been found,' Athair snapped. 'And not by you.' His thin golden lips curled. 'You handed the search over to a teenage girl. A *child*! And now she has found the gold that I carefully placed for you!'

Every word vibrated with fury but it was my sudden fear for Amy that made me shiver.

'You have spat on my gift and thrown it away with no thought or care for my feelings!'

I didn't give a flying fuck about Athair's damned hurt feelings.

'If you've hurt Amy,' Hester shouted, 'if you've done anything to that girl—'

'Then what?' Athair asked. 'What could *you* possibly do to *me*?' Unfortunately, he had a point.

'*Did* you hurt her?' I asked fearfully, trying to draw his attention back to me and away from Hester.

'Not yet,' Athair snarled. 'But be assured she is on my list. Eloise has been watching the events in Staffordshire and she has reported back to me. Once I am done with you all, I shall take care of the girl.'

Hester stiffened and turned to glare at Otis. 'I told you we couldn't trust that blonde brownie nincompoop!'

Athair ignored her. 'Do you think I am stupid, daughter?'

I didn't say anything but I didn't look away from his fury-filled gaze; I wouldn't give him that satisfaction.

'Did you think I wouldn't have my creatures tracking your associates in case you tried something like this?' He waved his hand towards the Fachan with a derisive sneer.

My knees suddenly felt strangely weak. Cumbubbling bollocks. He'd had somebody – or something – watching Gordon. That was how he knew we were here.

'Do you think,' he continued, 'I don't know why you have come to this place?'

My stomach dropped into my shoes. Oh no. Things were even worse than I'd thought. We'd only just learned of the scep-tre's existence and Athair would do everything he could to stop us finding it. We'd failed before we'd even started.

Athair pointed to Gladys, who was on the cave floor beside my feet, then at the Fachan and the huge sword he was still holding. 'You thought this troglodyte could teach you the skills necessary to attack me.'

Huh? My mouth dropped open. Athair laughed coldly at my astonishment. 'You underestimate my intelligence, daughter. You underestimate everything about me.'

Actually, all of a sudden I was starting to think that I'd *over*estimated him.

He wasn't finished. 'He is skilled with a sword, that much is true. But he could never teach you enough to beat me.' He thumped his chest. 'I am Athair.' He yelled the last three words, injecting so much drama that I was surprised not to hear an accompanying clash of cymbals.

To be fair, he'd drawn a logical conclusion. The Fachan was better with a sword than any other creature I'd met and he'd gifted Gladys to me; it made sense that I might have come here to learn from him. But no matter how good the Fachan was, or how impressive a teacher he might be, I agreed with Athair. I'd never learn enough to engage successfully with my father in a sword fight. In fact, it hadn't even occurred to me to try.

The Fachan, who still hadn't moved an inch and who had been watching Athair with little more than mild interest, hefted his sword and spun it in the air. 'I am told,' he said, directing his words towards the golden-skinned fiend, 'that the best teaching starts with a demonstration. Let us do battle and prove that.'

I started forward: that was the last thing I wanted. It was a horrific idea.

Athair, however, was already a step in front of me. He bared his teeth and answered the Fachan with grim delight. 'I thought you'd never ask.'

CHAPTER

EIGHTEEN

'No!' My voice echoed loud and clear across the cavern, but it could have resembled a foghorn for all the attention Athair or the Fachan gave me.

Hugo marched forward and inserted himself between the pair of them, but this was far more than a mere bar fight that required intervention. Athair snarled at him to get out of the way, and when Hugo held his ground he received a swift blow to the side of his head. As soon as it became apparent that Athair was prepared to follow up that blow with a lethal bolt of lightning, I jumped in and hauled Hugo away.

'Stop it!' I shouted. I appealed to the Fachan, aware that Athair wouldn't listen to me. 'Don't fight him. This is my battle, not yours.'

'It is too late, Daisy Carter. The challenge has been accepted. We must duel.' The Fachan smiled. 'This is a challenger worthy of my sword, if not my regard.' He nudged me out of his way.

'I do not suppose, daughter, that you will lend me your sword for this fight?' Athair enquired. He had to be fucking kidding me. 'I guess not,' he said. 'Do not worry. My bare hands will be more than enough.'

The Fachan blinked expressionlessly. 'Regardless of my opponent, I always fight fairly. We can delay the battle while I retrieve a suitable weapon for you, if that is your wish. No use of magic is permitted. The battle must be on an equal footing.'

Athair paused and appeared to consider, then he snapped his wrists and used air magic to raise three of the larger loose stones into the air and throw them at the Fachan. The first one struck him from behind, smacking him between his shoulder blades. The second bounced off the Fachan's skull, leaving a glistening smear of blood. He staggered and managed to avoid the third one through sheer luck.

'Nah,' Athair replied. 'I don't need any hand-me-downs.' He grinned. 'And I don't fight fairly.'

The Fachan grunted but didn't appear surprised or annoyed. Despite his wounds and the pain he was doubtless experiencing from the hefty blows, he twisted his sword and lifted his chin. 'In that case *en garde*,' he said.

I clenched my jaw. Suddenly I was more than prepared to do exactly as Hugo had done and step between the pair of them to stop the Fachan getting hurt. This time, however, it was Hugo who stopped me. 'The fight is underway. The best we can do is keep out of the way.'

I gave him a helpless look and Hugo returned it. 'I know,' he muttered. 'I know.'

Otis fluttered up to my shoulder while the Fachan swung at Athair, arcing his sword over his head as if it were made of paper then slicing it through the air with a powerful swing that made it appear to be stone. Athair dodged the blow – but only just.

'What do we do?' Otis wrung his hands. 'What do we do, Daisy?'

'You and Hester stay as far back as possible,' I said. 'You

keep out of the way.' I pointed upwards. 'If you need to, you fly up there and get the hell out of here.'

'We're not leaving you,' Hester said, although she'd already found herself a sheltered spot well away from the fight.

I nodded: their choices were their own. I licked my lips and desperately wished I had some spider's silk. I could certainly have done with its cold comfort right then. Instead, I nudged Otis away.

Athair was focusing solely on magic; the Fachan was only using his sword. His long, gleaming blade was far more useful against Athair's conjurations than I'd expected; it helped, that his reflexes were faster than Athair's lightning bolts. He blocked one after the other, swinging his blade left, right, up and down.

On three separate occasions the Fachan angled his sword so that Athair's magic bolts were sent back towards him, bouncing off the steel in a boomerang-like fashion. Under any other circumstances I'd have cheered to see my fiendish fucker of a father struck by his own lightning bolt, but I was too scared to do anything but watch.

The Fachan blocked another arc of lightning, sidestepped to his right and spun round with a roar. The tip of his sword scraped against Athair's bare chest and I saw a flash of pain and rage in my birth father's blood-red eyes. He responded with a blast of fire, trying to engulf the Fachan in flames, but the Fachan was ready and leapt several metres into the air to avoid it. He landed to the side with a soft, almost cat-like thump, twirled his sword and advanced on Athair again.

'Your kind is wholly evil,' the Fachan said. 'You should not exist.'

'Neither should you,' Athair returned. 'How long have you been hiding in this hole? What kind of existence is this?'

The Fachan responded by executing a series of jabs, slicing with more delicacy than I'd have thought his massive sword was capable of, and nicked Athair's skin several times. Blood was seeping from both their bodies now. Although I knew that the Fachan didn't have the ability to kill Athair outright, I realised that they were evenly matched. The Fachan could beat Athair and maintain his honour, then I could use Gladys to execute the killing blow.

I had to be ready. I knelt down and picked her up, gripping her hilt while she buzzed with anticipation. My action didn't go unnoticed. While Hugo nodded approval, the Fachan called out, 'Do not involve yourself, Daisy Carter. It is not noble to interfere.'

He had barely finished speaking when Athair lifted his hands and took full advantage of the distraction I'd mistakenly provided. He directed a powerful jet of water at the Fachan's exposed throat.

It was an intelligent – and nasty – move. The police employed water cannons to disperse unruly crowds for a reason; it was akin to being hit with a missile. The jet of water didn't break the Fachan's skin but it stopped his breath and sent him stumbling backwards. His pain must have been immense.

Athair swung his head towards me and winked. 'Feel free to clap at my prowess whenever you like, daughter.'

My face contorted and I couldn't disguise my hatred. Athair's eyes narrowed and, as if to punish the Fachan for my feelings, he attacked him with a second jet of water. Although the Fachan was still choking and gasping for air, he was prepared and managed to dodge it by ducking.

Otis gave a shrill cry as he narrowly avoided being hit by the magicked water cannon. If the jet had hit the brownie, it would have killed him. The force when it smacked into the cavern wall was terrifying.

Athair was already preparing another magical attack and I

cried out to warn the Fachan. My impotence as I stood on the side lines clawed at me – perhaps I should get involved, regardless of the Fachan's instruction.

I lurched forward – but I was already too late.

The Fachan ran at Athair, his enormous sword high above his head. Despite his injuries, he sprinted with such speed that his movements were a blur. He feinted to his right, drawing Athair's magic in that direction then swung to his left, his blade slicing far lower than expected. He pierced the flesh of Athair's calf with such force that he exposed the bone.

Athair's scream of pain was high-pitched. He spun towards his opponent and stretched out his weaponless hand. It connected with the Fachan's flat stomach, and for a moment the fighting seemed to stop.

I couldn't see what had happened. The Fachan's back was to me and Athair was angled so that all I could glimpse was his arm reaching forward, but I heard the noise that Hugo made and saw his face turn grey.

Athair stepped back, blood still gushing from his leg wound and spilling onto the cave floor. That was when I saw exactly what he was holding: the Fachan's intestines. Bile rose into my mouth and my knees felt weak. Athair had used his bare hand to claw open the Fachan's stomach and yank out what lay inside.

A groan escaped the Fachan's lips. In slow motion, his long fingers unfurled their grip on the hilt of his sword and it fell with a loud clatter that echoed around the cavern. That action alone answered my question. The Fachan would never allow his sword to drop, not unless the fight was over.

Athair laughed with genuine amusement and pulled harder, his fingers tangling with the bloody innards. The Fachan fell to his knees, his yellow eyeball wide and unblinking. 'Uhhhhhh,' he groaned.

Athair raised a bloodied hand and cupped his ear. 'What was that?'

'Uhhhhh.'

I gave a strangled cry. 'Stop it!'

Athair's lips tightened. He let go of the bloody mess and glared at me. 'How about a little sympathy?' he yelled. He gestured to his leg. 'I'm injured here!'

The Fachan's hands went to his belly and clung on to what remained inside him. I rushed forward just as he fell back and landed face up. His eyes were glazing over. 'Hang on,' I said desperately. 'Just hang on. We'll get you some help.'

Hugo had already ripped off his T-shirt and was by my side, pressing the fabric across the Fachan's wound. It was immediately soaked with blood.

'Stay,' I begged the Fachan. 'Fight. It'll be okay. You can still heal.'

Athair laughed again. 'No, he can't.' Sickeningly, I knew he was right.

The Fachan smiled up at me. There was no fear in his expression; in fact, I'd have described his face as peaceful. His cracked lips moved and I leaned in to listen. 'Pathetic,' he whispered. And then the light faded from his single eyeball and his body went limp.

He was dead.

Pain and horror stabbed at my chest and my eyes grew blurry with tears. *No. Oh no.*

Athair tutted. 'Finally! I do not understand why so many creatures take so long to die. It's impolite. He lost the fight – he should have displayed more honour and died with the speed and silence my victory deserved.'

The moment his words penetrated my grief and shock, cold fury ripped through me. I leapt to my feet and threw myself at him. There was no thought behind my actions, no plan. I simply wanted to kill him.

He was prepared for me. He thrust out his hand, slamming it into the centre of my chest and sending me flying. I landed on my back with a painful thud. Hester and Otis cried out and zipped towards me, while Hugo growled and conjured up a blast of white-hot fire magic.

Athair blocked it with nonchalant ease then grabbed Hugo by the throat, hauled him up until his feet left the ground and started to squeeze. My anger was immediately replaced by yet another surge of terrified horror.

I pushed myself up to a standing position. 'Stop!'

Athair only increased the pressure on Hugo's throat.

I snatched up Gladys and raised her high, preparing to slice down on Athair's outstretched arm. He didn't even look at me as he blasted a jet of air magic that forced my sword from my hand. 'Stand back, daughter,' he said, 'or I will kill this one too.'

Hugo's face had turned a nasty shade of purple and his blue eyes were bulging. I hissed. Hating myself for my lack of skill and strength, I stepped back. Athair loosened his grip slightly but he didn't let go of Hugo's throat.

'You told me that you wouldn't kill anyone for forty days,' I spat.

Athair tilted his head. 'So I did.' He considered this for a moment. 'It appears I lied.' He grinned. 'But it's all your fault. You provoked me. I have shown you nothing but patience and restraint. Do not forget, daughter, that I have been waiting for you for thirty years. I can only wait for so long.'

'Says the fucking fiend who's all-but immortal,' I snarled.

In response, Athair tightened his fingers around Hugo's neck again. 'It is time that you learned to show some respect for your elders. Speak to me like that again and the one-eyed cave dweller will not be the only death you cause. I have bent over backwards for you, shown kindness, been generous. In short,' he said, almost sadly, 'I have not been a good parent. Spare the rod and spoil the child.' He shook his head. 'I only have myself to blame.'

I looked from Hugo's pained eyes to Hester and Otis. The brownies were ten feet away, perched on top of one of the fallen boulders. Hester's hands were curled into fists and her face was full of rage; Otis had wrapped his arms around her waist and was trying to hold her back because she seemed determined to engage Athair in battle all on her own.

Athair would destroy her in a second with complete indifference. He'd destroy all of us.

'I apologise,' I said, dragging the words out of my mouth. 'I will do better in the future.'

Athair's hand squeezed harder.

I licked my lips. 'I apologise,' I repeated. And then, because it was the only card I had left, I said, 'I am sorry, Father.'

And with that, Athair released Hugo. I started to rush forward but Athair snapped his fingers and an arc of lightning flashed towards my feet. 'Stay where you are,' he commanded.

I did as he said. I had no choice.

'I have tried the carrot and that method has failed,' he said. 'There is no recourse now but to use the stick. Cross me again in any way, daughter, and the lives of everyone you hold dear shall be forfeit. It is time for you to fulfil your true destiny. I created you for one purpose alone – you only exist so that you can join me. It is time for you to do so. Come with me and I will spare your friends and family.'

His red eyes shone with terrifying fervour. 'Together you and I will rule the world. Nobody else matters.'

'I can't,' I whispered. 'I won't.'

Athair's mouth twisted. 'Wrong answer.' Magic flared up again and he flicked his fingers towards Hester and Otis, conjuring up a bolt of fire. This time I managed to react and countered it with a blast of water that extinguished it before it reached them.

I jumped into the breach, the words falling out of my mouth and tumbling over each other in my haste. 'Not yet,' I said. 'I can't do this yet. I need time to decide.'

Athair smirked. 'Time to decide whether their lives are worth your sacrifice?' he asked. 'I like it, daughter. You are not yet a lost cause.'

I shook my head. 'This isn't about them, it's about me. Give me time. Either I will join you or you can kill me, but leave them alone. This has nothing to do with them.'

'Fuck you, Daisy! This has everything to do with us!' Hester yelled.

From his crumpled position at Athair's feet, Hugo wheezed in agreement. Even Otis assented. 'Hester's right! We're all in this together!' Goddammit. This would be so much easier without their interference.

Athair looked as if he were enjoying himself. 'Three days. You have three days to decide. If you try to run, I will kill everyone you've ever cared about and a whole lot of other people, too. If you refuse my offer, I will do the same. Only if you agree to join me will I let them live. You will present yourself in front of the Royal Elvish Institute by midnight on Friday and give me your answer.'

I opened my mouth to speak.

'And,' Athair added, 'I will not negotiate further.'

Without another word, he tossed out a burst of powerful magic and rocketed up through the hole in the cavern roof.

He was gone, the Fachan was dead and we were all screwed.

CHAPTER

NINETEEN

I closed the Fachan's eyelid and stroked his forehead. Hester kissed his right cheek then dropped her head in silent acknowledgment of his death. Otis sniffed loudly and wiped away several tears.

'He died a warrior,' Hugo murmured. 'In battle.'

I bit my lip and nodded. I couldn't profess to have known the Fachan well – this was only the third time we had met – but I was certain this was the death he'd have chosen. If only that same thought would help ease the pain and guilt stabbing at my heart. This was on me: the Fachan's death was a direct result of my own actions.

'I'd do just about anything right now for some drugs,' I admitted quietly.

'Spider's silk won't help.' Hugo's voice was soft, without censure. 'You need to allow yourself to feel the pain. Numbing yourself won't alter the fact of his death. He deserves better than that.'

He wrapped his arms around me and, for several moments, I buried myself against his chest. It would be nice to hide away from the world in Hugo's arms while I grieved for the Fachan but there wasn't time. We only had three days.

'We can't linger here, Hugo,' I told him. 'We have to leave.'

'I know.' He glanced behind him. 'We can probably still get out the same way we came in. Only this cavern seems to have been damaged.'

As I nodded and turned towards the narrow tunnel, a tentative voice called down from above, 'Hello? Daisy? Hugo?'

I exhaled with relief. It was Gordon; he was alive and thankfully had escaped Athair's wrath. I looked up towards the hole in the roof that led to the open sky and squinted. 'We're here!'

'Don't move!' he shouted. 'I'm drawing a rune to pull you out of there.'

Bless his striped sorcerer's socks. I reached for Hugo's hand and gripped it tightly, while Hester and Otis managed brief grins and flew upwards of their own accord. A moment later Gordon's rune started to work and we followed them, our bodies rising through the cavern and the deep folds of the earth. It was an extraordinary way to leave the cave but sadly I was in no mood to enjoy the experience.

'Thank you, Gordon,' Hugo told him. 'You saved us a great deal of time.'

I nodded, though I couldn't smile. At that moment, I wasn't sure I'd ever smile again. 'Yes, thank you.'

The lanky sorcerer dropped his gaze. 'I don't deserve your gratitude,' he said. 'When I saw Athair, I could have tried to stop him but I didn't. I hid as soon as I caught sight of him. I'm a coward.'

'No.' My voice was harsher than I'd intended and I grimaced when Gordon flinched. I tried to soften my tone. 'You did the smart thing, Gordon. He'd have killed you stone dead if you'd tried to intervene. You can't win against him.' The ache in the centre of my chest deepened; even the Fachan hadn't been able to win against my father.

Hugo looked around. 'We're quite a distance from the entrance to the main cave.'

'There was a brownie,' Gordon said. 'A blonde female. She found me and directed me to this spot. She was here a moment ago.' He glanced about him. 'She vanished when I started drawing the rune. I don't know where she went.'

Hester snarled. 'Eloise.'

Otis flinched.

'Leave it, Hester,' I said tiredly. 'She's not the problem here.'

There must have been something in my tone of voice because Hester dropped the subject without an argument. She flew towards me and, with uncharacteristic affection, nuzzled the base of my neck. 'Three days,' she whispered. 'There are only three days. Please, Daisy, tell me you have a plan.'

I didn't say anything. The only thing filling my head at that moment was the Fachan's dead body lying in the hidden cave so far below our feet.

Hugo cleared his throat. 'Give Daisy some time.'

'We don't have time,' Otis whispered.

When Hugo smiled, the ghost of his dimple appeared in his cheek. 'Don't worry,' he said. 'Three days is plenty of time. *I've* got a plan.'

I was convinced he was lying. I gazed at him and he caught my look. 'Well,' he amended, 'the beginnings of a plan.' He held out his hand. 'If you're still willing to fight?'

I snorted. No matter how much I was hurting it was a ridiculous question, and Hugo knew it.

I took his hand. 'The only person I'll ever surrender to is you,' I whispered.

THERE WERE a lot of phone calls to make and some people took a lot more convincing than others.

My adopted mum and dad already had their bags packed. They'd known for several months that there would be a day when they would have to run and hide. I cursed Athair another thousand times for doing this to the people I loved, then I got down to business. 'I've been in touch with Rose,' I told them. 'She's made arrangements. All you have to do is get to King's Cross by ten o'clock tonight.'

'We're on our way out of the door as we speak,' my dad said briskly. 'Don't worry about us.'

'Is Hugo with you?' Mum enquired. 'Has he popped the question yet?'

'Believe me, this is not the time for romance,' I said firmly.

'Daisy-Pop, there is always time for romance.' It was easier not to argue.

Mr McIvanney, my old boss at SDS, took more persuading. 'What do you mean?' he demanded. 'I can't shut down the business and tell all my employees to go into hiding!'

I kept my patience; it wasn't his fault he didn't understand. 'Anyone connected to me is in serious danger – mortal danger. Send an email to all your customers in the next hour with your apologies and shut everything down until Saturday.'

'But—'

'Do it.'

'Is this a drug thing, Daisy?'

I sighed. 'Mr McIvanney, it doesn't matter what it is. Just do what I say and nobody will be hurt.' I hoped.

It took more than an hour to contact everyone. When I finished the last call, my whole body was shaking with exhaustion. It had been a long day, but the last thing I could afford to do was sleep. I couldn't waste any precious minutes, not even on a cat nap.

Hugo took one look at my drained expression and grimaced. 'Transport will be here shortly. You'll get a chance to rest, Daisy.' He gave me a meaningful look. 'And you *will* rest.' There was more than a hint of command in his voice. 'You need to be alert for what's to come.'

Rather than waste energy arguing, I simply nodded. 'What do you mean?' I asked. 'Transport? The Jeep is still in the car park. It's ready to go.'

He flashed me a grin. 'It would take us twelve hours to drive to Lincolnshire from here. That's precious time we can't afford to waste.' He folded his arms smugly. 'Fortunately, I'm Lord Hugo Pemberville, minor celebrity with major connections.'

I raised an eyebrow. Then I heard the faint whirring of an approaching motor. 'Is that—?'

'A helicopter. It'll get us to where we need to be in a few hours.'

I wasn't prepared to start celebrating yet. 'We don't know where we need to be, Hugo.'

As if on cue, his phone started ringing. He glanced at the screen then held it up so I could see who was calling. It was the Primes back at Pemberville Castle. 'Have faith,' he said, and then he answered the call. 'It's me. Daisy's here and you're on speaker.'

Rizwan's voice immediately responded. 'Good. She'll want to hear this, too.'

A sudden optimistic surge flooded my veins. If anyone could help us now, it was the Primes. 'It sounds as if you've actually found something,' I said.

'Hugo told us what the Fachan said about the sceptre and the other items. Once we had that information, the rest was easy.'

'Go on,' Hugo said.

'Two words for you, buddy,' Rizwan said. 'King John.'

Hugo's expression immediately cleared. 'Bad King John?'

'The one and the same.'

I gulped in air. 'From Robin Hood?'

This time it was Miriam who answered. 'That's the one. Robin Hood as a single entity didn't exist, but King John certainly did and he was certainly a bastard. He was unbelievably cruel and frequently starved his citizens to death – and also his friends and family.'

My body tensed with anticipation. That fit with what the Fachan had told us, so far at least.

Becky's voice filled the line as she picked up the thread. 'He was obsessed with his own self-importance and desperate to maintain his power. There are several independently verified histories that state he gathered a group of craftsmen and sorcerers to create a set of crown jewels for his own enjoyment. There's no information about the individual pieces because he had everyone who was involved in their creation executed immediately the jewels were completed. And the crown jewels themselves were subsequently lost.'

Hugo's body vibrated with tension. 'Lost?'

'In 1216 King John and his army crossed a tidal estuary. They hadn't planned particularly well, and according to some documents they were surprised by the incoming tide and nearly drowned. Although they escaped with their lives, they lost many of their baggage wagons. One of those wagons contained King John's crown jewels.'

My heart was in my mouth. 'Which estuary?' I asked.

'It's known locally as the Wash,' Miriam said. 'By a village called Sutton Bridge, which isn't far from King's Lynn.' She paused. 'Sutton Bridge is in Lincolnshire.'

That was it. That had to be the place.

'What are the chances,' Hugo asked, 'that it wasn't the

natural incoming tide that caught them unawares but a fiend who was determined to ensure the sceptre was never used?'

'It's certainly possible,' Rizwan said. 'We might never know for sure. It couldn't have been Athair, though. His birth was still generations away.'

I nibbled on my bottom lip. The passage of time was a huge problem. 'It's been eight hundred years and nobody has uncovered any of that lost treasure?'

'Not yet,' he answered.

Hugo and I gazed at each other and he smiled. 'Not until the country's two greatest treasure hunters went looking for it,' he said.

Hope surged in my chest; it was a desperate long shot but perhaps not all was lost after all. Athair knew of the treasure's existence, he knew where it had disappeared and he probably knew about the sceptre's powers. But King John had died decades before Athair was born and the crown jewels had already been lost. Athair didn't know enough to retrieve the treasure for himself and probably believed that it wasn't a danger to him as long as it remained lost in Lincolnshire. If we could find that sceptre in the next three days and use it against him... I was almost too afraid to allow the thought to form properly.

Hugo ended the call just as the air around us started to whip up. My hair flew in several different directions, and Hester and Otis started to shriek from where they were hovering beside Gordon. I tilted my head back and watched a sleek black helicopter as it started to descend.

'Shall we?' Hugo asked.

I didn't have to say anything. We both knew there was nothing else left to try.

CHAPTER

TWENTY

Dawn emerged on Wednesday morning without any fanfare: there were no rose-pink tendrils or golden-hued shafts of light indicating the start of a new day on the outskirts of Sutton Bridge. The darkness of the night slid into dull grey – and there was rain. Lots and lots and lots of rain.

'I thought Scottish rain was bad,' Hester muttered. 'This English stuff is horrendous.'

'Rain is good for the plants, Hes,' Otis said in a vain bid to keep her spirits up.

She pointed to a waterlogged fern that had certainly seen better days. Its long leaves were drooping forlornly into a muddy puddle. 'Tell that to that poor bastard.'

For my own part, I wasn't bothered by the slate-coloured skies and wet weather; they seemed appropriate. I was concerned, however, that the rain would hamper our efforts to locate King John's treasure. That task was hard enough, given the vast area and the time frame, and localised flooding would hardly aid our cause. The helicopter had helped enormously but we were still under extraordinary pressure.

Stretching inwards from the coast, the land here was flat. Shrubby grass covered a large area of it, patchy, marshy and doubtless treacherous, especially in these current weather conditions. There were few people around. I spotted a couple of dog walkers in the distance and a trio of witches collecting salt-drenched plants for their own supplies, but most sensible people were staying indoors. At least that meant our search wouldn't be interrupted.

'The River Nene used to be called the Wellstream,' Hugo said. 'A lot of the land has been reclaimed since King John's time and the landscape is very different to what it was eight hundred years ago.' His mouth set in a grim line. 'It's no surprise that the lost crown jewels have never been located. Slim found some old documents that suggested King John attempted to make the crossing not far from the Crosskeys Bridge.' He pointed to his left. 'It's about half a mile that way. The baggage carts were lost in – and I quote – "whirlpools and quicksand".'

I grimaced. 'I don't suppose that there are any thousand-year-old creatures living around here who we can ask for guidance?'

Hugo waved a hand around the open, empty landscape. 'I'm afraid not.'

I sighed. What I wouldn't have given for a monster-sized spider right about now.

At least all the Primes had joined us; there was no longer any reason for them to stay at Pemberville Castle as decoys so that Athair believed we were still following his treasure hunt. With Duchess's delighted help, they'd killed the vampires lurking outside Pemberville then driven straight here.

This was a no-holds-barred, all-hands-on-deck situation, so the Primes weren't the only new addition to our group. Amy hadn't taken as much persuading as I'd expected. Athair had been correct: she'd found a small chest of gold buried in the garden of the old cottage. It was already being assessed for its connection to the rest of the Staffordshire Hoard.

Despite her sudden newfound wealth, Amy wasn't resting on her laurels. Essentially, I'd asked her to join us for her own safety because Athair had indicated that her life was in danger, even if she wasn't a priority for him. She hadn't appeared particularly concerned about the mortal threat; she was young enough to still believe in her own invincibility. But when I'd suggested that she could join in our latest treasure hunt so that I could keep an eye on her and help keep her safe, she'd jumped at the chance. She said her mum would be thrilled to have her out of the house for a few days and that she was sure she could help us.

As soon as we picked her up at the train station, I recognised the gleam in her eyes. Amy had been well and truly bitten by the treasure-hunting bug. I wasn't sure whether to be thrilled or dismayed to be the cause of that. 'There's a lot of ground to cover,' she said, eagerly bouncing on her toes.

That was an understatement. There were miles of shifting sands and marshy lands to search.

'You'd think that old King Johnny would have been smarter.' She snickered. 'What a dickhead. Thinking he could beat the tide? I've eaten sandwiches that have more intelligence than that.'

Hester gazed at her with wide-eyed admiration. 'You're going places, girl.'

'Not today,' Otis pointed out. 'For the next four hours we're all staying right here, until the tide comes in again.'

Amy smirked. 'Not if I find that treasure before the sea shows up.' She rubbed her hands together. 'Let's get started.'

We fanned out across the vast estuary in a long line like a crime-scene team scouring for clues. Soon the boggy ground was throbbing with bursts of earth magic as we searched for large items buried beneath the shifting, salty earth.

Unfortunately for us, experts believed that even if the location of the drowned crown jewels could be pinpointed the hoard would probably lie under at least twenty feet of mud, sand and silt. We only had two and a half days; there certainly wasn't time to dig up the entire estuary.

My first blast of magic sent several ricochets of pain through my body, indicating the presence of unnatural items. I squelched over to the nearest one and crouched down: a discarded water bottle lay wedged in a spot of bare, sludgy sand. I hauled it out and dropped it into a black rubbish bag I was carrying for that very purpose.

I side-stepped to the next point and had to scrabble in the wet ground before I located a length of rubber hosing. I added it to the black bag and continued. Another water bottle. A disposable cigarette lighter. A large number of barely recognisable cigarette butts. Three empty crisp packets. The now-hairless pink head of a discarded doll. There was plenty to be found but none of it counted as treasure.

I moved to the next section and repeated the process. The results were depressingly similar.

Miriam was searching to my immediate right; Hugo was to my left. Amy was next to him and the other Primes stretched out beyond her. Every so often one of us would pause and investigate the ground more closely. With depressing inevitability nobody found anything of real note, but none of us were prepared to quit. We kept going, scouring every inch of land for hour upon hour until it was only the incoming tide that caused us to stop.

'We can't stay any longer,' Hugo said, just as I uncovered a straggly length of old rope that was knotted at one end. 'If we do, we'll end up being washed away like King John.'

'I'm not that dumb,' Amy said. 'I'm not drowning. Not today, not ever.'

'King John survived his encounter with the sea,' Slim pointed out. 'It's only his magical crown jewels that were lost.' He gazed at the incoming water. 'But, yes, we have to get out of here until low tide returns. In six hours or so we can start again. We'll have more time to search then.'

What he didn't say was that it would be night time when the tide receded. Our treasure hunt would be even more difficult in the dark but we couldn't afford to wait for daylight and low tide; they wouldn't coincide again until Thursday morning and I had to face Athair on Friday night.

I didn't look at the shore line and the fast-approaching sea, I looked at the tense, frightened expressions on the faces of my friends. My gut twisted. Our earlier optimism had vanished in the face of the reality of our situation.

Only Hester was brave enough to say the words aloud. 'What do we do when we don't find these magical crown jewels?' she demanded.

'*If* we don't find them,' Otis hissed. 'Not *when* we don't find them.'

She gave him a long, measured look and his head dropped. 'All I'm saying,' she said, 'is that we need to come up with a plan B.'

Everyone nodded their agreement but, alas, nobody had any suggestions to offer.

~

Although Sutton Bridge was the nearest settlement, it was a small place and there wasn't much in the way of accommodation. The relentless rain and driving wind meant that camping would be unpleasant, but the larger town of King's Lynn was just across the county border. Mark had managed to secure us a whole floor of rooms at one of the hotels where we could dry off properly and rest before the tide receded and the next round of searching began.

There was a certain poetic symmetry to staying in the historic town because Bad King John had started his own ill-fated journey there more than eight hundred years earlier. The shiver of history ran through these streets, co-existing easily with modern shop fronts and the hustle of twenty-first century life.

Once we'd checked into the hotel, I went for a shower then lay down on the pristine white sheets of the double bed and closed my eyes. Not much later, Hugo stretched out beside me. I appreciated the warm, reassuring touch of his body next to mine but I still couldn't relax. Troubled thoughts tumbled one after the other, precluding any real rest or relaxation.

We lay together for several long minutes, neither of us speaking. Despite the comfort of his silent company, it was clear that this would be one of those rare occasions when sleep eluded me.

Eventually I opened one eye. Hugo was as wide awake as I was and his velvet-blue eyes were watching me carefully. 'It doesn't seem that either of us can sleep,' he said.

I sighed. 'No. I know I should get some proper rest.' I tapped my forehead. 'But there's too much going on in here for me to settle down.'

'Tell me about it.' He offered me a wan smile. 'There is still hope, Daisy. We might still uncover the lost crown jewels and find the sceptre that will help us get rid of Athair and all his kind for good.'

I estimated the odds of success at around a million to one. If

I were optimistic. 'I shouldn't have gone looking for the Fachan,' I said for the umpteenth time. 'If I hadn't done that, he'd still be alive and Athair wouldn't have imposed his impossible deadline. We wouldn't be in this situation.'

'Hindsight is always twenty-twenty. Besides, we made the decision together. We've gone through this. It was a better idea than going through every book in every library in the country.' He cupped my face and stroked my cheek with the base of his thumb. 'We can still run.'

'Athair would track us down eventually and you know he'll cause havoc until he does.' I gazed into Hugo's eyes. 'By havoc, I mean mass murder.'

He didn't disagree. 'We might get lucky, Daisy.'

We needed a lot more than luck, though I didn't say that aloud. My skin itched and I felt the painfully familiar scratch of my lost addiction. It would have been easier to give myself completely over to spider's silk, safer for everyone I loved if I'd surrendered to it.

I pulled away from Hugo and sat up. 'I can't lie here,' I said. 'I'm going for a walk.'

He nodded. 'That's a good idea. I'll come with you.'

'No.' I touched his hand. 'Stay here and get some rest. I checked online earlier and there's a meeting nearby. It would help me to go to one.'

Thankfully, he understood. 'I can come with you and wait outside until you're done.'

'I appreciate it but I'd rather go alone. Besides, it'll cause problems if anyone recognises you.' I gently mussed his tawny hair before kissing his cheek. 'Try and get some rest. I won't be too long.'

Then I quickly dressed, put on my coat and shoes and slipped out of the hotel room.

CHAPTER

TWENTY-ONE

I might have managed to persuade Hugo to stay behind at the hotel but I had no such luck with Hester or Otis. They'd taken up position in the hotel lounge and they immediately spotted me when I tried to sneak past and go outside.

'Brilliant!' Hester zipped towards me with a beaming grin. 'This is the kind of Plan B I'm talking about!'

I gave her a blank look. 'Huh?'

'Running away,' she said. 'Fleeing the country and leaving Hugo and the Primes to deal with Athair.'

My jaw dropped as I stared at her.

'You're finally going to take your revenge on him for being a better treasure hunter than you are,' she crowed.

Otis joined her and glared angrily. 'Hes! That's not what Daisy is doing!'

'And he is *not* a better treasure hunter than me,' I muttered before I stalked outside. Unfortunately, both brownies followed.

'There's Amy!' Hester waved vigorously at the teenager, who was leaning against the hotel wall with a vape in one hand

and her phone in the other. 'Amy!' she called. 'Come join us! We're running away!'

I rolled my eyes. 'Nobody is bloody running away. I'm going to a meeting.'

Amy pushed herself away from the wall and joined us. 'Meeting?'

I felt a twitch of discomfort. 'I'm a recovering drug addict,' I said. 'It helps me to go to support meetings, even when I'm away from home.' I hesitated. '*Especially* when I'm away from home.'

She stared at me and my discomfort grew. '*You* were a drug addict?'

'Technically I still am. It never goes away, no matter how long it's been.'

'But you're so ... so ... so...'

'Annoying?' Hester asked. Otis glowered at her.

Amy's nose wrinkled. 'So *together*. You're a Lady. You've got screeds of magic at your fingertips. You're rich and smart and confident.' She pointed to the brownies. 'You've got underlings. Hugo freaking Pemberville worships the ground you walk on.'

It was quite extraordinary to see yourself through someone else's eyes. 'Anyone can be a drug addict, Amy.'

'I'm beginning to get that.' She examined me more carefully. 'What kind of drugs? Heroin? Meth?'

'Spider's silk.'

She recoiled and her expression changed. 'What's wrong with you?'

'That's what we keep asking,' Hester said.

'I hate spiders,' Amy hissed.

I shuffled awkwardly. 'We know. Anyway, I ought to—'

'Can I come with you? Not to the meeting,' she said hastily. 'I don't mean that. I'm too amped to sleep and I could do with a walk if you don't mind me tagging along.'

'We're thrilled to have you,' Hester said.

'We are,' Otis agreed.

So much for my alone time. I yielded to the inevitable. 'Sure,' I said, doing my best to smile. 'Let's go.'

We wandered down the street in the direction of the building where the meeting was due to take place. The rain had paused and there were chinks of sunlight appearing through the grey clouds. King's Lynn was much brighter with the change in the weather, and the pedestrianised high street, with its busy shops and pretty plants, was lovely to walk through.

Otis and Hester garnered several wide-eyed stares from the passers-by, which prompted Amy to stare pointedly in return and force them to look away.

Eventually we turned left between a bank and an outdoor clothing store. I checked my phone. 'It's only another five minutes' walk,' I said. 'Up that way then around the corner.'

'Cool,' Amy said. 'I'll walk with you there and then I'll—' She broke off in mid-sentence and grinned. 'Look! That's got to be him, right? Old King Johnny himself?'

I blinked, flummoxed for a beat until I saw what Amy was referring to. Less than twenty metres ahead of us was a large statue. The other pedestrians were ignoring it, veering around it without a second glance, but I couldn't prevent myself from stopping and staring at it.

Hester flew straight for it and flicked its nose. 'Take that, you fucker!' she yelled.

A passing woman scowled as if she thought Hester's gibe was directed at her. I hastily jogged over and mumbled an apology. As soon as the woman had continued on her way, I turned to gaze at the bronze figure again.

The statue was perched on a low-lying plinth rather than a tall pedestal so that it was possible to look Bad King John in the eyes. I had no way of knowing whether it was a true likeness of the long-dead monarch but I liked to think so. There was a crown on his head and he sported a neatly trimmed beard. The sculptor had included a sword and chain mail, alluding to King John's military background, but it was difficult to think of him as a heroic figure even when he was a life-size statue and within touching distance.

Amy joined me and reached out to touch his outstretched hand and then his chest. Three lions were carved onto his bronzed cassock. As she traced the outline of each kingly animal, my heart rose into my mouth. She said something but her words didn't register.

I took a step back, blood thumping in my ears. Hester frowned and waved at me in confusion as I took another step back. This was not the first time in recent days I'd seen three lions carved like that: there was a corpse inside Culcreuch Castle wearing a gold signet ring with exactly the same motif. A corpse that we suspected was a metal detectorist from this very area.

Otis tugged my earlobe. 'Daisy?' he asked anxiously. 'Are you alright?'

I swallowed hard and nodded. 'Yes,' I managed. 'Yes. I'm good.'

'We should go. You'll be late for your support meeting if we don't hustle.'

I gave a half-hearted nod. 'The meeting will have to wait.'

Alarmed, he started to flap his wings vigorously. 'It can't wait! You can't ignore your recovery, Daisy! I know there's a lot going on and you're distracted right now, but this is important.'

He was right about my recovery; however I was in control and attending a meeting could keep for later. Besides, I didn't need spider's silk – I didn't want any when my blood was buzzing with the start of a real plan that relied on more than luck and tide times.

I dug out my phone and jabbed in a number, impatience making my fingers fat and clumsy. Mark didn't answer on the first ring or the second or the third. In fact, the phone rang for so long that I was already striding in the direction of the hotel, determined to thump on his door to wake him. Fortunately, he finally picked up and mumbled blearily, 'Hullo?'

'Mark, it's me.'

'Daisy?'

'Uh-huh. Listen, what happened with William Hausman? Did you get any further identifying him as the dead body in Culcreuch Castle?'

There was a rustle of fabric as, presumably, Mark sat up in bed. 'You might have noticed that we've been rather distracted lately.'

I didn't take offence at his short tone; we were all under pressure. 'Anything you found would be useful,' I said.

He sighed. 'Hang on. We don't have much. We put him on the back burner when everything else kicked off.'

I waited. Hester, Otis and Amy were watching me with identical expressions of puzzlement.

'Alright,' Mark said, after a beat or two, 'I've found the right piece of paper. There's no guarantee that this is the same man, though. We don't have much evidence to go on.'

'I understand.'

'In that case, William Hausman resided at 62 Glynn Close here in King's Lynn. It was a rented property, which was cleared out around six months after he went missing. His parents are deceased and he has one sister. She moved to Australia more than a decade ago.'

Cumbubbling bollocks. There wasn't a lot there so it wouldn't be easy tracking down people who knew him. 'When did he vanish?' I asked.

'February 2012.'

My stomach dropped further. Twelve years was a long time.

'He was thirty-three at the time. If he had any partners, we've not found any mention of them.'

My optimism was evaporating by the second. 'Anything else?' I asked. 'Anything at all?'

'I think Rizwan found an old Twitter account belonging to him. I've got the handle here.' He read it out loud. 'I'm afraid that's all I've got.'

'Can you text me the sister's details?' It would be night time in Australia but I could always leave her a message.

'We didn't get that far, I'm afraid. All I have is she went to Melbourne.'

Fuck. 'Alright,' I said. 'Thanks anyway.'

'What is it, Daisy?' Mark asked. 'What's the rush?'

'We're searching for a sceptre, right?'

'Right.'

'What *is* a sceptre?' I asked.

It was Hester who answered. 'It's a big stick that I'll hit you over the head with when we find it.'

I wrinkled my nose. 'Maybe a better question is what does a sceptre represent?'

Mark's voice was filled with doubt. 'Power?'

I smacked my lips together. 'Exactly,' I said. 'Power.'

Amy found William Hausman's old Twitter account within seconds. There had been no activity on it for years but his old tweets remained visible. We huddled together in the middle of the street as she scrolled through them. 'There's not a lot. A complaint about the council, a plug for some local pub, a link to a cat video...'

Otis brightened immediately. 'A cat video?'

'Yep. Do you want to see it?'

He clapped his hands greedily. 'Of course!'

I interrupted. 'Which pub?'

She pursed her lips. 'The King's Head. It looks like a dive.'

I didn't care what it looked like, I only cared that William Hausman had liked it enough to tweet about it. There might still be people there who remembered him. I jabbed the name into my own phone and found it – it wasn't even a mile away from where we were standing. My earlier enthusiasm was already returning.

I orientated myself, located the side street and jogged towards it. 'Hey!' Amy called. 'Where are you going?'

Otis sounded concerned. 'Daisy, what's wrong?'

'She's finally lost it,' Hester said. 'All that stress was bound to get to her sooner or later.'

I ignored them and picked up speed. The faster I got to that pub, the faster I could find the answers I wanted. I crossed the street, sprinted around the corner – and came to a sudden halt.

Hester was the first to catch up to me. 'For fuck's sake, Daisy. What's going on with you?'

I didn't move. I barely even breathed.

Hester buzzed in annoyance – then she looked up and saw what was in front of us. 'Oh,' she whispered.

Otis flew to my shoulder. 'Thank you for waiting,' he said. 'What is—?' He stopped abruptly in mid-sentence and his body stiffened.

A moment later, Amy jogged up. She reacted faster than either of the brownies. 'What the fuck is that?'

I gazed at Arbuthnot looming in front of us a few metres away. 'That is a bogle,' I said. And there were no prizes – not even a raffle ticket – for guessing who had sent him here. 'Get behind me, Amy.'

'But—'

'Get behind me,' I snapped.

Thankfully, she obeyed. I tensed my body and prepared for an attack. I'd scorch Arbuthnot and the ground he stood on if I had to.

'I didn't mean for you to see us,' the huge bogle rumbled.

Us? My anxiety ratcheted up another notch as I squinted, trying to see who was hiding behind him and what other threat I'd have to deal with. But Arbuthnot's companion wasn't standing behind him; she'd been concealed inside the breast pocket of his oversized tweed jacket and only became visible when she poked out her head to blink at us.

'Eloise!' Otis tumbled forward from my shoulder, his fear disappearing at the sight of the blonde brownie. 'Are you alright? Has this beast harmed you?'

Insulting Arbuthnot, even by accident, was not a good idea but neither Arbuthnot nor I had the chance to react. Hester flashed forward, flying past her brother to grab Eloise's hair.

The blonde brownie shrieked. Hester shrieked back. 'Traitor!' she yelled. 'Honourless bitch!' She yanked harder on Eloise's hair. 'Where is the bastard? Where is Athair?'

Before Eloise could reply, Otis barrelled forward and slammed into Hester, forcing her away. 'Leave her alone!' he yelled furiously.

Hester elbowed her brother. 'Get it through your thick skull that she's our enemy, Otis! She's with that bastard drug-dealing bogle. She works for Athair! Just because she's pretty doesn't mean she's not evil!'

To be fair Hester had made a good point, but one look at Eloise's miserable expression told me that she was horrified by what was happening. Nothing about this was good. I would have to do something – anything – to defuse the situation. 'Let's all take a moment, shall we?' I said. 'We're in a public place. We don't want anyone to get hurt.'

Unfortunately, as soon as I'd finished my sentence Amy jumped out from behind me, her face a mask of contorted rage. It wasn't her expression that concerned me, though: it was the knife that she was holding in her right hand. Its blade was only three inches long but it glittered in the afternoon sunlight, implying lethal menace.

Gladys, who was still sheathed at my side, buzzed loudly. Something flashed in Arbuthnot's eyes and I knew beyond a shadow of a doubt that all hell would break loose if I tried to slide her out. I hushed her. There had to be a way out of this without resorting to bloodshed. The only thing that sprang to my mind was flattery.

'I am impressed. The two of you have done well,' I said.

Amy snarled and stared at me as if I were crazy. I stepped forward, angling myself in front of her outstretched knife in a bid to negate its threat. Arbuthnot also stepped forward. 'Well?' he asked.

'I knew Athair would try and track us down,' I said, choosing each word carefully. 'But I didn't expect him to find us so quickly. I doubt he would have managed it on his own. He's lucky to have such skilled people working with him.'

Hester growled. Before she could react, I snapped out my hand and grabbed her. Otis smirked and opened his mouth to speak but I silenced him with a glare.

'Lucky?' Arbuthnot hawked up a large ball of phlegm and spat it on the ground. I supposed I should be thankful he'd not directed it at us.

'Ewwww. You ought to see a doctor, mate,' Amy said. 'It's not healthy having that sort of green sludge inside you.'

'Not your mate,' he rumbled.

Eloise, who had been rubbing her head after Hester's hair-pulling attack, frowned at him. 'Hey, we've talked about this,' she said.

She sounded as if she were scolding him and, despite the tension, I was genuinely surprised. The sight of a blonde brownie the size of my thumb berating the likes of Arbuthnot, a hulking drug dealer whose body was so broad and solid that I'd heard he was once mistaken for a small car, was astonishing.

A deep grumble escaped his mouth then he sniffed. 'Fine. Not your enemy either.'

My astonishment grew.

Arbuthnot laughed, a short, unamused sound. 'You think I'm happy about being a fiend's slave?' he asked. 'One minute I'm enjoying life in my own little corner of Edinburgh keeping my punters happy and avoiding the polis. Next minute I've got that bastard dangling me on a hook.' He nodded towards me. 'And that's all your fault, girlie. He wouldn't be interested in me if it weren't for you.'

'Remember what we talked about, Buthy Baby,' Eloise said.

The bogle scowled. 'Fine,' he huffed. Then he said eight little words that changed everything. 'The enemy of my enemy is my friend.'

TWENTY-TWO

One bogle, two elves and three brownies strolled into a coffee shop and ordered tea and cake. I doubted anything stranger had been seen in the eight hundred years since King John had taken a small army and foolishly left King's Lynn only to be attacked by the tide.

At least Arbuthnot managed to find a chair that was large enough to accommodate his bulk. Amy and I perched on smaller stools nearby while the brownies sat on the small table. Hester's arms were folded and her glare was terrifying.

Otis, on the other hand, was thrilled to be spending more time with Eloise even under such bizarre circumstances. 'I like your dress,' he said, gesturing at the pink frothy concoction she was wearing. Hester snorted derisively.

'Thank you, Otis,' Eloise said. 'I have a matching hat but it's impractical for travel.'

'I can imagine. And anyway, it would be a shame to hide your pretty hair under a hat.'

Eloise blushed and Otis shuffled closer to her. 'So how did you end up with Athair?' he asked. 'Was it awful?'

'Yes,' she said, hanging her head. 'It still is awful. He killed my former master and forced me and—'

'Can we get down to business?' Hester interrupted. 'I don't think any of us has time for small talk.'

Arbuthnot rolled his heavy shoulders in a shrug. 'We've got time.'

Amy pointed to the watch on my wrist. 'Perhaps you do, but we don't.' She was right: there was little more than an hour before we needed to return to the estuary to resume our search for King John's crown jewels.

'What are your orders?' I asked.

Eloise and Arbuthnot exchanged glances. 'To follow you,' Arbuthnot said. 'And to inform Athair immediately if you're about to flee the country or go into hiding.'

I exhaled. 'That's it?'

'Pretty much.'

Eloise took up the thread. 'We're not supposed to approach you, and we're definitely not allowed to harm you.'

'You?' Amy raised a sceptical eyebrow. 'Harm Daisy?'

Eloise had the grace to grimace. 'Obviously not me, but Buthy is strong.'

Arbuthnot didn't say anything, but from the look in his eye he was doubtful about his ability to beat me in a real fight. He was right to be dubious: I'd kick his ass to Kingdom Come if I had to. He was enormous – but so were my magic skills. A bogle was someone I could beat.

'We were trying to hide from you when you came around the corner,' Eloise continued. 'We didn't want you to see us and we weren't expecting you to come that way.'

I didn't comment on my sudden mad dash; I hadn't forgotten about William Hausman but I didn't trust Eloise or Arbuthnot enough to mention him. Not yet. 'Is he angry? Athair? Is he pissed off?'

'Furious.' Arbuthnot chewed at a dirty hangnail with his yellowing teeth. 'He thinks you're an ungrateful child.'

That part I already knew. 'I mean, is he angry that I'm here?'

'He doesn't know you're here. We've not told him yet.'

'We're only supposed to contact him if you try and run,' Eloise said. 'You don't look like you're running to me.' She squinted. 'So why *are* you here?'

Hester grabbed Otis's lapels. 'Don't tell her,' she said. 'Don't you say a damned word.'

Arbuthnot's eyes widened. 'You have something? You have a way to beat him? Or you know where to find one?' I didn't reply. He leaned forward, his chair creaking dangerously. 'You do not trust us.'

'Shocker,' Hester said sarcastically.

'You should know that I am sorry about what happened at the restaurant,' Arbuthnot said. 'I did not want to be there. I did not want to shove spider's silk into your face. I had heard about you and what you've done.' He gestured to my eyes. 'And I know you're clean. There are very few who free themselves from silk. Well done.'

Anyone else would have sounded patronising but for some reason, even though Arbuthnot had often supplied me with spider's silk, his words sounded both genuine and heartfelt. It didn't mean I trusted him, of course, but I could be gracious. 'Thank you.'

He nodded. 'I sell plenty of alternatives. Weed, of course. The usual pills. An aficionado like yourself might appreciate...' He registered the hard look in my eyes and stopped. 'Sorry,' he mumbled. 'Old habits die hard.'

He was certainly right on that account. 'Let's stick to what's important, shall we?' I said coolly. 'What's the deal with you and Athair?'

Arbuthnot flushed. His fingers started to twitch and his shoulders drooped. 'You can tell her,' Eloise said. 'It's okay.'

He passed a hand in front of his face. Although the temperature inside the coffee shop was ambient, Arbuthnot had started to sweat. He shuddered, then he seemed to compose himself and his eyes met mine. 'He killed my entire crew,' he said in such a direct, pained manner that I felt truly chilled. 'Then he told me I could work for him or die. I don't want to die.' He gave a sad smile. 'Until a few months ago, I didn't even know that fiends existed.'

'It's a common problem,' I muttered.

'Are you really his daughter?' Eloise asked.

'Yes.'

She eyed me. 'You're not very similar.'

Thank fuck for that. I drummed my fingers on the table top and came to a decision. 'What can you tell me about the corpse in the oubliette at Culcreuch?'

Arbuthnot frowned. 'Huh? Culcreuch?'

So he wasn't part of the inner sanctum and didn't know about Athair's castle hide-out. Eloise, however, had turned pure white. 'How do you know about that?'

I didn't answer her, just waited.

'I don't know who he was,' she whispered. 'He was already dead when Athair first became my master. He's always been there.'

'You must know something,' I said.

She shrugged helplessly. 'Athair spits on his body whenever he walks past. One time when he was feeling chatty, he said that the man had been an idiot who'd thought he was smart and could succeed where nobody else had. Athair realised what he was doing and punished him for even trying.'

In one fell swoop she'd answered my main question about

William Hausman. There was no longer any need to question the regular punters of the King's Head pub.

'Why would he tell *you* that?' Hester sneered.

Eloise looked down. 'It was a threat in case we tried to do something similar.'

We? I watched her carefully but she didn't say anything more.

Suddenly Arbuthnot reached across the table and I stiffened automatically, my magic bristling defensively. All he did, however, was take my hands in his. In all the years I'd known him, he'd never touched me and he'd certainly never acted like that.

Despite the ingrained dirt and lack of a tidy manicure, his skin was far softer than I'd expected and his massive fingers were callus free. They were, I thought sardonically, the hands of a drug dealer.

'If you don't show up at the Royal Elvish Institute on Friday night,' Arbuthnot said, 'Athair will raze the city. He's threatened to do it – I'm sure he's capable of it.'

I had no doubt that he was capable of it. 'Don't worry,' I said. 'I won't shirk my responsibilities.' Because Athair *was* my responsibility, whether I wanted that burden or not.

Arbuthnot swallowed. He did a good job of concealing it but I knew in that moment that he was truly terrified of my father. I'd always suspected that the bogle was smarter than he looked. 'I'm hoping that you came here for a reason,' he said quietly. 'I'm hoping that you're sifting through all that sand near Sutton Bridge because you're looking for something that will stop Athair.'

Amy stiffened but I wasn't surprised. If Arbuthnot had tracked us to King's Lynn, he knew where we had been a few hours ago. With a pair of cheap binoculars, he and Eloise could have watched what we were doing from a safe distance even if they couldn't work out why.

'It's true,' I told him. 'We're hunting for a precious object that we've learned is powerful enough to destroy all fiends.'

Hester hissed. 'Daisy! What the fuck are you doing?'

Otis apparently agreed with her. 'Don't say anything else,' he warned me. He gave Eloise an apologetic look. 'I'm sorry,' he said. 'But—'

'It is fine,' she told him. 'I understand. It is better that you stay quiet.'

'Indeed.' Arbuthnot swung his large head up and down. 'You should not tell us what you're looking for. You have no reason to trust us and you know that I am not a good man. I do not pretend to be.'

'I think you're good, Buthy,' Eloise said.

Arbuthnot looked at me. 'There's room for improvement,' I told him. 'But that's the case with all of us.'

He smiled slightly then repeated his words. 'I am not a good man.' He lifted his chin. 'But the evil that your father presents is on a completely different level. It is not something I can countenance." Both his words and his tone were uncharacteristically formal, as if their weight deserved a greater level of propriety than Arbuthnot usually employed. "If there is any chance you can beat him, I will do anything I can to help you. We will not tell him we followed you here, or that you have been anywhere near Sutton Bridge and know of an object that could destroy him. It is not much, but we can at least offer you our silence.'

For the first time since I'd knelt by the side of the Fachan's body my lips curved into a genuine smile. 'I don't want your silence,' I said. 'In fact, I want you to tell Daddy Dearest exactly where I've been.'

'What?' Hester spluttered.

I leaned forward and picked up my teacup, raised it towards

her then took a sip. 'You wanted a Plan B,' I said. 'Now I've got one.'

~

'Where did you get that damned knife from?' I asked Amy as we waited for the others to join us in front of the hotel.

'My mum's kitchen.' She shrugged insouciantly, as if wandering around with a dangerous weapon was the most natural thing in the world.

'You can't keep it.'

'Why not? You've got a sword. I've got a knife.'

'I've had training.' Some, at least.

Amy raised an eyebrow. 'So have I. Four years of Food Technology classes at Biggleswith Secondary. I'm the fastest onion chopper in the school's history.'

I folded my arms.

'I need to protect myself,' she said. 'You told me my life is at risk from your dad. That's *your* fault, not mine. Really, this is all on you, Lady Daisy.' She smiled pleasantly.

Cumbubbling bollocks. It was difficult to fault her logic but I wouldn't be defeated. 'A kitchen knife won't do you any good against a fiend – or a bogle, for that matter. You're more likely to end up hurting yourself.'

Gladys hummed loudly in agreement.

'I made a leather pouch for it. I won't stab myself by accident. I'm not completely stupid.'

'Carrying that thing will cause far more problems that it could ever solve, Amy. Hand it over.'

There was a mutinous tilt to Amy's chin. 'No. If I'm going to hang around with you, I need some sort of protection of my own.'

'No, you don't.' I said, 'And you won't be hanging around with me for much longer. There's a change of plan.'

Her eyes narrowed. 'I want to find King John's treasure.'

'You still can. But not right now.' I managed a smile. 'I've arranged for you to take a lovely holiday in the south of France. I've spoken to your parents and they're sending over your passport. It's all arranged. After everything you've been through lately, I think a holiday will do you the world of good. As you said yourself, you need some protection. Leaving the country is the best protection you can get.'

Amy didn't look particularly impressed. 'Oh yeah? And what will you be doing while I'm being forced out of England to sunbathe?'

My smile widened, but it was neither amused nor happy. 'Embarking on a hunt of a different kind.' I swallowed. 'It's only temporary, Amy. You're in danger and it's my fault. I need to know that you'll be safe while I'm dealing with the situation.'

Her suspicion didn't lessen. 'You're not just trying to get rid of me so you can keep King John's crown jewels for yourself?'

'I'm not. I promise.'

She gazed at me, but she must have seen something in my face that convinced her because she sniffed. 'Fine,' she muttered. 'I'll go to France – but not for long. I'll come back here as soon as I can. I'm going to find this treasure.'

'I'd expected nothing less.' I exhaled. 'Thank you, Amy. And, please, give me the knife. You can't travel abroad with it.' I held out my hand.

She sighed but thankfully she did as I asked. I examined the makeshift pouch, determined it was safe enough, and slid the knife into my pocket. Teenagers carrying sharp weapons was never a good idea.

Hugo came up behind me and slung an arm around my waist. I instantly felt a flood of tension leave my body as I leaned into him. 'What's going on?' he asked as the rest of the Primes gathered around.

I cleared my throat. 'We're not going to find King John's crown jewels.' The only person who looked unhappy was Amy. Her face was still twisted into a frown and her hands were on her hips.

'What's the alternative?' Rizwan asked. 'We have to keep searching, there's no other choice.'

Miriam's clever eyes flashed. 'There's always another choice, dear.'

'The other choice is that Daisy hands herself over to Athair and agrees to become a fiend just like him,' Becky said.

'And then,' Slim continued for her, 'we'll end up having to fight Daisy to the death as well as Athair.'

Hugo growled, 'That won't happen.'

'No,' I assured him, 'it won't.'

'We've got a maximum of thirty-six hours before we have to leave for Edinburgh. There are three more low tides between now and then, so almost eighteen hours of search time left.' Mark sounded earnest. But we all knew that eighteen hours wasn't enough; eighteen years might not be enough.

'We are talking about a vast tract of land,' I said. 'Land that's constantly shifting. King John couldn't retrieve his treasure after a single tide. There have been hundreds of thousands of tides in the intervening years.'

'Almost six hundred thousand,' Hugo muttered. 'I did the arithmetic.'

William Hausman flitted into my mind. 'First of all, we have to assume that the treasure hasn't been found by anyone else. It might have already been dug up and taken elsewhere or melted down. We can't ever know for sure.'

Amy scowled. 'We would know. Somebody would have blabbed if they'd found it.'

I glanced at her. 'Okay. Even if we imagine that nobody *has* managed to find it, we have to believe that we're not only the best treasure hunters in the country today but that we are the best treasure hunters in the last eight hundred years.'

'Works for me,' Hugo said.

I grinned but I knew that even his ego wasn't that large. 'And that we don't have days or weeks or months or years to find this long-lost treasure.' I swept my gaze across the group. 'We've only got hours.'

Slim sighed. 'We know all that, but there's no alternative.'

They all looked at me and I straightened my shoulders. 'Some new information has come to light.' I felt imbued with a strange new confidence; we were no longer on the back foot or playing catch-up. Not any longer. 'We need to get back to Scotland.'

CHAPTER

TWENTY-THREE

I had only ever been in the vicinity of Culcreuch Castle once, when I'd time-travelled back to 1994, lurked in the nearby woods and spied on the old building from a distance. Thirty years later, those woods looked much the same. There was a bit more litter caught in the undergrowth but the trees remained in place and were only slightly taller and leafier than I remembered.

We hadn't travelled all the way by helicopter; after all, stealth from this point on would be vitally important. We'd managed to fly to the nearby city of Perth from Sutton Bridge, however, and Slim had driven us the rest of the way so we could approach Culcreuch without being noticed. We waited until daylight in order to avoid Athair's vampires and then he'd dropped us a mile from the castle. We'd walked the final section but, before we arrived in the castle grounds, I made a silent promise. If I made it to Saturday morning, still alive and still free, then I was definitely taking flying lessons. I was a high elf now – hell, I was practically royalty. At the very least I ought to live up to my newfound status and zip around the countryside in my own helicopter.

'Hours,' Otis said, checking the time and causing my brief daydream to evaporate. 'We've got mere hours until we need to meet Athair in front of the Royal Elvish Institute.'

'Plenty of time,' Hugo said.

'Screeds,' I agreed.

'We'll be in and out by lunch time.'

I nodded. 'By noon, we'll be in a warm, welcoming country pub and eating a hearty lunch. There will be hours left to prepare for tonight's showdown.'

'It'll be great.'

'We'll be heroes.'

Hester and Otis gazed at us. 'Will you say it?' Hester asked her brother. 'Or will I?'

'It'll sound better coming from me,' he replied without missing a beat. 'You're both fucking crazy.'

'And,' Hester added, 'we're all going to die.'

I sucked on my bottom lip and my eyes met Hugo's.

'At least we'll die fighting,' he said. He smiled and his dimple appeared. 'In case it's not clear, Daisy, I have lots of regrets about what happened when we first encountered each other but the one thing I will never ever regret is that we met. My life is inordinately richer because you're in it. No matter what happens today or later tonight, don't forget that. I will always be yours. You told the Fachan that I belong to you and it's completely true.' He paused. 'And I couldn't be happier.'

'That will be from the adrenaline caused by facing imminent death,' Hester said.

I ignored her and kept my gaze on Hugo. 'I feel the same. You're the best thing that's ever happened to me.'

He smirked. 'Naturally.'

I matched his expression. 'Now you can admit the whole truth, darling.'

'The whole truth?'

'That you desperately love me.'

He nodded. 'I do.'

'Your desire for me is ardent.'

'Yup. It is.'

I reached up and brushed a lock of his tawny hair away from his forehead. 'And,' I breathed, 'I'm the best treasure hunter this country has ever seen.'

'Let's not be *too* enthusiastic, Daisy,' he said, while the brownies rolled their eyes in exasperation.

I kissed him briefly, grinned and stepped back.

'Is all the soppy shit out of the way now?' Hester enquired.

Hugo's hand reached for mine. 'Never.'

She sighed. 'Come on. Let's get a move on and meet our gruesome death.'

We picked our way through the woods, doing what we could to stay well behind the tree line. There was every reason not to rush: we didn't want Athair to know we were there – not yet, anyway. We wove in and out of the bushes and foliage until there was a break in the trees and we could see Culcreuch Castle

.

Last time I'd thought the building and its surrounding landscape were awesome, but now the lush splendour I'd seen during that visit had vanished. 'Wow,' I whispered. 'There's no denying that a fiend is in residence.'

There was still a lake in front of the castle. Last time it had been a sparkling expanse of aquatic serenity complete with lazy ducks and shimmering blue water, but now it was a murky hole. The water was black rather than blue, there were oily ripples on its surface and certainly no quacking ducks.

The lake wasn't the only difference: the once perfectly manicured lawns were a quagmire. I couldn't see a glimmer of natural life; the landscape looked as dead as if we'd walked onto the set of a dystopian film. Unfortunately, this wasn't Hollywood. Far from it.

Close to the grand front door of the castle was a battered wooden crate. It was empty now but I knew without asking that it was the same crate Hugo had mentioned that had contained chickens to feed Athair's small army of vampires. There were bloodstains around it and, if I squinted, I could see trails of feathers and bones. The poor chickens hadn't had an easy death.

Given the time of day, at least the vamps weren't in evidence. There was a makeshift barn structure on the eastern side of the castle that definitely hadn't been there before; the bloodsuckers were doubtless inside, sleeping away the day until it was safe to emerge. I shuddered slightly and told myself to be grateful that they were tucked away.

The castle building, which had stood for enough centuries to prove that it was made of strong stuff, was in better condition. There were some dark red stains on the stonework that I tried not to think too closely about, and a couple of broken windows on the upper floors, but it was mostly intact.

'He's not very houseproud, is he?' I murmured.

Otis's mouth was turned down in disapproval. Hester's hands were on her hips.

'It looks far worse in daylight than I realised,' Hugo agreed. 'He's taken more care inside – it's cleaner in there.'

'Apart from the random corpses shoved into handy dungeons,' I muttered.

'Yeah.' Hugo's mouth flattened. 'Apart from those.'

I shook my head; nothing Athair did would surprise me. 'At least there are no signs of life. We should be able to get to the rear of the castle without too many problems.'

We'd already planned to enter the building the same way Hugo had done. It was the one known weak point in the castle's defences. The only real problem was Athair's current where-abouts. We couldn't risk running into him.

'Let's go.' Hugo led the way through the trees until we could go no further without crossing open ground. It was at least four hundred metres from here to the castle with nowhere to take cover but it was the only route. We had to take it.

I looked at Hester, who had already made a show of rolling up her sleeves and glaring at the castle like she was a thumb-sized seize engine, then I checked on Otis. He was grim faced but determined. 'Ready?' I whispered.

'We were born ready,' he said without a trace of humour.

'We've got this,' Hester agreed, and a moment later they were off.

My hand sneaked towards Hugo's and I entwined my fingers with his. With my heart in my mouth I watched the brownies flit through the open air towards the looming walls of Culcreuch Castle. Their small bodies would be far less likely to attract attention if Athair or anyone else inside glanced out of the window at the wrong moment, but neither brownie was invisible. Someone with sharp eyes would still see them.

I tracked their progress, my stiff-necked tension only easing when the pair flattened themselves against the stone wall of the castle. The danger wasn't over but step one was complete. That had to count for something.

I inhaled deeply; by the time my lungs were filled with air, Hester had flitted towards the first window on the ground floor and Otis was at the next window above. There were thirteen windows in total, which posed a risk to our venture. Hester and Otis were going to check inside each one before Hugo and I ventured across the open ground. It was a far from foolproof method of avoiding detection, but short of making ourselves the same size as the brownies it was the best we could come up with.

Hugo and I watched in tense silence as the small siblings moved from window to window, stopping by the edge of each frame before peering inside. They were surprisingly fast and it was less than a minute before they beckoned us forward. I nudged Hugo and, after briefly squeezing my hand, he abandoned the relative safety of the trees and darted forward. I stayed behind, scanning the windows and guarding the rear on the off-chance that someone appeared. If the worst happened, I could create some sort of diversion from where I was hiding.

In contrast to Hester and Otis, Hugo's progress was desperately slow; instead of sprinting, he trudged forward. The loud squelches that accompanied his every footstep explained his lack of speed: the mud was thick and gloopy. Without a pair of wings, and needing to avoid using magic that might alert Athair to our presence, there was no choice but to move slowly. I held my breath for most of his journey, my gaze nipping between his back and Hester and Otis, who were still zipping from window to window to check that the coast was clear.

The relief I felt when Hugo finally reached the foot of the castle walls was immense. He turned around and offered me an ostentatious wink but I was too nervous to respond. I simply nodded, glanced at the brownies who waved their agreement, and followed in his footsteps.

The moment I was out in the open, I felt the cold breeze blowing in from the west curling around my body and making me shiver. I did my best to ignore it and focused on my feet. The mud was worse than I'd expected, and with every step my feet sank deeper and deeper into the foul-smelling goop. It required considerable effort to yank each foot out and proceed but I pushed on, determined to make it to the first wall as quickly as possible.

Squelch. I stepped one foot forward. Suck. I yanked my trailing foot out of the mud. Squelch. Forward. Suck. Out. I was wearing trainers and it wasn't long before the mud seeped through and I could feel it between my toes. It was remarkably unpleasant, but at least it spurred me on and encouraged me to keep moving and extract myself from the quagmire as quickly as possible. Squelch. Suck. Squelch. Suck. Squelch. Su—

Cumbubbling bollocks. My right foot was stuck. I yanked my leg, trying to free it. When that didn't work, I used both hands to grab my calf and provide extra oomph, but the mud was like quicksand. The more I tried to extract my foot, the deeper it seemed to sink.

I cursed aloud. I could use magic. A small, directed blast of earth magic would likely free me in an instant, or I could use water magic and draw the moisture out of the mud, but any magical power of any sort would be a terrible risk. Athair was inside those walls and he would no doubt sense even the tiniest flicker of my power. Magic had to be a last resort.

I gritted my teeth and tried again to free my trapped foot then, out of the corner of my eye, I spotted Otis waving at me in panic. He was by a window on the second floor, pressed against the frame where he couldn't be seen from inside. His frantic gestures could mean only one thing: somebody had entered the room he was looking into. All they had to do was glance out of the window and they'd see me.

Hugo started forward. I hissed and waved him back as I pulled on my foot with all my might. Come on. *Come on.*

Otis moved slightly and peered through the glass into the castle. When he drew back, his signals were even more panicked. I had seconds at best, and I was still more than a hundred metres from the relative safety of the exterior walls where I would be hidden.

With little choice, I drew in a breath and threw myself to the ground. I landed face down, gaining a mouthful of foul wet dirt for my effort while the thick gloop started to encase my sinking body. I couldn't worry about that; I could only hope that the sticky mud would be enough to hide me.

I held my breath and waited for as long as I could, only moving when my lungs were burning. When I reared up and gasped for air, I couldn't see a thing – but neither could I hear anything. Nobody was shouting an alert.

As I heaved in another desperate breath, I heard Hester's voice in my ear. 'It's okay. He's gone. You can keep moving.'

Every inch of me was covered in thick mud. I tried to wipe the worst of it off my face but all I managed to do was spread the sludge around. I couldn't see a damned thing and, with my hands covered in the stuff, I couldn't clear my vision. At least my fall meant that my foot was free, although I'd lost my trainer. Attempting to retrieve it would be a wasted effort.

I grimaced then, caked in yuck, moved forward with my arms outstretched until I felt the hard stone of the castle walls and heard Hugo's reassuring voice by my side. 'You made it! You're here.'

'Mmmph,' I said and spat out a mouthful of mud. It didn't help much. 'Mmmph?'

'It was Athair,' Otis said. 'He walked right into the room. I don't know what he was doing but he got very close to the window. I was sure he was going to see you.'

My heart skipped a beat. 'Mmmph?'

'No,' he assured me. 'He didn't notice a thing.'

Thank fuck for that. I spat again, finally clearing my mouth of the last of the muck while Hester snickered. 'You look like the creature from the black lagoon,' she scoffed.

I smelled like it too.

'Are you okay, Daisy?' Hugo asked.

I'd had better days but I wasn't going to complain. 'Yep.'

I felt something rub at my face. I stayed still as he wiped away the worst of the mud before using the water in his bottle to clear the rest. It was a relief when he came into focus and I could see again.

'Well,' he said, 'you're certainly well camouflaged now.'

I stuck out my tongue. 'I'll have to get cleaned up before we go inside. I can't leave a trail of mud.'

Hugo nodded. 'We'll sort it out. I've got a spare T-shirt you can wear.'

It would be better than nothing, I supposed. I looked down at my mud-caked body. 'Still love me?' I asked.

'More than ever.'

'Want a hug?'

His mouth crooked up. 'I'll pass.'

CHAPTER

TWENTY-FOUR

We hugged the castle walls and kept our bodies low to the ground and, within a few easy minutes, reached the rear of the large building. There were very few windows around this side so there was far less chance that we'd be spotted, but we continued to take care; we only stopped when we found a nook beside the old tower.

Hugo rummaged in his bag while I located a small expanse of tall grass that had managed to escape being transformed into a mud bath. I stripped off my clothes and rolled around on the ground to wipe most of the mud on my body then pulled on Hugo's T-shirt, which was easily long enough to reach mid-thigh. I'd be barefoot and cold for the rest of this incursion, but at least it was now Hugo's scent against my skin.

I discarded my mud-caked clothes behind a bush and looped my belt with Gladys and her sheath around my waist. It was an interesting fashion statement as well as a necessary precaution.

By the time I rejoined Hugo, he'd taken his coil of rope and snagged one of the tower's jutting parapets. I shielded my eyes against the glare of the weak sun. 'We're going old school, huh?'

'The trapdoor to gain access to the castle interior is at the top of that tower. We can't use magic to get up there for fear of alerting Athair. We'll have to climb.'

I was suddenly glad I'd eaten a hearty breakfast. I cracked my knuckles. 'Betcha I'm faster at climbing up there than you.'

Hugo raised an eyebrow. 'Game on, princess.'

'Does everything have to be a competition?' Hester complained.

'It's a healthy distraction from our impending doom,' I said cheerfully.

She exhaled noisily. 'At least you're acknowledging this is a suicide mission.' She glanced at Otis. 'First one to the top is a stinky nincompoop.' She zipped upwards before her words could even register.

Otis glared after her. 'Does everything have to be a competition?' he said, repeating her complaint.

From the uppermost edge of the tower, Hester grinned down and blew him a kiss. 'You're right, Daisy,' she called. 'Competition is a very healthy distraction.' She smiled smugly. 'I'm better than you, Otis. Stronger, faster, smarter.' She paused. 'Better.'

Bickering from the brownies wasn't what I'd been aiming for. To forestall any more sniping, I grabbed the rope, tested that it was secure and slowly hoisted myself up. Being barefoot actually helped. Although I was sweating by the time I climbed over the parapet, I had even impressed myself.

I rolled onto my back and allowed myself a few moments to catch my breath as I waited for Hugo to catch up. 'I was faster,' he said, when he finally appeared.

'I don't believe so,' I told him.

'You know that you two are worse than we are?' Otis said,

I opened my mouth to tell him he was being ridiculous then

closed it again. Perhaps he had a point. Hester laughed and high-fived her brother.

'We're not worse than them,' Hugo muttered.

'Of course not,' I said. I flicked him a side glance. He did the same to me.

'Perhaps we ought to continue with our suicide mission,' he said.

I grinned. 'It's probably safest.'

Although the banter was a pleasant distraction, it didn't prevent the nauseous churn in my stomach when we edged towards the trapdoor and prepared to enter Culcreuch Castle. This was the perfect moment to swallow down several pills of spider's silk but I didn't need drugs to be successful; I knew that to my very core.

I drew in a deep breath of fresh air instead and nodded at Hugo. The teasing twinkle in his deep-blue eyes had been replaced once more by steely determination. Hester flew closer to Otis and reached for her brother's hand. Suddenly they looked as nervous as I felt.

Hugo tensed his body and lifted up the trapdoor.

A part of me had been expecting to see Athair's coldly smiling face greet us, so when I saw there was nothing below the trapdoor but an empty room, I sagged with relief. So far so safe. I stepped forward and quickly lowered myself into the building, clambering down a rickety ladder to reach the stone floor. Seconds later, Hugo followed together with the brownies.

The first room contained nothing but an old rickety chair that looked as if it might collapse at any moment. The second room wasn't much different except for a few old paintings stacked against a wall. I squinted at them though I didn't dare touch them for fear of disturbing the dust and leaving a trail. They looked pretty enough. I spotted a naval scene with an old gallant warship leaving a stormy harbour, and a still-life oil painting of some drooping flowers. I guessed Athair didn't much care for art.

I wondered if he truly cared for anything or whether his longevity had sucked the joy out of everything. Soldiers grew inured to violence, medical professionals got used to blood. Maybe Athair had experienced too much of life to appreciate anything anymore. I could almost feel sorry for him. Almost.

Hugo took the lead, walking silently down the next flight of stairs. He opened the door to the third room. I peered past him and glimpsed the large pinboard that he had photographed on his previous visit. The carefully marked map of the British Isles was no longer there.

We exchanged glances before I tiptoed inside. The Billy bookcase was in one corner and the books lined up on its shelves looked untouched. In fact, the entire room appeared the same as it had when Hugo had sneaked in here in every way bar one: the stone floor was littered with scraps of ripped paper.

I bent down, picked one up and smoothed it out. It was from the map. Suddenly I could imagine the scene: as soon as Athair had realised I'd passed over the responsibility for the first treasure hunt to a teenager, he'd thrown a tantrum. He'd stormed in here and ripped up his map. He might be ancient, but maturity was not his strong suit.

Otis flapped around, picking up the bits of paper as if he were on a cleaning mission. I reached out to him and wagged my finger to tell him to stop. He paused, gazed down at the scraps and immediately released them. His face flushed.

'It's information about treasure,' Hester whispered in my ear. 'New treasure.'

That was not why we were here; it wasn't treasure I wanted. I shrugged to indicate that to Hester. 'Gold is gold,' she muttered.

I shook my head. No, it wasn't.

I scanned the room again, satisfying myself that there was nothing else of note. When I rejoined Hugo, we continued our descent to the basement of the old tower. My stomach was already tightening in wary anticipation: I knew what was coming next. Or rather who. It was why we were here.

The moment I stepped onto the uneven stone floor of the windowless tower, my claustrophobia stirred back into unwelcome existence. I told myself that I wasn't trapped; there was a door to my right that led into the rest of Culcreuch Castle and the staircase next to it went up to the top of the tower. There was more than enough space to move around and there was certainly no lack of air. But the dank smell, the miserable atmosphere and the corpse in the hole by my feet were more than enough to encourage my old fears.

Hugo sensed my anxiety almost immediately. He reached for my hand without speaking and gave me a look laden with meaning. I swallowed and nodded to indicate that I was fine; I had things under control. William Hausman, whose dead body lay in that terrible pit, deserved far more than my illogical panic.

I calmed my breathing then turned to Hester and Otis. They were both pale faced and Otis was trembling. I wasn't going to force them to do this. I mouthed, 'You don't have to.'

Hester glared and set her chin in a stubborn line whilst Otis lifted his head. 'We do,' he mouthed back. Then without hesitation, and with Hester hot on his heels, he dive-bombed into the oubliette.

I didn't have a lot of experience with dead bodies – almost none, in fact. There was the Fachan and the fiends I'd killed, but I'd been there when they'd died. This was different.

I had expected more smell, but although the odour in the room was unpleasant and it contained a definite tinge of death it wasn't overpowering. It didn't make me gag. William

Hausman had been dead for such a long time that his body no longer emanated the reek of decomposition. To be honest, there wasn't much left of the poor man. With any luck, that would make Otis and Hester's grisly task much easier.

Hugo and I kept away from the edge of the oubliette so as not to block what little light there was. The brownies were already by Hausman's body and I could clearly see his gold signet ring from where I was. There wasn't much flesh clinging to his finger so it wouldn't take long to retrieve it.

I gazed at the ring while the brownies did their best to remove it without disturbing the body. The three tiny lions etched onto the golden surface were exactly the same design as the ones carved onto the statue of King John in the centre of King's Lynn. *Exactly* the same.

'It's a perfect match,' Hugo breathed.

I smiled. 'Power,' I whispered.

Unfortunately, that was the exact moment when Gladys buzzed in warning and the door to the tower started to open.

I froze in shock. Although I'd known that Athair was inside the castle, it was a big building and our success at staying unnoticed so far had lulled me into a false sense of security. We'd located Hausman's ring and I'd let my guard down, a mistake that could well prove fatal.

Beside me, Hugo braced himself and gathered his magic. I reached for Gladys and drew her out. A beat later, I heard Athair's voice from the other side of the tower. 'Get a fucking move on, Horace!'

I didn't know who Horace was and I didn't care – not until a brownie flapped through the gap in the door. Eloise clearly wasn't Athair's only indentured servant.

The little man with dark wings and tattered clothing halted in mid-air. His jaw dropped as he stared at us, his eyes flicking from me to Hugo to Hester and Otis in the depths of the dark oubliette. Then he somersaulted in the air and sped out the way he'd come. My terror increased tenfold.

'What the fuck are you doing, Horace?' Athair growled. 'Get into the tower.'

'I've had enough of waiting for answers. Where is my sister?' It was unmistakably the brownie's voice. 'She's been gone for ages.'

My stomach dropped. Horace – whoever he was – was putting his life in danger by delaying Athair. He was helping us in an extraordinary fashion.

Athair's rejoinder was clipped with anger. 'It's no concern of yours where she is.' There was a crack of magic followed by a sharp, high-pitched scream. 'And I do not appreciate your attitude.'

My hand clutched Hugo's arm. He understood: he knew exactly what the brownie had done for us and how vital it was that we took advantage of the extra seconds we'd gained as a result. But he also grimaced and gestured helplessly at the stairs. He was right: Athair was less than two metres away. If we tried to leave via the staircase, there was every chance he'd notice us: the door was already ajar by a good four inches.

Alas, there was only one place for us to hide. It would be a tight, unpleasant squeeze but there was no choice.

I spun around and jumped feet first into the oubliette, narrowly avoiding landing on William Hausman's decomposed body. Hester and Otis had pressed themselves against the damp walls of the narrow dungeon and were holding Hausman's golden ring between them. I hoped that all the work they'd done to retrieve it would be worthwhile.

I scrambled to my feet, moved to the side to make more space, and a moment later Hugo jumped in and joined us. His white teeth flashed in a humourless grin.

There was a loud creak as the tower door opened fully and

Athair strode in. Don't look down, I prayed. Please don't look down.

'Stop snivelling, you whining shite.'

I wrapped my arms around my body and tried not to breathe, blink or twitch but it was easier said than done, especially when my nose started to itch. A sneeze was approaching. Cumbubbling bollocks.

'I'm sorry,' Horace croaked, his voice filled with pain. Whatever Athair had done to him as punishment for his question must have been truly horrible. I squeezed my eyes shut for a long, agonised moment. I couldn't repay Horace's sacrifice by sneezing. *I couldn't.*

'One more inappropriate word from you,' Athair muttered, 'and I will rip the wings from your body.'

Hester's eyes widened with horror.

'Be more mindful of your place.'

Horace's response was a whisper. 'Yes, master.'

Athair started to ascend the staircase and I risked raising my hand to pinch my nose and stop my sneeze from escaping. It was enough. I breathed out and glanced at Hugo and the brownies. They gazed back at me. We all knew we were lucky to still be alive.

Hugo pointed upwards. There was only one way out of the oubliette and that was the same way we'd entered it. Escape would be impossible for anyone non-magical.

There was a reason why William Hausman had died down here: bottle dungeons were impossible to get out of without help, whether that was of the magical variety or a helping human hand. The walls that surrounded us tapered upwards in such a way that nobody could climb out; there was no point even trying. Air magic would provide us with the boost we needed but we couldn't try that until Athair was far away and couldn't sense our power.

I took out my phone and checked it: no signal, not even a flicker. For the time being we were trapped. I pulled a face to indicate that to Hugo and he nodded grimly. We were stuck – but the brownies were a different matter.

I didn't dare speak aloud so I gestured to Hester and Otis. They could fly out of the bottle dungeon with Hausman's signet ring. It would take them some time to travel to the rendezvous point with Slim but they'd manage it. They'd be free and they could take the ring with them.

Hester and Otis watched my attempt at silent communication then looked at each other. An unspoken agreement passed between them. A moment later, Hester shrugged and Otis, obviously confused, pursed his lips. I gritted my teeth. They knew exactly what I was telling them to do but they were pretending not to understand.

I nudged Hugo, indicating that he should try sign language with them but he raised his eyebrows dubiously. They were no more likely to pay attention to him than they were to me, but their lives might depend on it. At least if they were safe, I'd feel better.

Hugo embarked upon a complicated mime and this time the brownies' confusion was genuine; frankly, so was mine. Charades were not his strong suit. I tried to add my own fluttering hands into the mix but I didn't get far before we were interrupted.

'What the fuck are you lot doing here?' The harsh hiss came from overhead. I looked up and immediately spotted Horace hovering above us. He lowered himself until he was level with Hester and Otis. The large welt across his face was still bleeding. My jaw clenched. Fucking Athair. Fucking bastard.

'We came to get that,' I whispered as quietly as I could and pointed to the gold ring that Hester and Otis were hanging onto. 'From him.' I nodded at William Hausman's body beside us.

If anything, Horace's disbelief only increased. 'Why?'

'It's important,' Hugo told him. 'Very important.'

Horace shook his head in dismay. 'You must know what he will do to you if he finds you here.'

I opened my mouth to answer.

'And, yes,' Horace continued, 'I know who you are. Your shared blood won't mean a damned thing. He's already furious with you. Your heritage won't save you.'

Good: I didn't want it to save me. I didn't want Athair's attention and I didn't want to be continually reminded that he was my birth father. It had proved easier to escape drug addiction than Athair.

'Eloise told you who we were?' Otis said. Horace nodded. 'You're the reason why she wouldn't leave Athair?' Horace nodded again.

Otis threw a triumphant look in Hester's direction but she barely noticed. She was staring at Horace with two high points of colour on her cheeks. And she was being unusually quiet.

'I'm the hostage,' Horace said sadly. 'Athair keeps me by his side to force her to do whatever he wants. I've told Eloise to leave but she won't go.'

Hester finally spoke. 'That's incredibly heroic of you.'

Otis choked.

Horace looked at them. 'I know who you are, too. You're Otis. And you,' he bowed, 'are Hester. From what Eloise told me, you're the heroic one around here. You do just about everything you can to keep your brother safe. You even attack your mistress when the situation calls for it.'

'Sometimes Daisy needs to be kept in line. I only do it because I care.'

Hugo was grinning as I glared at Hester. Unbelievable. 'Let's stick to what's important, shall we?' I hissed. 'Does Athair know where you are?'

Horace bobbed his head. 'He sent me to the kitchen to get him some food. He's going to be up there for hours.'

My stomach sank. That was not the news I wanted to hear.

'What's he doing?' Hugo asked.

'Sticking his big map back together.' Horace gave me a pointed look. 'He believes you'll jump ship tonight and he wants to give it to you as a welcome gift. My master has to feel that he's in control at all times. He won't be happy when he finds you're already here.'

'He won't find us here,' I said.

Horace didn't say anything but he didn't need to: his expression spoke volumes.

'Don't underestimate Daisy,' Hester said earnestly. 'She often falls in shit and comes up smelling of roses. She might surprise you. She's going to defeat Athair. That's why Otis and I are staying by her side until the bitter end, no matter how many times she tells us to leave.'

Horace's answer was stark. 'Nobody can defeat Athair. In the end he will destroy us all.'

TWENTY-FIVE

Horace didn't stay for long; he didn't dare give Athair another reason to punish him and none of us wanted to raise his suspicions. The little brownie didn't believe that we'd escape from the oubliette, let alone defeat Athair, but he wished us luck and I believed he was being sincere.

Eight hours later, as we continued to hide in the damp dungeon with William Hausman's corpse for company, Hester was still talking about him. 'I like the way his eyes twinkled,' she said. 'And did you see the way his hair made those cute curls on the nape of his neck?'

Otis gave a long-suffering sigh. He'd done remarkably well to keep his mouth shut until then but even his patience was starting to ebb.

I massaged the back of my neck and tried to stretch my limbs, an almost impossible task; there wasn't enough space in the dungeon for one full-sized person to be comfortable, let alone Hugo, me and a dead body.

Time was ticking away. I had hoped to get to Edinburgh and take up position near the Royal Elvish Institute long before

Athair arrived, but we couldn't get out of here until he left Culcreuch. I wouldn't just be stiff and tired when I arrived for the final showdown, I'd also be late.

I knew it would be too dangerous to confront him here on his own territory, though the thought was becoming more and more appealing. If we didn't manage to get out of the oubliette soon, we might *have* to face him.

I was shifting position for the umpteenth time, manoeuvring carefully around Hausman, when Hugo's head reared up. His hearing was far keener than mine. My eyes flew to his and he nodded grimly. As if on cue, my nose started to itch again. I ignored it and stayed very, very still.

'I will be leaving within the hour,' Athair said, his voice growing louder as he walked down the stairs towards us. 'Make sure the car is waiting out front.'

I wondered if slashing his tyres and delaying his arrival in Edinburgh would aid our cause. Probably not. It would be entertaining, though.

'My vampires are already gathering,' he continued.

Hugo's gaze sought mine; they were filled with warmth, love and reassurance.

'It will be a glorious night in Edinburgh. I have been waiting for this moment for a very long time,' Athair said.

'Master?' Horace squeaked.

'What is it?'

'What will you do if she chooses not to join you?'

Athair's footsteps reached the ground floor and once again I prayed that his eyes didn't stray towards the oubliette. 'My Daisy will make the right decision,' he said. 'She will be by my side before the next dawn arrives.'

'But if—'

'Enough!' Athair roared. There was a pained squeak from rusting hinges as he yanked open the door leading out of the tower. 'If she chooses to remain as she is, there will be no choice. I will kill her – but not before I kill everyone she has ever loved. She will watch them suffer and then she will die. Painfully.'

He cleared his throat and his voice returned to normal. 'That will not happen. She is not stupid. There will soon be another fiend joining our ranks.' The tower door thudded closed. If my fiendish fucking father added any further dark promises, I didn't hear them.

'Is it too late to make a Will?' Hester enquired once several beats had passed.

I forced a smile in her direction. There was nothing more for me to say; I didn't even have any misplaced humour to offer her.

'Whatever happens tonight, history will be made,' Hugo said quietly. 'People will be talking about this night for generations to come.'

I considered his words then I reached behind my neck and fumbled for the clasp on my pendant necklace. Once it was unfastened, I dropped it to the dungeon floor. 'For posterity,' I whispered. 'And future treasure hunters who might venture through here one day.'

Hugo smiled and his dimple flashed. 'Amen.'

WE WAITED for as long as we dared before we conjured up enough air magic to boost us out of the oubliette. Although there was no time to celebrate, the relief I felt at escaping the dark hole was wonderful. I allowed myself a long luxurious stretch before I turned back and glanced down at William Hausman, bowing my head in brief, silent prayer. Only then did I speak.

'We have to get out of here,' I said. 'And fast. Athair will already be on his way to Edinburgh and if we don't hurry we'll be late.' The hours spent inside the oubliette had been necessary but they could cost us, lethally so.

'I should be able to get a phone signal as soon as we're outside,' Hugo told me. 'Slim will be waiting to pick us up. But we'll have to take care – the sun will have already gone down and those bloodsuckers out there are a real threat.'

Hester blanched. 'We can do this,' I told her.

She swallowed. 'Yes.'

We gazed at each other. Then, without another word, we ran for the stairs.

It was far easier to leave the tower than it had been to enter it. Hester and Otis swooped across to the front of the castle and quickly established that Athair had definitely gone so there was no longer any reason to worry about detection. We ignored the rope in favour of another blast of air magic then skirted the castle by avoiding the muddy quagmire at the front and heading for the open driveway.

By the time my bare feet hit tarmac, Hugo had already messaged Slim. In less than fifteen minutes, the battered Jeep stopped beside us and we jumped in. Slim gunned the engine and accelerated away. 'I was beginning to get worried,' he said. 'I didn't think you'd take this long.'

'Neither did we,' Hugo said. 'But we got what we needed and we got out safely. That's what's important.'

'You have the ring?' Slim asked.

'Yes.'

'And?'

Hugo looked at me.

'It's what we expected,' I said.

Slim exhaled. 'Okay,' he said. 'Okay.' He licked his lips

nervously. 'I don't suppose there's any point asking why you've lost your shoes and clothes?'

'Not really.' I'd already retrieved the bag I'd taken to King's Lynn and was searching for the cleanest set of clothes I could find. I couldn't face Athair dressed as I was, but there was no time to stop off at home first. I had to make do with what I had – although I kept on Hugo's T-shirt.

When he raised an eyebrow, I told him the truth. 'It smells of you.'

His lips curled up with a hint of possessive delight. 'Good.'

I dropped my head onto his shoulder. 'Don't die tonight.'

'I'll do my best. Don't you die, either.'

I smiled softly but I didn't say anything. Slim put his foot down and we sped towards the city – and whatever fate awaited us.

It didn't matter how fast Slim drove, we were playing catch up with Athair and he had a good head start. I spent most of the journey staring at the clock on the dashboard. Any traffic problems and we would be late. I dreaded to think how Athair would react if that happened.

We were approaching the Queensferry Crossing, with the Forth Road Bridge to the left, when the phone calls and text messages started. I checked the time again. It was 11.31pm. We could still make the midnight deadline.

Sir Nigel was first. 'Good evening, Daisy.' Even under the most extreme circumstances, he remained perfectly polite.

'Good evening,' I said. I didn't bother with any preamble. 'Is there a problem?'

'I thought it would be prudent to inform you that there are a number of vampires descending on Charlotte Square.' He coughed delicately. 'In fact, there are more than I've ever seen before in any one place.'

My mouth dried. The Royal Elvish Institute was on Charlotte Square. 'Are they attacking anyone?'

'Thus far, they are remarkably well behaved.'

Truthfully, I would have preferred the reverse. The Royal Institute was more than capable of battling vampires. Bloodsuckers weren't smart and they were almost exclusively driven by bloodlust; the only thing that could hold them back from an attack was the control of a fiend. Athair had told Horace the vamps were gathering, so it appeared that he was in control and he had a plan. I just had to pray that my plan was better.

'Are they entering the square itself?' I asked.

'No, but they appear to be encircling the area. They have left the George Street entrance clear, but the remainder of Charlotte Square is blocked off.'

I swallowed. 'Okay.'

'Are you in the vicinity?' he asked hopefully.

'We're twenty-five minutes away.'

There was a beat of silence. 'Tell that dear chap to put his foot down, will you?'

I looked at Slim's grim expression. 'I heard,' he said. 'I'm going as fast as I can.'

'We'll be there, Sir Nigel,' I told him. 'We'll make it.'

Two minutes after I hung up on him, Miriam called. 'We're all here, dear, waiting for you.'

'We're not far out.'

'I'm pleased to hear it. Everything is in place.'

I exhaled. 'Good. That's good.'

The next phone call was unexpected. 'Are you fucking coming or not?'

My brow furrowed, then I realised who was calling. That

growl was unmistakable; it was one of the doormen from the Royal Elvish Institute. 'Huey?' I asked.

'My name is Lewis.'

'If you say so. We're ten minutes' away. We won't be long.'

'Uh-huh.' He sniffed. 'You might want to try moving a bit faster.'

'We're doing our best.'

'Your dad is here. He's waiting for you out front.'

'Already?'

Lewis was telling the truth; Hugo's phone was chiming with message alerts and so was Slim's. Cumbubbling bollocks.

'Yes,' he snapped. 'Already.'

Hugo nudged me and held up his phone, showing me a photo of Athair standing smack bang in the centre of the square. He was leaning casually against the statue of Prince Albert as if he were waiting for a friend. This was no casual social appointment, however.

'I'm on my way,' I said. 'Don't worry.'

Lewis snorted derisively.

'Don't worry?' Hester asked. '*Don't worry?*'

Yeah, alright. It wasn't my most impressive attempt at a stirring speech. I shrugged helplessly. What else was there to say?

I ended the phone call and turned off my phone. The stream of calls wasn't conducive to calm, and anyway I had nothing useful to offer any of the callers. We were coming. That was all.

The seconds and the minutes ticked by. It helped that most of Edinburgh's streets were empty and silent; it appeared that most people had learned that something terrible was going down and had taken the wise decision to stay indoors away from the action.

At two minutes to midnight, Slim swung the Jeep onto the

city's main thoroughfare, Princes Street. We were almost there. He twisted the steering wheel and the tyres squealed onto George Street. Charlotte Square was dead ahead – I could see the lights. And I could certainly see the vampires, who were six deep. But Sir Nigel had been right: they'd left a gap so we could get through. How very thoughtful.

The Jeep screeched to a halt. There wasn't time for any final words and we'd said everything already. I straightened my shoulders, jumped out and started marching past the rows of waiting vamps. Hugo flanked my left and the brownies flew through the air by my shoulder to the right.

But Athair had already started to shout, his voice so loud that I felt the ground vibrating beneath my feet. 'Where is Daisy? Is she nothing but a coward after all? Has she run away? Is she too afraid to face me? Where the fuck is my daughter?'

If anybody answered I didn't hear them as I passed through the waiting vampires. Their ranks immediately closed behind me, effectively sealing off the square; there was no turning back now.

Glancing round, I spotted Athair. He was sitting astride Prince Albert's statue, straddling the horse with his arms around Albert's bronzed-green waist like a drunk university student looking for attention.

'I'm right here,' I said as calmly as I dared.

Athair's head whipped towards me. 'You're late.'

A nearby clock started to chime midnight. I raised my index finger. 'Nope. I'm bang on time.' I eyed him. 'I thought you didn't like that statue.'

'I don't.' He leapt off and landed on the ground next to it. His gold-skinned, sinewy body was almost cat like. 'But I was bored and it turns out that old Albie is surprisingly huggable.' He leered at the statue then returned his attention to me and folded his arms across his chest. 'So let's get to it and not waste any time. What is your decision? Will you join me? Or,' he licked his lips, 'will you die?'

TWENTY-SIX

I didn't answer him immediately. I was intent on creating a very specific atmosphere and I didn't want to rush into the denouement. I swivelled around, surveying the scene and taking stock of the hundreds of vampires who were encircling Charlotte Square. There were a lot of fangs on show.

'You've come with an army,' I said softly.

'You could call it that, daughter, or you could call it an honour guard. It all depends on you.'

'Their presence is problematic. There are too many of them and they pose a considerable risk to life.'

Athair shrugged. 'So?'

I smiled pleasantly. 'Would it upset you if I arranged for them to be dispersed?'

A gleam lit his scarlet eyes. 'You want to see bloodshed.'

'I want to see *their* bloodshed,' I corrected.

Athair crooked his little finger and snarls rippled through a section of the watching vamps. One of the ragged figures detached themselves and limped forward. A child: of course it was. Ice filled my veins but I maintained my smile.

The bloodsucker was small, perhaps only four feet high.

There was no indication as to how she had died, but she clearly hadn't been dead for long. Although she had the pallid, bloodless skin of the undead, her clothes were immaculate and there were few signs of decomposition. She didn't deserve this afterlife. None of those vamps did.

'Here you go,' Athair said with a friendly grin. 'You can take this wee one's blood if her existence bothers you so much.' He raised his hand and patted her head gently.

As if on cue, a tear leaked out of her dull, glazed eyes. I knew it wasn't as a result of any emotion she was feeling but just a physical irregularity; even so, it tore at my heart.

I set my jaw, slid Gladys out of her sheath and gazed at the undead child. 'I will give you peace,' I said, then I swung my blade and sliced off her head. It was a gruesome act to witness and it was even worse to be the instigator, but it was the fastest and least cruel method of sending her to oblivion where she belonged.

Athair pursed his lips and made a show of assessing my work. 'You didn't hesitate,' he said. 'I'm impressed.' He paused. 'But I remain concerned that you are too soft-hearted. That side of you will diminish when you become a fiend.'

'And if I don't become a fiend?' I asked in a deliberately casual tone.

He smirked. 'Your soft-hearted nature will make you suffer even more when I slowly torture and kill everyone you care about.' He glanced over my shoulder at Hugo. 'The blue-eyed boy you pretend to be in love with will be first.'

I put my hand in my pocket then turned my back on Athair. I withdrew my hand and released Hausman's golden ring into Hugo's palm. 'Time for you to go,' I said. 'Take the brownies with you.'

He grinned, leaned forward and planted a brief kiss on my

mouth. 'See you soon, Daisy,' he murmured, before turning away and jogging off towards the Royal Elvish Institute. The doors opened as he approached and within seconds he'd been swallowed into its depths with Hester and Otis trailing behind him.

'He's pleasingly obedient,' Athair commented. 'But that won't save him.'

I turned back to face him.

'What did you give him?' he asked. 'What did you take out of your pocket and hand to the boy?'

'A souvenir,' I replied. 'From our recent trip.'

'A romantic interlude before you abandon his side for mine?'

'It was more business than pleasure,' I said. 'We went to Lincolnshire.'

There was no obvious reaction from Athair but I fancied I saw a fleeting shadow cross his face.

'Well,' I said, 'it was actually Lincolnshire *and* Norfolk. We spent some time in King's Lynn and a small village over the county border. Sutton Bridge. Do you know it?'

Athair gazed at me with his unblinking red eyes. He didn't answer – he didn't need to because a moment later, a voice boomed out from amongst the vampires on the right-hand side of the square. 'She's telling the truth, boss,' Arbuthnot called. 'They were in Sutton Bridge first and then in King's Lynn.' He lumbered forward, shoving several mindless vamps out of the way.

'You didn't mention this before,' Athair growled.

Arbuthnot hefted his vast shoulders into a shrug. 'You said only to tell you if it looked like they were running away. It didn't. As far as I reckoned, they were only searching for something.'

I kept my gaze fixed on Athair's face but his expression

remained impassive. 'And did they find what they were looking for?'

I jumped in before Arbuthnot could answer. 'You could ask me, your daughter, instead of your drug-dealing henchman.'

Neither Athair nor Arbuthnot paid me any attention. 'I don't know, boss,' Arbuthnot said. 'I don't think so.'

'You don't think so?' Athair sneered.

I interrupted them again. 'We didn't find anything in Sutton Bridge,' I said loudly. 'There wasn't enough time.' This time I caught the flicker of a smile on my fiendish birth-father's face. 'But,' I added quickly, 'we also realised that the true object of our search had already been found. It wasn't in Sutton Bridge at all.'

The smile vanished. This time it was replaced by a snarl. 'Enough!' Athair spat. 'Enough talk and enough delay! I don't care about your stupid little treasure hunts. Tell me your final decision, daughter. Are you with me? Or are you against me?'

I was grateful that he'd allowed me to babble on for as long as I had. I considered prevaricating and spinning out this dance for longer but there wasn't really any need: I was only delaying the inevitable. I drew in a deep breath and filled my lungs to breaking point. Then I exhaled. 'You already know what my answer is.'

Athair's expression grew stonier. Yeah, he knew. His golden hands curled into tight fists. I saw with a brief jolt of shock that he'd dug his fingernails into his palms with such force that blood was dribbling through his fingers and splashing onto the ground.

'Say it,' he bit out.

I would if he insisted. 'I'm not going to join you,' I said aloud. 'I am not your daughter, not in any sense that actually matters. I will not use blood magic. I will not become a fiend. I have no desire to be a soulless, friendless creature that cares for naught but herself. I don't need more power or more wealth or a longer life. It's quality, not quantity, that counts. You are on your own. Forever.'

Athair's tone was devoid of emotion as he whispered, 'Then you have signed your own death warrant. Yours and everyone else's that you've ever cared for.' He raised his hand and there was a spark of flame above our heads. It flickered and started to grow. Within seconds it was big enough to swallow up several bogles.

He laughed coldly then snapped his fingers and sent the gigantic fireball flying at high speed towards the front of the Royal Elvish Institute. I held my breath – but the vast ball of flame didn't reach the grand building. Two metres before it hit the stone façade, it jerked, sizzled and vanished.

I gazed at the spot where the fireball had been. 'Aw.' I pursed my lips. 'Where did it go?'

Athair's eyes narrowed. He flicked his fingers and repeated the process. The second fireball was larger and hotter than his first one, but when he threw it at the building exactly the same thing happened.

I smacked my lips in satisfaction. 'It so happens that I'm friends with a couple of very powerful sorcerers,' I said. Boonder was skilled at modern runes and Gordon was an expert in ancient ones; when their skills were combined, their ability to draw an effective ward was extraordinary.

'No ward will stand against the might of my magic for long,' Athair snarled.

I sniffed. 'I seem to recall that my mother managed to create one that kept you out of the Assigney mansion for weeks.'

'That was blood magic.'

True.

'And at the time I didn't want to hurt your mother,' Athair said. 'Or you. These circumstances are very different. I'm going to raze that fucking elvish building to the ground.'

He raised his hands in the air then thrust them downwards as he conjured up a wave of rumbling earth magic. The manicured grass across Charlotte Square ruptured as the tremor blasted towards the Royal Elvish Institute. Even though the magic was directed away from me, I was still thrown off my feet. I landed on my back with a thump, just in time to see the forceful earthquake shudder to a halt.

As I heaved myself back upright, a voice called out from one of the upper windows. 'Mud McAlpine has established root magic beneath this ground! No earth magic shall penetrate it!'

I grinned and waved at the witch. 'You know, Mud is an incredibly powerful witch,' I said to Athair. 'He banished the fiend called Zashtum all on his own.'

If this was news to Athair, he didn't show it. 'Zashtum was weak. No witch can banish *me*. As I've already proved.'

That part was probably true. Unfortunately. 'There's more than one way to skin a cat.'

Athair smiled nastily in response. 'Indeed.' He sprang upwards, landing on the backside of Prince Albert's bronze horse. For a centuries-old prick, he certainly was nimble.

From his high vantage point, he moved his arms one way and his hands another. It took me a moment to realise what he was doing: he was conducting his own orchestra. There were no violinists or cellists, and certainly no woodwind section, but there were dozens upon dozens of cumbubbling vampires.

He drew upon one group, which comprised around fifty vamps, and they broke away from the others to advance upon the institute. Athair twirled his wrists and flicked his fingers. The vampires immediately screeched a loud response and threw themselves towards the ward. They bounced off it then picked themselves up and threw their bodies at it again. I realised they would repeat that movement over and over again with no regard for their soft, rotting flesh.

'Worth a try,' Athair muttered, then he called down to me. 'I might not be able to get into that building just yet, daughter, but it won't hold out against for me long. Besides, this is Edinburgh.' He grinned toothily. 'You can't ward every building in the city. It's a shame there are no longer any orphanages in existence – still, I'm sure my fanged darlings can find some tasty families to snack on while your friends cower inside the elves' shithouse. Watch this, darling Daisy. Watch the power you could have enjoyed for yourself.'

He twirled on the back of the horse, flinging out his arms and directing those blasted bloodsuckers away from Charlotte Square towards other streets, other doors and other homes.

I licked my lips as fear scorched my veins – but then there were several loud screeches as vehicles skidded through the streets towards the square.

Unable to see what was happening, I took a few steps backwards, just in time to spot an armoured car approach one group of marauding vampires. It spun to the side, halted and a window lowered enough for one of the vehicle's occupants to point a weapon. The muzzle of a gun appeared but it didn't fire bullets; instead it jetted out a spray of liquid.

I watched the arc of fine droplets mist through the air. They looked innocuous; to anyone who didn't know better, they could simply have been water. But I knew better, and when the liquid hit the stampeding vampires they knew better, too.

Their screams echoed through the night sky as the enhanced vamp spray ate through their flesh in seconds. The first wave fell to their knees and pitched forward; the second wave collapsed, writhing, onto their companions. Each droplet ate through hair, skin, flesh and bone; as soon as it hit their rotting brains, it was game over. It was incredibly satisfying to watch.

Athair howled in rage, though not because he cared about his army of undead warriors. It was simply that he hated not being in full control. He directed his anger at the armoured car, sparking out magical lightning in its direction. When that didn't work, he blasted it with air magic.

The vehicle could withstand a barrage of bullets but it couldn't repel a powerful fiend's magic. I grimaced as it overturned, hoping the occupants would be alright.

At least half the vampires had already been decimated and the remainder were spreading through other streets.

'Arbuthnot!' Athair yelled. 'Get to that fucking car! Kill whoever is inside!'

There was no answer: the bogle had disappeared. Arbuthnot had seen his chance and taken it – he must have run off at the first opportunity. Good for him. I'd be very, very surprised if we saw him again.

If Athair realised that Arbuthnot had vanished, he didn't react. Instead, still balanced on top of the bronze horse, he spun towards another of the departing group of vampires. I heard a muttered hiss and I followed his gaze.

We'd lost one bogle but we'd gained another. At the far end of the street on the southern side, I spotted a large female. A battle to the death wasn't where I'd expected to see a museum director but at least Agatha Smiggleswith wasn't alone; she was flanked to her left by Duchess. A troll and a bogle fighting together was an incongruous sight, but they looked as if they were enjoying themselves. They wore matching grins of ear-splitting proportions.

They didn't remain alone for long, either. Uniformed police

officers poured in from the side streets to join the fray. Those vamps were toast.

'For fuck's sake,' Athair yelled. 'For fuck's sake!'

He ought to wait for the finale. I glanced to my right, towards the Firth of Forth estuary. The water wasn't visible because there were too many grand buildings and staggered rooftops to see it from where I was standing, but I could see the dark sky above it.

And I could see the large shape wheeling in the air and flapping towards us.

Aine the dragon reached us in seconds. She might be far from home and possess far more motherly concerns than anything that elves might conjure up, but she could certainly fly fast when she put her mind to it.

Athair tilted his head upwards. As soon as he caught sight of her, he flicked a lightning bolt towards her that I knew was designed to kill. She dodged it easily and turned her attention towards the remainder of the vampires.

'You're losing, Father!' I shouted. 'Why don't you come down off your high horse and give in to the inevitable?'

The words had barely left my mouth when a bank of fire left Aine's massive jaws. In seconds she scorched a hundred vampires, charring their bodies beyond all recognition. They certainly wouldn't be rising again.

'You think killing a few bloodsuckers means you've won?' Athair called back. 'This fight is only just beginning. You've not seen anything yet.'

Aine turned and attacked another group of sprinting vamps. She fixed her slitted dragon gaze on the final few; soon there would be none left. In less than an hour, we'd managed to destroy Edinburgh's entire undead population. If nothing else went right this night, I could at least be proud of that.

Gladys buzzed, her impatience growing. I couldn't blame

her. 'Soon,' I whispered. I tightened my hand around her hilt, wishing my palms weren't so sweaty. 'Soon.'

Athair jumped down from the horse and landed a metre in front of me. 'How about now?'

I raised my chin. 'I'm game if you are.'

TWENTY-SEVEN

I wasted no time. Drawing on all the training I'd received, I danced forward on delicate toes and then I slashed at Athair with brute force. Gladys's blade caught his shoulder, slicing through his white shirt and his golden skin until bright-red blood oozed forth.

He hissed and responded with magic, tossing out a casual burst of air that would have flattened me if I hadn't immediately countered it with my matching power. We pushed at each other, air against air. I knew that Athair's magic was stronger and so did he, but I wasn't the underdog I'd always been. It would take more than power to win this fight. Play smarter, Daisy, I reminded myself. Not harder.

As I gritted my teeth and threw out screeds of powerful air magic, a few sweat beads formed on my forehead despite the cool night air. I didn't test my limits and empty myself of all I had, however; I gauged my energy levels and watched Athair's expression. When I was certain he was least expecting it, I dropped to the ground and stopped my attack.

Athair's magic faltered momentarily – perhaps he thought

I'd collapsed because of his strength – but he didn't pause for long. He gathered his air magic and swirled it around my body.

A tornado, I realised: the bastard was conjuring up his own damned tornado.

I ducked my head and, mindful of the tricks that Mud had employed, focused on earth magic. I told the ground to hold me: we were one, we belonged together. The wind screamed and spun around me but I remained in place, rooted to the spot. Just.

I waited, my eyes screwed shut to guard against the whipping wind but my other senses on high alert. As soon as the wind started to drop and Athair's magic loosened, I tensed.

Glady was ready. I held myself for another beat and then, at the very moment when I knew I wouldn't be blown away, I rose up and thrust Gladys towards Athair again. I swiped to my right and to my left, cutting into his skin for a second and a third time. More of his blood spilled forth. Even though his wounds were healing in front of my very eyes, my minor success spurred me on. I had this. I *could* do this.

I swung Gladys towards him again, aiming for his exposed neck but this time he was waiting for me. He lashed out at my stomach with his foot. I pulled back instinctively and, as I did, Athair hit me with fire. Flames engulfed my right hand – the hand that I was using to grip Gladys's hilt.

The pain was excruciating. I shrieked aloud and automatically dropped the sword before I conjured up ice-cold water to treat the burn. As I did so, Athair casually bent down and picked up Gladys.

No. Oh no.

She buzzed with hatred, making no attempt to disguise how she felt at being handled by a fiend. Sentient or not, though, she couldn't prevent Athair from using her against me.

She altered her buzz to a high-pitched whine but he only chuckled.

'Killed by your own father with your own sword.' He clicked his tongue. 'And to think of all you could have been.' He raised her blade, angling it towards my chest.

I sucked in a breath as time seemed to stop. Then a loud voice boomed out across Charlotte Square. 'Wait!'

Hugo. I looked up and saw him standing on the roof of the Royal Elvish Institute in exactly the same spot where I had been when I'd confronted Athair up there. Suddenly a huge grin spread across my face. 'He's got it,' I said. 'He's ready.'

'What?' Athair asked. 'What are you babbling on about?'

'Hugo's got the ring. The one we took from William Hausman's corpse in Culcreuch Castle.'

As my words sank in, Athair's eyes widened a fraction and he lowered Gladys an inch – but he didn't let go of her. 'You've been to Culcreuch?'

I almost laughed. 'You think we don't know where you live? You think we're stupid?' I shook my hand free of the remaining water and winced. The skin was already blistering; unfortunately there was only so much the water could do.

'We didn't find King John's crown jewels at Sutton Bridge because we realised we didn't have to,' I said. 'William Hausman had already been there. You punished that poor man for hunting for the treasure that could destroy every fiend in existence, treasure marked with the emblem of three lions to signify the power and might of England, King and country.'

I paused for no reason other than dramatic effect. 'The ring that was on William Hausman's finger when you threw him into that dungeon has the same emblem. That's what I gave to Hugo earlier and that's what he's holding aloft right now.'

Athair hawked up a ball of greenish phlegm and spat it on the ground. His disgusting show of defiance didn't fool me because I'd seen the way his fingers had tightened around Gladys's hilt. He believed me, believed every word because everything I'd said was the truth. Athair could scent a lie in a heartbeat and I hadn't lied.

He growled, 'I don't know how you learned about King John's jewels, Daisy, but the item you're talking about is a sceptre, not a ring.'

I rolled my eyes. 'Please. You're six hundred years old. You know better than anyone how fluid language is, how words change shape and meaning. You understand that words become metaphors and vice-versa. According to the stories, it was the sceptre in Bad King John's crown jewels that possessed the power to get rid of all enemies and kill all fiends. But you also have to think about what a sceptre is and what it symbolises.'

Athair whispered the words. 'The power of a monarch.'

'The power of a *country*,' I said in a near shout. 'You weren't alive when those jewels were lost and you took the old stories at face value. But don't beat yourself up for being wrong. You don't have the time.'

A strange blue light was emanating from Hugo; his hand – and the ring he was holding – were glowing bright blue and lighting up the rooftop. He looked like an ethereal vision from heaven. Hell, Hugo looked like a *god*.

As if to complete the image, Athair slammed out a fork of magical lightning but it didn't even get close to hitting Hugo. The ward around the Royal Elvish Institute included the rooftop; we'd made sure of that.

'What will it be, Daddy Dearest?' I asked. 'You can strike me down, you can kill me – we both know you're capable of that. But if you delay then Hugo will use that ring long before you can get to him and prevent its true power being invoked.'

I affected a brief sigh. 'If you let me live, you still might not make it to him in time. The ward around that building is strong and it won't be easy to break, no matter how much magic you fling at it. The choice is yours. Sweet revenge – or complete annihilation?'

Athair's red eyes flashed. 'Pathetic,' he hissed. 'You're fucking pathetic.' He turned away, already gathering his power as he prepared to throw everything he had at the magical barrier.

Something inside me hardened. 'You do not get to call me that,' I said icily. I reached into my pocket, found the little knife I'd taken from Amy and leaned forward, then I stabbed it into Athair's broad, golden neck.

He threw his head back and screeched as his hands scrabbled at the knife that was embedded in his flesh. In the process, he dropped Gladys. I didn't waste a second. I scooped her up and she offered me a welcoming hum in return.

Athair grunted as he yanked the knife out of his neck. With blood spurting from the wound, he turned and threw it at me. His intent was obviously to hurt me in the same way I'd hurt him but I was ready for him. I raised Gladys up and the knife bounced uselessly off her blade.

'Hang on, Daisy!' Hugo cried. 'It's almost there. A few more seconds...'

Athair snarled. Still bleeding copiously, he slammed his hands forward and threw everything he had at the Royal Elvish Institute – and Hugo. Fire. Wind. Lightning. Air. Earthquake. Athair tossed each violent blast of magic in quick succession.

The ward around the building was stronger than any other potential barrier except against blood magic, but it wasn't foolproof. Not against a fiend's powers and certainly not against Athair's. A loud crack filled the square and the air in front of the institute glowed bright green. Then there was a wild gust of warm air as the ward finally snapped.

'It's happening, Daisy!' Hugo shouted. 'Now!'

The bright blue that surrounded him increased in intensity and Athair covered his head with his hands. I tensed, adrenaline shooting through my veins. My bones quivered and my hands trembled. Gladys hummed loudly.

Nothing else happened.

Athair slowly dropped his hands and looked up. 'It didn't work!' He laughed aloud. 'It didn't fucking work! Screw you, King John! Screw you, elves! And screw you—'

I twisted Gladys and thrust her into his back. She pierced his body, sliding through bone and gristle and muscle and heart.

He choked and then he fell to his knees. 'Daisy,' he croaked.

I kept my hands on Gladys's hilt. It was down to her now, but I was right there with her.

'The ring...'

I crouched down to his ear. 'The ring is just that,' I said. 'It's a ring, nothing more, nothing less. We *did* go to Culcreuch Castle and we *did* take it from William Hausman who *had* been hunting for King John's treasure. But that ring is not connected to the sceptre. It's cheap gold, probably purchased from a market stall. You fell for the oldest trick in the book.' It wasn't the first time he'd fallen for an imitation but it would be the last.

He wheezed. 'You ... could ... have ... had ... everything.'

'I've already got everything,' I told him.

And then I twisted Gladys for a final time and ended it.

MY KNEES HAD GIVEN way and I was sitting in a puddle of something wet. It might have been water or it might have been blood. I was too drained to check.

'You went off script,' Hugo's chided me mildly.

I looked up. He was standing over me; his stance was casual but the look in his eyes was pure concern. I managed a flicker of a smile to indicate that I was alright. He reached down and pulled me up to my feet. 'Minor improvisation,' I told him. 'At best.'

His arms wrapped tightly around me. 'Improvisation that worked,' he whispered. 'You did it.'

'*We* did it. That blue goop from Baudi worked a treat.' The will-o'-the-wisp I'd met several months before couldn't abandon her marshland home to join the fight, but even so she'd insisted on helping.

'It did feel like I was in The Beatles performing a rooftop concert,' Hugo admitted.

'Which Beatle?'

He grinned. 'All of them rolled into one.'

There was a click of footsteps as somebody approached. Hugo released me from his hug but from the way his fingers continued to grip mine, he wasn't planning on ever letting go again. That suited me.

I pushed back my hair with my free hand and glanced at the two women in front of me.

'This will be quite the clean-up operation,' DI O'Hagan said. 'But I can't deny that I'm impressed. You've done a lot for the city tonight. I had no idea there were still so many vampires lurking around.'

'I suspect Athair brought a lot of them in from other places.'

'Then it's not just Edinburgh that owes you a debt of gratitude, it's the entire country.'

I shifted uncomfortably. The praise felt misplaced; after all, I had mostly been saving myself.

'I will make sure that you are not billed for the damage this time,' the other older woman said.

I felt a squint of confusion and I gazed at her more closely.

Then I blinked. 'WPC Hurst?' I asked. Was this the fresh-faced police officer who'd tried to help me when I'd time-travelled to 1994?

'It's Detective Inspector Hurst these days.' She smiled. 'You've not changed much, Lady Daisy.'

I swallowed. Uh-huh. 'Apart from the blood and gore, I suppose.'

'I suppose.'

Hugo nudged me. 'She's not the only face from the past who'd like a word.'

I raised an eyebrow then I spotted Tracey Coles, ex-homeless entrepreneur. The last time I'd seen her had also been in 1994, outside Waverley Station. She might be thirty years older since the last time we'd spoken but she certainly looked good. I didn't need to ask to know that she'd done well for herself in the intervening decades. She'd been on the cover of *Time* magazine, for goodness' sake. 'Your vamp spray was extraordinary.'

Tracey dipped a little curtsey. 'It's a new recipe. I always thought it would be hard to improve upon the original but I'd say it's working out well.' She winked at me. 'The sprinkling of fresh thyme makes a difference.'

I grinned. 'So I've heard.'

There was a loud thud and I flinched, my eyes inadvertently trailing to the body of my own father. He was still dead, however: the thud had come from the overturned armoured car. Several muscled men dressed in tight black clothing were emerging from it and brushing themselves down.

'Is that...?' I started.

Hugo nodded. 'John Thurgood and the rest of his team. When he heard what was happening, he got in touch and asked to be involved. He reckoned, rightly, that he owed you for saving him from Bella the giant snake.'

That felt like a lifetime ago. Hell, it *was* a lifetime ago. 'So many people came and helped.' I shook my head, scarcely believing how many were there. They had all put their lives on the line.

'One good turn deserves another,' a familiar voice said and I turned to Sir Nigel. Somehow he was still immaculately dressed in a pristine white shirt and a perfectly knotted bow tie; not a single hair of his waxed moustache was out of place. 'And you, Lady Daisy, have completed a lot of good turns. You're a very special person.'

Heat rose in my cheeks; I wasn't convinced I deserved all this praise. 'I'm just a junkie,' I mumbled. Strangely, it had felt easier when everyone disliked me.

Hugo stiffened. 'No, you're not. You're not an addict any more and, even when you were taking spider's silk you were never just a junkie, Daisy.' His voice grew quieter. 'Nobody is.'

'Indeed,' Sir Nigel said in an avuncular fashion. 'Indeed.' He smiled proudly at me. 'Now, Eleanor is inside making tea. She and I were not equipped to join the battle, but there's a lot to be said for those of us who stay behind the scenes making the brew. She has asked if you'd like to come inside and partake of some refreshments.'

'Is there cake?' I asked.

'Of course,' he answered.

'That explains where Hester and Otis are,' I said ruefully. I reached for Gladys. 'We'll get you properly cleaned up,' I told her. Then I lowered my voice. 'The Fachan would have been so proud of you.'

Her hilt trembled in my hand. I patted her and we all ambled towards the open door of the Royal Elvish Institute. Lewis and James, the two doormen, were already back in their usual spots and a part of me hoped they would refuse me entry but they were falling into line with everyone else. They stepped back and even bowed as I passed by.

'I don't like this,' I muttered to Hugo. 'I prefer it when everyone glares at me.'

'Get used to it,' he said. 'Your days of being glared at are over. It's pure adoration from here on in.'

There was a loud snort from behind me. 'Don't be too sure about that, girlie,' Duchess said. 'I'll glare at you as often as you like.'

Hugo sighed. 'There are exceptions to every rule.'

Thank goodness.

I walked across the threshold into the Institute. The place was a mess, although that was hardly surprising given all that had happened not just today but a few weeks earlier too. I felt a nervous twitch. Even if Edinburgh Council didn't bill me, there was a chance that the Royal Elvish Institute might. Then again, I could always give them Culcreuch Castle as compensation. After all, I was Athair's sole heir and there were only so many castles and grand buildings a girl could own before she started to look greedy.

I turned left, preparing to turn into the drawing room. Eleanor, however, quickly ducked her head out of the main dining room. 'In here,' she said. 'It's best if you don't go in the drawing room right now.'

I frowned. 'Why not?'

She pulled a face. Curiosity got the better of me and I glanced into the room. Oh. *OH*.

Hester was at one side of the room. Otis was at the other side. They weren't alone. Horace was passionately kissing Hester while Otis was gazing adoringly at Eloise.

'You're amazing,' I heard Horace say.

'Say that to me again with your clothes off,' Hester told him.

I nodded quickly. 'You're right, Eleanor. The dining room is better.' I changed direction.

The Primes, who had gathered inside, were already cheering.

CHAPTER

TWENTY-EIGHT

I lay on one side of the bed, Hugo lay on the other. We were facing each other, our hands and feet touching.

'I love you, Lady Daisy Carter Assigney.'

'I love you too, Lord Snoot-Face Pemberville.'

His eyes danced. 'Say that again. Go on. I dare you.'

I smirked but before I could risk repeating my words, the bedroom door opened a fraction.

'You have to knock first, Hester!' Otis said.

'He's right!' Eloise agreed. 'Horace, you have to wait until you're granted admittance! Manners cost nothing!'

I rolled my eyes at the intrusion. 'We ought to send you lot to minion finishing school,' I told them.

'I'd like to see you try,' Hester snorted. She flew over to the bed and hovered between us. Horace was practically glued to her side. 'Are you going to stay in bed all day?'

'It's not the worst idea in the world,' Hugo murmured.

'You won't say that when you see what's happening on the news,' she said ominously.

I sat up straight. 'What?' I asked. 'What's wrong?'

'You've worried her now.' Otis scowled at his sister before

also flying over. 'It's nothing. You and Hugo should stay here and enjoy yourselves. There are no problems and there is nothing whatsoever to be concerned about.' Unsurprisingly, his words only ratcheted up my anxiety.

'Tell us what's going on,' Hugo said.

Eloise bit her lip. 'It's better if you see it for yourselves.'

Hugo and I exchanged glances then we sprang out of bed and bolted downstairs. The television in the lounge was already on and all the Primes were grouped around it. They started guiltily when we entered. Even Miriam looked nervous. 'Hello dears,' she said, then she looked away.

'What's going on?' Hugo asked.

'It's nothing,' Becky chirped.

'Absolutely nothing,' Rizwan agreed.

Slim was already nodding. 'Nothing whatsoever.'

Uh-huh. I folded my arms across my chest. Hugo glowered. 'If anyone else says the word nothing I'm going to rescind our wedding invitations with immediate effect.'

'I'm glad you mentioned your upcoming nuptials,' Slim said. 'There are some details that I'd like to go over with you concerning the flowers. The wedding planner is already in the ballroom setting up the first of the table arrangements, but I'm not sure about the roses she's selected for the ceremony.'

'And the hair stylist called,' Becky said. 'She wanted to confirm the time with you. She's planning to be here from eight o'clock tomorrow morning.'

Mmm. I drummed my fingers against my arms. 'Back away from the television.'

Hugo tapped his right foot. 'Do what she said.'

They glanced at each other then they moved away. Hugo took the remote control from Mark and turned up the volume.

The news anchor smiled out from the screen. 'And so we come to our final news item of the day concerning Amy Aurum, a teenager from Hammerwich in Staffordshire, who's recently made an extraordinary discovery. Our reporter, Edward Dixon has been catching up with her. She's not in Hammerwich right now, is she, Edward?'

The camera cut to a windswept man. 'She certainly isn't,' he said. He gestured to the wide-open landscape around him.

'I recognise that place,' I said.

Hugo's eyes narrowed. 'Me too.'

The reporter continued. 'Amy Aurum is here with me in Sutton Bridge, and it would be fair to say she's made a most extraordinary discovery.' He held out a microphone towards her. She was rosy cheeked from the wind and the sun and beaming from ear to ear. 'Tell us about what you've found, Amy.'

'Only the greatest treasure that's ever been uncovered,' Amy told him. 'I have located the lost crown jewels of King John. They've been buried beneath these sands for eight hundred years but they're buried no longer. I've dug up a large number of gold coins, a crown, a sword, a chalice, a helmet, an orb and a sceptre. In fact, I have the sceptre right here.' She held up a heavy-looking golden object.

Yep: that was definitely a sceptre. A *real* sceptre. Its surface was dull from the centuries it had spent in the ground but I knew it would soon be cleaned up and restored to shiny brilliance. Its magical power already seemed to sparkle even through the television screen.

'It's extraordinary,' the reporter breathed. 'Do you have any idea of its worth?'

'Its monetary worth is in the millions. But,' Amy added, 'its historical worth is even greater.'

'People have been searching for this treasure for hundreds of years,' he said. 'It's amazing that you've found it. You're barely eighteen years old!'

She smiled modestly.

'In fact, you're something of a prodigy when it comes to treasure hunting, aren't you? You come from Hammerwich, which is the location where the Staffordshire Hoard was found. And you recently dug up some of the original Hoard that had been moved to a different spot, didn't you?'

'It's true,' Amy said. 'I did.'

'Not only is this treasure the greatest that's ever been found, but you must be the greatest treasure hunter that's ever existed.'

She giggled slightly. 'That's something of an exaggeration.'

'No,' the reporter said. 'I don't believe it is.'

I took the remote control out of Hugo's hands and turned off the television before I looked at him.

'What are you thinking, Daisy?' he asked.

I drew in a deep breath. 'Amy is very talented.'

'Indeed.'

'She's a great treasure hunter.'

'She is.'

I shrugged. 'I'm not sure you could say that she's the *greatest* treasure hunter.'

'Definitely not.' He paused. 'Full kudos to her, she's done incredibly well. But there's a lot of treasure out there that's yet to be found. There's a lot of history bound up in this sceptred isle. It would be foolish to give her the title of greatest treasure hunter when there's still so much to discover.'

'We could pack our bags,' I suggested. 'Leave this afternoon? Head out and see what we can find?'

'Sounds like a plan,' Hugo agreed.

Otis tentatively raised his hand. 'Um, what about your wedding? You're about to get married.'

Eloise's expression was worried. 'Tomorrow,' she said, in case we'd forgotten.

I looked at Hugo. 'I mean,' I said slowly, 'we can get married *any* time.'

His blue eyes gleamed. 'Yep. We can easily postpone the ceremony until later. If you're alright with that, Daisy.'

Wedding-schmedding. 'First one to the Jeep,' I said, 'is a rotten egg.'

Author's notes

Culcreuch Castle made it into *Skullduggery* first and it receives a brief mention in the author's notes for that book. It is located in Perthshire but, as it's no longer open to the public, I've not visited it. However, it is stunning in all its photos and any descriptions of muddy quagmires or penned-up vampires destroying the scenery are pure fiction. There is a tower with a bottle dungeon (also known as an oubliette); however, I have taken considerable creative licence in describing it and most of the castle in this book comes from my imagination.

The Staffordshire Hoard is also based in reality, although there has never been any indication of a witch who found some of it and buried it in her garden! The real Staffordshire Hoard is the largest collection of Anglo-Saxon treasure ever discovered and includes more than four thousand items. It was discovered by a metal detectorist in 2009 in a field near Hammerwich and was eventually valued at more than three million pounds. It was bought jointly by the Birmingham Museum and Art Gallery and the Potteries Museum and Art Gallery. The proceeds were divided between the metal detectorist who found it and the landowner.

The tale of King John's lost treasure is true. In 1216 he attempted to cross the Wash estuary with baggage wagons containing his crown jewels. He misjudged the tide and only narrowly escaped with his life. Historians agree that King John was a truly terrible and cruel monarch but there is indeed a statue of him in King's Lynn, and there are lions carved onto the statue's breastplate. The lost crown jewels have never been found – but they must be out there somewhere.

Although there is no Royal Elvish Institute in Edinburgh, Charlotte Square is real and contains many examples of great architecture including Bute House, the official residence of Scotland's First Minister. There is indeed a large statue of Prince Albert seated on a horse in the centre of the square. Until recently Charlotte Square was the location for the annual Edinburgh International Book Festival, which is held in August.

ACKNOWLEDGMENTS

There have been so many people involved in the creation of both this book and this series. I owe a huge thank to them all. Firstly, Clarissa Yeo and JoY Cover Designs, who created the wonderful covers. I've worked with Clarissa almost from the very beginning of my writing career. She's moving onto pastures new and I cannot thank her enough for all that she has done in the past twelve years. Her art is extraordinary and I wish her all the very, very best for the future.

My wonderful editor, Karen Holmes, has worked her own particular magic on all of my words, ironing out my messy repetition of 'just', 'raised eyebrows' and 'shrugging'. Oh, so much shrugging! Deeply felt thanks must also go to Ruth Urquhart for her continuing audiobook narration, alongside the team at Tantor. I know how lucky I am to work with such a great team.

There are many ARC readers whose contribution throughout the series has been invaluable. Some are new advanced readers, and some have been helping me out for years. If someone had told me back in 2012 that this would be my career twelve years later, I would never have believed them.

I truly hope that you've enjoyed Daisy's adventures. Although her treasure hunting days are far from over, this is her last novel. There will, I hope, be many more books from me to come with a host of new characters and shedloads of magic!

Helen x

9 781913 116453